The Wife's New Maid
Amora Sway

Copyright © 2025 by Amora Sway

All rights reserved.

No part of this book may be reproduced or transmitted in any form, including electronic or mechanical, without written permission from the publisher, except in the case of brief quotations embodied in reviews or articles. This is a work of fiction. Names, characters, businesses, events and incidents are pure product of the author's imagination. Any resemblance to actual persons, living or dead, or an actual event is purely coincidental and does not assume any responsibility for author or third-party websites or content therein.

Author's note: As this is a thriller there is some violence, and while it's not overly graphic, there are dark themes, nevertheless.

PROLOGUE

PRE-NUP AGREEMENT BETWEEN DORIAN AND LINLEY GUNN.

ARTICLE 1X – GROUNDS AND STIPULATIONS FOR DIVORCE

1. No Children Clause

1.1 Requirement of Childbirth: The parties agree that if no child is born to the Wife within four (4) years from the date of marriage, the marriage shall be automatically terminated unless mutually agreed otherwise in writing by both parties.

1.2 Settlement Upon Termination: In the event of such termination of the marriage under this clause, the Husband shall pay to the Wife a lump sum of two million dollars ($2,000,000) within sixty (60) days of the effective date of termination. This amount shall be considered the full and final settlement of any and all claims the Wife may have against the Husband.

2. Infidelity Clause

2.1 Husband's Infidelity: Should the Husband be found to have engaged in an extramarital affair during the marriage, the Wife shall be entitled to receive fifty percent (50%) of the Husband's total net worth, calculated as of the date of discovery of the infidelity. This amount shall be paid to the Wife within ninety (90) days of such discovery.

2.2 Wife's Infidelity: Should the Wife be found to have engaged in an extramarital affair during the marriage, she shall forfeit any right to spousal support or division of the Husband's assets upon dissolution of the marriage. The Wife shall receive no financial compensation or property division from the Husband in the event of divorce due to her infidelity.

ONE

THE BAR HUMS WITH a medley of whispers, elongated vowels, chuckles, and raucous belly laughs, creating a constant buzz around me as I try to grasp something intelligible. It's sad, I know, having to rely on strangers' conversations for some sense of belonging. But hey, I can't help it if my drinking partner rushed off to meet her new 'possible' relationship. Her bubbly vibe was so overwhelming that I welcomed her quick exit after just one margarita. I know that sounds uncool and like sour grapes. I should be happy for her, and I am, but what about me? Why aren't I getting all silly and giggly over some new guy?

My second martini offers little relief after another interminable week of fixing everyone's issues at the publishing house. From the wrong type of milk in someone's coffee to a bestseller turning up with typos after it's sold a hundred thousand copies, everyone's been racing around in a panic, talking over each other, and coming to me as though I'm the only person on the planet who can make things right.

My boss, the queen of tantrums, has just gone through a messy divorce and is now turning everything into a drama. I do feel for her; it can't be easy losing a thirty-year marriage to a younger, prettier woman.

At least loneliness doesn't cause heartbreak.

I brush a loose ginger strand away from my cheek. My hair, untamed and free, falls over one shoulder. During the week, I stick to buns and ponytails—carefully styled with not a hair out of place. But by Friday evening, I'm a disheveled wreck, especially after my boss demands I fix a last-minute problem that can't wait. There are always a ton of those, especially on Fridays.

Instead of heading back to my tiny Upper West Side apartment, I order another drink. Here I am, sitting at a bar alone on a Friday night. I might as well wear a 'Loser' neon sign over my head. I should be on a train to Greenwich to visit my parents, but I'm exhausted. It's been a trying week.

Suddenly, I feel a whoosh of air and catch the scent of pine with a hint of musk. I glance up and see a man in a well-cut suit that looks like it's been stitched onto his tall frame. He has broad shoulders on a lean body—the type of man who looks after himself.

He approaches me with a confident stride, as if this is his place and people step out of *his* way, not the other way around.

His light brown hair is short on the sides and sculpted on top, not a hair out of place despite its tousled style. His brown eyes meet mine, and suddenly we're alone; everything around me blurs.

Pointing to the seat, he asks, "May I?"

Wide-eyed and a little starstruck, I nod.

He slides onto the stool next to me, and the bartender is already there waiting for him. I sense this guy doesn't wait for anyone. "Manhattan," he says in a deep, smooth tone before turning to me.

Looking at my nearly empty glass, he asks, "Can I get you something?"

"I'm not in the habit of accepting drinks from strange men," I say, my voice trembling.

His well-defined mouth curls slightly. "I've been described as many things, but strange ain't one of them."

"I meant stranger," I correct.

"I'm Dorian." He holds out his hand, and I take it.

We're in a crowded bar, so aside from possibly spiking my drink, there's not much this man can do to me—other than mess with my hormones. I mean, he's hot with a capital H.

"Linley," I reply, clearing my throat. The heat in my neck rushes up to my face. I'm blushing. "Do you always buy drinks for strangers in bars?"

"Only the ones that appeal to me. And red hair is a weakness of mine." His eyes lock onto mine with such intensity that I nearly forget to breathe.

Is he hitting on me?

Lost for a coherent response, I say, "I'll have a martini, then."

He's magnetic, that's for sure, and incredibly confident—unlike me. I'm so riddled with uncertainty that when a man smiles in my direction, I glance over my shoulder to see if his attention's aimed at someone else.

It's been a lifetime, and I'm really out of touch when it comes to men, but this guy is coming on strong. He's a little sure of himself but not completely cocky; there's something quiet about him too.

It helps that he's handsome.

"So, Dorian, what do you do?" I ask as the bartender delivers my drink.

"Hedge funds." He shrugs as if it's no big deal. "Not so glamorous, but it pays the bills."

I play with my drink, unsure of what to say next. Am I shy? I never thought so, but this man is making my heart skip a beat.

Gulping down my drink as though that will help lower these sudden walls of insecurity, I remind myself it's either stick it out here or go home to an empty apartment. And small talk I can do, especially now that I'm on my third drink. I'm feeling a little light-headed, but what could go wrong here? I'm not exactly going to see this guy again.

"And what do you do?" His eyes land on my bag with a folder sticking out. "Let me guess. Publishing?"

"Am I that transparent?" I ask.

"No. But I noticed that." He points to the folder with Scribes Publishing House stamped on it.

"Yes, well... a little weekend reading," I respond with a chuckle.

"Do you always take your work home on the weekends?"

"Not if I can help it. But there's a deadline." I shrug. "Like always."

He raises an eyebrow. "That sounds demanding."

"Oh yeah. I usually work sixty-hour weeks. I had planned to go to my folks' place in Greenwich since it's quieter there and I could focus better, but honestly, I'm just not in the mood. It's been a long week."

"Downtime's important." He takes a sip and then looks around the bar.

"Are you expecting someone?" I can't help but ask.

He shakes his head. "Are you?"

"No. The friend I came with left in a hurry, and I thought I'd just stay for another drink."

"I'm glad you did." His eyes hold mine, and my hand tightens around my glass.

"I like this place. It's quieter than most bars," he adds. "Do you come here often?"

I can't help but grin.

"What?" he asks.

"That's a cliché question."

He shrugs. "It's a conversation starter."

"It is. Sorry. You're right." I smile.

After a bit more small talk, he studies me for a moment. "So…"—his voice lowers—"what do you say to dinner?"

"Um, like now?" I ask, hating how croaky my voice sounds.

"Sure. I could use a bite to eat, and I'd prefer to dine in the company of a…"

"Of a?" I prompt.

"Of an attractive woman." He smiles.

"Okay. Um…" Am I brain-dead? I can't believe how stupid I've become. *He's asking you out on a date, silly.*

Dorian's dark eyes meet mine, waiting for my answer.

"I am rather hungry. And I also shouldn't keep drinking on an empty stomach," I say at last. "But on one condition."

"What's that?" he asks.

"That you let me pay for myself."

"I just made a million dollars this week." His mouth curls at one end.

"Good for you," I reply coolly.

He sniffs, which is the closest he's come to laughing. "Hey, I wasn't bragging. I'm just saying I'd love to buy you dinner and that I can afford it. No strings attached. Promise."

I laugh at his scout's honor gesture and open my hands. "As long as you're not expecting anything more than just a dinner companion, then why not? Beats picking up a pizza on the way home."

"I'm sure we can do better than that," he says, rising from his stool. "Shall we?" He extends his arm to me.

I straighten my skirt, wishing I'd chosen something a little more flattering than a black skirt and a faux silk beige top. A bit drab for a dinner date with a man who has success woven into his bespoke jacket.

Even his confident stride is that of a man about to take over the world.

There's a debate raging, though, as I follow him out. Should I run?

For a thirty-two-year-old who hasn't been on a date in months, the answer is a resounding no.

It's not apathy that has led to my sad dating history; it's more that New York is full of commitment-phobic men. Not that he's said as much, but

I can only assume it's the same for Dorian too. When you look like that, you can get any girl you want.

It's about time I let my hair down and played a little, regardless.

TWO

Six months later...

Dorian is scrolling through his phone when I arrive. It's our six-month anniversary, and he suggested we dine at the same Japanese restaurant where we had our first date. It's such a romantic gesture, and I'm bubbling over with anticipation. He's the one who remembered; it hadn't even occurred to me to mark the calendar. If I'm being honest, I didn't expect that second date, let alone the many that followed. On our fifth date, we took things further, and I must say it's been nice having someone to cuddle with at night. I was about to buy myself a dog for that purpose when Dorian came along and swept me off my feet.

Lately, he's been asking where I see myself in a few years and what I'm seeking from life—big philosophical questions that warrant far-reaching answers. I kept it simple and said I'd like to start a family one day.

Like really soon.

Reluctant to sound desperate, I kept that part to myself.

So far, I've just been going along with things. He calls the shots, and I'm happy to be there as his smiling girlfriend. We're exclusive; he made that clear the first night we slept together when he stated that he didn't share.

I almost laughed at the insinuation that I might be running around with other men since he's the first man I've slept with in years. I shared that embarrassing detail, and he looked pleased, even admitting that he couldn't see himself staying with a woman who'd had many boyfriends.

I'd always viewed my lack of sexual experience as a sign of failure, but as an open-minded person, I found Dorian's intolerant views on past sexual partners a bit dated. I kept that to myself because I felt blessed that he'd chosen me.

Now, most nights I'm at his apartment, where I've even learned to keep things tidy given his aversion to clutter and mess.

Not a hair out of place, he looks up from his phone. Having removed his jacket, he's wearing a fitted shirt that shows off those well-defined muscles he works hard for. He's a gym junkie. I'm not. But hey, opposites attract, don't they?

Dorian sets his phone down. "I took the liberty of ordering."

"Yes, sorry. You got my message?" I take a seat.

He nods. "It's fine. I've had a few things to deal with."

His smile's tight, indicating that something's on his mind. To describe Dorian as intense would be an understatement. He always has some plan, which is to be expected since he's ambitious. At night, he works while I watch TV or read. Dorian doesn't mind; he says it relaxes him to be around a woman who isn't running around or glued to social media.

The waiter brings out our food, and we eat in hungry silence. It was yet another big day at work. I didn't even have time for lunch. It's getting me down, and I want out.

He looks up at me, and I smile. I'm in love. Who would have thought that six months ago I'd be admitting that?

Sure, he isn't the greatest communicator, but after a few drinks, Dorian loosens up and talks about his life working on Wall Street and how he's about to start a new business in the wellness industry. It's all interesting to me, I'm a good listener. I have, however, stopped asking questions about his childhood after he looked uncomfortable and quickly changed the subject whenever his boyhood home in Queens came up.

It take some effort to get him to share where he came from. Perhaps he's ashamed of his humble beginnings, especially now that he's a rising star on Wall Street. All I know is that he was raised by a single mother.

At some point, I hope to get a clearer picture, but I'm not pushy when it comes to people, even though Dorian is more than just a friend.

"I think we're doing well, aren't we?" he asks.

Munching on sushi, which suddenly triggers a volcanic reaction in my nasal passages, I nod and grimace simultaneously.

His brows knit together.

"Sorry. Wasabi." I chuckle. "And yes, I love being with you. I feel blessed."

That's me gushing a bit, but it's how I feel. While Dorian isn't great at expressing his feelings, I make up for it by telling him how I feel—almost daily. And as I mentioned earlier, opposites attract. We keep each other grounded. Sure, Dorian makes all the decisions about where to eat and what shows to watch, but as someone who's pathologically indecisive, I don't mind.

"I was just thinking, after our last talk, how we share similar values and ambitions. I want a family. I'm ready for that now. I enjoy being with you and you enjoy being with me." He takes a sip of wine and clears his throat.

My heart races, and anticipation flushes through me.

Is he about to propose?

It certainly sounds that way. I can already envision streamers, balloons, and champagne corks whizzing through the air. Though I'd prefer a more elegant reception, that's just my wild imagination breaking out into a dance.

He reaches into his pocket and hands me a small red velvet box.

I open the box, and there it is, glistening like one of those evening stars that takes my breath away—only this is tangible and mine.

The emerald is surrounded by a cluster of diamonds, embodying an exquisite classic style.

Left speechless, I finally manage to say, "It's beautiful."

"I thought it would match your eyes." He gives me a half-smile.

I love that he even knows my eye color, let alone that he bought me what looks like—cue internal gleeful scream—an engagement ring.

"Is this what I think it is?" I ask.

He nods and takes my hand. "I believe we make a good couple. You've mentioned wanting children sooner rather than later, and I feel the same. I want all of that. I want a family. I'm financially secure, and you won't want for anything. I'd like you to stay at home to raise our children. I don't want to marry a career woman."

Our eyes meet. He's unapologetic about what some might consider demeaning. But I'm too happy to object. Sure, I know women at work who would walk away in protest at such a proposition, but not me. Being a housewife sounds perfect; it's music to my ears. I love to bake, and I adore the idea of running a beautiful home.

I smile. "That sounds marvelous."

"Then it's a yes?" He cocks his head.

"It's a big, happy yes." I lean over and hug him.

On our way back to his apartment, he says, "I'd prefer a quick wedding. Nothing fussy. How does next week sound?"

My neck cracks as I turn to face him. "Oh? That soon?"

"You don't want that?" he asks.

Thoughts of the past decade—grinding away as a PA, earning crumbs for endless hours—flash through my mind.

I smile back. "I'm more than ready for this."

He takes my hand and kisses it. "So am I."

I cuddle up to him and link my arm to his. "I love you. I'm so happy."

He squeezes my hand, and I'm nearly in tears. Life is smiling at me. This is all I've ever wanted. And to think I almost declined his dinner offer six months ago.

THREE

The honeymoon suite feels like something out of a dream—a secluded luxury resort nestled amid the pristine turquoise shores of Cancun. Floaty curtains flutter in the breeze as the salt air mingles with the scent of jasmine, while the crash of waves echoes in the background. The resort sprawls across acres of lush tropical gardens, where palm trees sway in the gentle ocean breeze, and a floral scent fills the air.

Shirtless and barefoot, Dorian pads around in off-white drawstring linen pants, looking tanned and healthy. I can't take my eyes off him, and I find myself smiling a lot.

"Hey," he says, taking a swig from a water bottle.

"Everything okay?" I ask, watching him move around the large room decorated in blue and white. He fits the scene perfectly and would make an excellent model for a 'Holiday in Heaven' advertisement.

Dorian runs a hand through his hair. "No." He gives me a strained smile.

"Oh? Do you want to talk about it?" I open the glass door to let, in a gentle breeze. It's only morning, but the humidity is thick.

Dorian hates air conditioning. He says it dries out his sinuses. I'm fine with the sea breeze, and he's right—it is healthier.

I go to hug him, and at first, his body stiffens, but soon he relaxes. I suppose this whole work thing is stressing him out.

He pulls away from me and lifts his finger. "Just a few calls."

Before I can respond, he pulls out his phone and heads outside toward the pool.

I decide to go for a dip in the ocean and change into a bikini and a silky cover-up.

I call out to him, "Just off for a swim. I can't tempt you?" I give him a flirtatious smile.

He shakes his head. "I'll stick to the pool, I think. But hey, enjoy." He looks down at his phone again.

An hour later, after a refreshing swim in the crystal-clear turquoise sea, I enter our room through the gate and use the outdoor shower to wash off the sand. The sun beats down on my pale skin, reminding me to cover myself in sunscreen for the afternoon sunbathing. I try not to stay out in the sun too long, but I do love the warmth on my skin. It must be all the serotonin release, something Dorian alluded to yesterday while he sunbathed. Opting for the sensible route, I'm inclined to remain in the shade given my lily-white skin.

Rubbing my hair with a towel, I enter through the balcony door only to find the room empty.

Dorian is in the other room, still on his phone. I go to the fridge, remove the glass container of fruit salad, and dish some out. Since my husband, who gets jittery over sugary snacks, isn't here, I indulge in the ice cream.

Dorian walks in and nods. "Good swim?" he asks, heading for the fridge to grab another bottle of water. I've never seen anyone drink this much water, but according to him, it's a good way to flush out toxins.

Before Dorian, I never really thought much about healthy eating. I always had home-cooked meals growing up, so I've always eaten well. And although I enjoy sugary snacks, I don't seem to gain weight for some reason—must be my nervous disposition. I read somewhere that thinking burns calories. That explains a lot. While others bound about in activewear, I tend to overthink.

"The water is so warm, and it feels wonderful. You should try it," I say.

He shakes his head. "I'm good. I prefer the pool."

Dorian is scared of sharks, something he hinted at after a few drinks. But he hates showing weakness or fear, so I don't dwell on it, having learned the hard way. A few days ago, when we arrived, I joked about his shark phobia, and his mood soured; he went quiet.

"How about lunch at that nice café we spotted yesterday?" I ask.

"Sure." He drains the bottle of water and wipes his mouth. "Just give me an hour or so. I've still got a few calls to make."

My shoulders slump. I hope I don't have to eat alone, like yesterday. "Dorian, it's our honeymoon."

He smiles and strokes my arm. This is his first hint of affection today, other than the early morning sex, which was more athletic than tender.

"I'll make it quick." He returns to the other room, where I hear him speaking in hushed tones.

The little I know involves a business colleague and legal issues. Dorian has kept it vague. I sense he isn't in the mood to share.

Our wedding was rushed and bare—no friends, just us and the officiant in an empty room. Our vows echoed off the walls like hollow promises.

That's how it replays in my mind now.

At the time, I kept reminding myself that this was going to work. Those big, expensive, chintzy weddings with tons of friends cheering were something that twenty-somethings did, not mature couples. Whether thirty-two is mature is up for debate, but Dorian at forty certainly qualifies.

Even so, I would have preferred a bigger event, despite Dorian's insistence on keeping things low-key. There had been an issue at his firm—a colleague under investigation, someone he worked with on Wall Street. I sense that's what all these recent calls are about.

It had been a difficult month, I admit, but still, a wedding would have been nice, as my disappointed mother expressed.

As I stare out the floor-to-ceiling windows at our infinity pool that seems to spill into the vivid blue horizon, I push away negative thoughts and envision a bright future, setting up a beautiful home I can call my own.

And now here we are at this five-star resort nestled right on the beach, where time feels like it has stopped. We hopped off the endless Ferris wheel of life in New York, where I escaped a job I had grown to despise. In many ways, Dorian saved me because I never saw myself as a ladder climber.

This is our third night here, and it has been dreamy, to be sure. I've enjoyed sleeping in—at least I have. Dorian is an early-morning kind of guy who loves to jog. Having turned over a new leaf, he's into his routines.

Marriage. Healthy food. He has ditched the heavy drinking and partying, all part and parcel of working on Wall Street.

It's now early evening. I glance over at my new husband, who is sitting on the edge of the bed, tapping away on his phone. Deep in concentration, he furrows his brow. He has spent the past few hours pacing, holding the phone to his ear, looking stressed about something. To be honest, it's the first time since arriving that I have begun to question things.

That thought passes quickly, though, because I want this marriage to work. I love my new husband.

I just need to ensure he stays happy, as Dorian has a long list of needs—some of which I am only just beginning to learn about. These include not swearing, dressing modestly, and maintaining a pristine, clean house.

He hates mess. He's always moving my things into a neat little pile, which leaves me searching for items I thought I had placed elsewhere. The benches need to be constantly wiped, and coasters are essential. He keeps setting my glasses on one, and those pesky watery rings make him twitch. But then again, we all have our quirks, and I can learn to be tidier. After all, I'm not being asked to memorize the periodic table.

I'm hungry. It's after eight, and I'm wondering about the candlelight dinner he promised.

Right now, Dorian is on his phone again.

I get he has responsibilities but on our honeymoon?

Isn't this meant to be our time? Our beginning to forever?

Okay, that might be a tad idealistic, but my parents have been married forever, so it's not an unrealistic expectation.

Pushing away my doubts, I remind myself of Dorian's commitments. A millionaire doesn't just get rich from working nine to five.

But on his honeymoon?

I walk to the balcony and indulge in a massage from the balmy night air. Stars sparkle in the early twilight like diamonds sinking into a silky turquoise sky.

I breathe deeply, asking the spirits what awaits me. I'm excited about my future. I'm sure that this is just a blip.

This troubled colleague of Dorian's is hopefully in the past. I never liked Brendan. He talks endlessly about himself and is always looking for his next big deal, shamelessly networking with anyone willing to listen.

Now I'm wondering if he sold any of his shady investment schemes to people I know. He was always around.

I pray not.

He even met my parents. Oh my god, I hope not.

I push that disturbing thought aside and soak in the idyllic beach scene around me as a pair of lovers, probably newlyweds—this *is* the honeymoon resort, after all— walk barefoot on the sand hand in hand.

Dorian also has an aversion to sand, which I discovered after he refused to remove his deck shoes and spent a good amount of time wiping off every speck of sand.

I turn my attention back to the room, studying my husband and hoping that he'll look up and give me one of his rare smiles. He doesn't smile much and isn't very affectionate, but I've grown accustomed to initiating hugs.

He's focused intently on his feet, deeply engaged in a conversation, speaking in a strained tone as if he's trying hard to keep from yelling.

My stomach tightens a little, robbing me of my appetite.

I'm not one to create a scene, but I can't help thinking, yet again, "What about me?"

Instead, I walk over and tap his shoulder with a teasing smile to remind him I'm waiting.

He lowers his phone. "Just a second. It won't be long. This is important."

Sitting beside him, I rub his back. His skin feels warm, and his shirt is slightly damp. I can't tell if it's sweat from stress or just the humidity.

He ends the call and forces a smile.

"Is everything okay?" I ask.

"Just another call. I promise it will be the last one."

Before I can respond, he presses a button on his phone, and I feel like I've lost him again.

Resigned to more delay, I return to the balcony and gaze up at the dark blue sky, where a silvery crescent moon shines like a jewel in the galaxy.

A cold wind sweeps through me, despite the warm night.

After a late-night dinner and some rushed lovemaking, I'm awakened early next morning by Dorian talking on his phone outside on the balcony.

I rise, take a quick shower, and help myself to coffee.

On the table lies a newspaper with the headline, "Leading Wall Street Investment Guru Convicted of a Ponzi Scheme." I read the first paragraph and discover that he owes people over a hundred million dollars.

Dorian ends his call and joins me, giving me a gentle peck on the cheek. It's not a passionate greeting, but it's nice nonetheless. I'll take what I can get from my reserved husband.

I lift my coffee cup, which has left a wet ring on the table, and just as I pull an apologetic smile, he slides over a coaster.

"Is everything okay?" I ask.

He swiftly removes the paper from the table.

"I see Brendan's been convicted," I continue, despite his obvious reluctance to discuss it.

"Let's not talk about that." He rubs his neck. "There's a bike trail I've discovered. How about some bike riding?" Though the sudden shift in subject is a bit jarring, at least he seems more upbeat.

I shrug. "Sure." I would have preferred lounging by the pool or taking another dip in the ocean, but I keep reminding myself that it's fine for married couples to enjoy different hobbies.

He opens his laptop. "Hey, come and have a look."

I lean over his shoulder and peer at a stunning two-story colonial home, similar to my parents'.

"Do you like it?" he asks, scrolling through more images of the house. "The back has a modern wing attached."

I nod as I study the square, ultramodern minimalist design that overlooks an infinity pool, a stark contrast to the house's classic wooden façade. "It's lovely."

"Good. I just bought it. For us." He wears a bright smile like we've won the lottery.

"Oh?" I thought that was something we could decide together. "Where?" I finally ask.

"LA."

This is news to me. During dinner last night, our conversation was about health supplements and favorite movies—not about moving to LA.

"But what about New York and your career?"

"I'm over the finance industry and hedge funds." He removes a bottle of water from the fridge. "I'm setting up a company with a new business partner."

"Oh?"

He gulps down half the bottle, wipes his lips, and says, "In the wellness industry."

As I nod pensively, he adds, "Don't worry. I've got enough stocks and blue-chip investments to keep us going for ten lifetimes."

Yes, well, I know he's worth half a billion dollars. When Dorian proposed, he showed me his account, which I thought was strange, but I just went with it. I wasn't sure what to say. Then he took me into his arms, and that was all that mattered to me.

I fell in love then, and I plan to stay in love, despite our obvious differences.

FOUR

Three years later

Tonight's *that* night. The time of the month when the magic of conception might happen.

Who would have thought getting pregnant could be so stressful?

It seems that the stork has forgotten our address.

Where's Dorian? I'm wearing my new green lace lingerie, which is scratching into me. But I'm ready to do what it takes to get my husband aroused. He's not that easily aroused these days.

Positioned on the side of the bed, doing my utmost to look alluring, I'm tired. I just want to go to sleep.

When did sex become such a chore?

Blame it on that pesky four-year clause.

We have a prenup. And yes, I get it; my husband's a multi-millionaire, and they're all the rage. But still, it hurt a little. As a romantic at heart, I see a marriage contract as more of a business arrangement.

Don't get me wrong, I love my life. I love being married and my beautiful home here on Marigold Boulevard.

Time's ticking, though, and the weight of expectation hangs heavily on me.

When Dorian proposed, I had stars in my eyes. I was marrying a rich, handsome, ambitious guy. What else could matter? Well, sure, affection, but I was in love. Am I still in love? Some days I am.

The little affection Dorian showed then has all but disappeared.

He never talks about his mother, and whenever I ask about his life growing up, he changes the subject. I sense something is broken there for sure, which is heartbreaking because I want him to be happy within himself.

He rarely smiles now, though he didn't exactly exude a jolly side when we first met either.

We're at least building a life together, I guess. As for the rest? We put on a good show when others are around.

I pad outside and head to my husband's study—Dorian's personal space. I go to knock on the door when I hear heavy breathing. The kind that should be happening in our bedroom.

Curiosity getting the better of me, I quietly open the door, and there is my dear husband masturbating to an image of a woman bouncing her very large breasts in her hands. If it weren't so shocking, I'd laugh. Instead, I bite my lip to stifle a gasp.

Tears burn in my eyes as I tiptoe away.

Yes, I could get all confrontational and storm in. But that's not my style. Any hint of a fight and I go and hide, which is not some emotional hangover from a sad childhood. I had a healthy upbringing if anything.

I return to the bedroom, bury my head in the pillow, and scream. I've been doing a lot of that lately.

Dorian suddenly enters the room, and I quickly readjust my position on the bed into seduction mode. Not something I'm feeling, especially after seeing the breasty brunette turning my husband on. I'm the absolute opposite of her.

He strips out of his gray Lululemon sweatpants, and I force a smile that is so plastic I might melt from burning frustration.

I pat the bed. "It's that time." My lips tremble. This whole fake act is twisting me inside out.

He comes toward me, fully erect, which has little to do with my lacy negligee. We all know what's gotten him all hot and steamy.

Dorian gestures for me to turn around, and I'm not about to complain. If entering me from behind produces that elusive super baby, then I'm happy to comply.

Huffing and puffing, Dorian charges in and pumps away. The sex borders on painful, but like a compliant fifties wife, I take all of him. At least he's not well-endowed—a fact that riles him. Among his eighty or so supplements that take up an entire cupboard, I've seen pills purported to lengthen a man's penis. It's laughable, if not a little sad.

After ten minutes of humping and pumping, much to my relief, he comes.

I go to lie down when he points to the wall. "Prop your legs up."

Stretching my legs against the cold wall, I grudgingly obey, though I'm smiling, of course. I always smile.

I'm stuck here for ten minutes, and my lower back starts to ache. A wife has to do what a wife has to do, especially when there's very little choice. And apart from this, my life is perfect. Isn't it?

I've made some close friends while living on Magnolia Boulevard, and while I don't mind people gushing over what a perfect couple Dorian and I make, deep down, I'd swap all of that in a heartbeat for the real thing.

So why am I still here?

As is the case with unhappy marriages, the answer is complicated.

Wait, wasn't I happy a minute ago? Well, yes, that's the version I stick to because I can't exactly walk around looking miserable, but this is me now talking. The real me.

After ten minutes, I lower my fatigued legs and join my snoring husband in bed.

I remove earplugs from my drawer and pop them in. I hate how they make me feel claustrophobic, but I've learned to tolerate them—just one of those petty annoyances you get used to when living in close quarters with someone.

The following morning, after a restless sleep, I wait until Dorian's out the door for his morning run before heading to his study. The door's locked, but I know where to find the key. I've done this before, after I heard him one night. At first, I thought he was having a stroke, but then I put two and two together, and well, surprise! My husband uses internet porn to get aroused. "Welcome to married life," a phone tarot reader said.

I hate sharing the unflattering details of my seemingly perfect marriage with friends.

Self-pity doesn't become me, and I'm not one to wallow. I always remind myself to look at the positives and not dwell on what's missing, as Hecate, my phone counselor, advised me to do in her soothing tone.

There are also my neighbors, who drool with envy whenever they see me with Dorian. We must be doing something right.

Acting was never my thing, but I'm a quick learner. The character I embody is a happy-go-lucky housewife. I've given them no reason to doubt that. So when things go sideways, I call a psychic. I know it sounds a little loopy, and it's something I would never have once entertained. I'm not heavily into the stars, though I'm an airheaded Libra, apparently, and yes, I do fit the profile—especially the part about giving people the benefit of the doubt due to persistent indecision.

Psychics, I've found, are more in tune with the emotional side of things, and they cut to the chase. None of that fiddling around with childhood memories and dream analysis. Though most of the time, the psychics' advice is so glaringly obvious it borders on cliché, I still walk away a little less stressed after a chat with Lunaria Starchild, Hecate Beltane, or some other pagan name. One even predicted Dorian's porn addiction.

Is it an addiction? He's certainly addicted to having everything perfect and in its place—wife included.

I walk into his study, decorated with sporting memorabilia, trophies, fake college certificates, and very little else. Volumes of health-related books sit on dark wooden shelves, no doubt informing his wellness fixation, which keeps the bank balance rising exponentially as he peddles all kinds of life-boosting supplements.

This snooping around Dorian's personal space isn't new for me. Despite that, adrenaline eggs me on as I approach the mahogany desk. I just need to see what my husband gets up to and what type of woman arouses him.

The PIN is easy enough to guess. It's the year of his birth, and—what have we here? He hasn't even cleared his browser.

I scroll down sites like "Busty Horny Babes" and "Hungry Hot Fucks." Wow, subtle.

The video comes up, and I click on the arrow. The woman is sitting with her legs apart, naked in every sense. The only body hair is on her head—thick, dark, and tumbling down her voluptuous backside.

She couldn't be more different from me. While I'm red-headed, a size ten, and small-breasted, she's brunette, olive-skinned, possibly a size twelve, with enormous fake boobs that resemble balls jiggling beneath a layer of skin.

As I keep scrolling through his browser history, I discover a ton of similar types.

I sigh. Now I know why he's not so aroused whenever I prance around in skimpy lingerie. Our sex life has always been a little beige. Don't get me wrong; I'm fine with vanilla. It's a nice flavor.

Oops, there's the sound of the door opening. He's back from his run.

I quietly sneak out and lock the door. My heart races in rhythm with Dorian's panting as he jogs up the stairs.

He sees me and nods.

He's not a "Good morning" sort of guy.

I paint a warm smile. "Good run?"

Nodding, he moves past me. "Just going to shower and then I'm off."

"Do you want me to whip up your green juice?"

Dorian's morning smoothie involves shoving a bunch of kale into the blender with two cups of berries. Maybe he was a rabbit in his former life, I tell myself, which always makes me chuckle as I watch the juice turn swampy green.

In the same way Dorian insists on keeping up his fiber intake, I keep my humor up for sanity's sake.

"How's the maid hunt going?" he asks.

"It's happening." I smile.

Off he goes. Short little sentences. We don't really do conversation—only at dinner parties. That's for show. Like me, he likes the world to see that he is living a perfect life in the suburbs.

FIVE

It is late evening, and Dorian's asleep in his study. I know he's working around the clock on some new super-supplement that's meant to renew cells and add years to our lives.

I peek in, and there he is, asleep in his chair, mouth wide open, laptop illuminated.

Unable to resist the urge to spy, I head for the history button. Dorian is hopeless at clearing his browser. I was never like this, but since I found him playing with himself while staring at some busty woman on the screen, I've found it difficult to stay away.

Festa Latina comes up, and I can just imagine.

Some busty brunette is being rammed from behind by a very large penis. The man's head is out of frame, though her face is exposed, groaning and moaning. If it weren't so sad, I'd laugh.

"What are you doing?" Dorian jolts awake.

I jump back. Why am I acting like the guilty one here?

"Just that you were asleep, and when your computer came on, I went to shut it down."

"You're spying." He snaps the laptop shut.

"Why can't you sleep in our bed? Am I that repugnant?" I ask. "And now I discover this." I point at the laptop.

"You shouldn't be snooping."

"But you're cheating." My heart clenches. I hate arguments.

Leaning back in his chair, he shrugs like I've accused him of something trivial, like leaving a wet towel on the bed. "It's the internet. Pop-ups and whatnot. You know how it is. It's not cheating. It's just porn. Everyone does it."

"Married men don't."

Shaking his head, he responds with a cold laugh, like I'm some naïve child who has yet to learn about the realities of life. "Maybe focus on something that matters, like getting pregnant."

My eyes burn as I fight back tears. I'm trying to remain calm, but the fire in my belly has turned me into a nervous wreck. Control and emotion are as compatible as a newly divorced couple. "This matters, Dorian. You getting off on porn fucking matters."

He points into my face. "Don't use that tone with me." He rises and rakes back his hair. "You like making problems when there aren't any."

Pushing past me, he leaves me standing there, stunned.

Why am I feeling like I'm the one that's in the wrong?

Shouldn't I be screaming at him?

The prenup flashes before me. That four-year clause is coming up, and my ovaries are not complying. It's me. Because Dorian had his sperm checked, and he's apparently virile. That put a smile on his face.

Of course, when I enter the bedroom, he's fast asleep. No apology for watching porn or even promising to not do it again.

The next morning, I'm in the kitchen making Dorian's favorite juice when he appears. The living area's a mess, and he's edgy.

Our last maid just walked out after Dorian complained about his juice. It's quite a fastidious process for sure. The drink must have the same amount of kiwi and açai, along with some twenty other ingredients.

"Have you called the agency for a new maid?" he asks.

I chop up some kiwi as he watches me, making me nervous. I forgot to put on gloves.

"I'm interviewing today."

"No males this time," he says.

I resist the urge to roll my eyes. The best helper we've had to date was a young guy who was gay and very much on the ball. I liked Pierre; he was also great for a chat. A little like our new gardener, Jarrad.

Jarrad is a bit nicer to look at and built like an Adonis, but I digress.

Dorian, who's homophobic, I suspect, protested, and poor Pierre was out the door within two days.

"I've requested women only," I say.

"Good, employ one. ASAP. The place is a pigsty. What do you do all day? Do I have to start making lists for you?"

I bite my tongue. He's treating me more like an imbecile than a wife.

I do plenty, I think to myself. I bake. I read. Catch up with the neighbors and chat with Jarrad while he's weeding.

Dorian sips his juice and nods. "Better."

"I'm glad," I say with a phony smile. I hug him, and he softens in my arms, which goes a long way to ease the rising tension between us.

He pulls away and says, "Look, about last night. It was from the past. I used to check out some porn sites." He wears a tight smile.

I knit my fingers. This is Dorian's first-ever apology. If that's what it is. "I get that a lot of men do it, but it did hurt."

"I'll be sure to remove it from my computer."

I could bring up how I caught him masturbating that time, but I hold back. He's at least trying, and apologizing doesn't come naturally to Dorian. Besides, I'm allergic to arguments and conflict in general. I'm that person who takes the blame if only to keep everyone happy.

But this situation is wearing me down.

Some days, I just want to walk away. Two million can do a lot. And sure, a good lawyer could argue that internet porn is cheating, but that's going down a grubby road.

The problem is that two million may not be enough. There is a fresh complication. I've only just discovered that my parents have lost everything to some shady investment scheme they bought into three years ago, peddled to them by Brendan Crib, Dorian's former colleague, who's now rotting in prison. They kept it from me because they didn't want to worry me. But it came out in a conversation with my mother, and now I'm sending money to keep them going.

"I won't be back until late." He looks down at his watch, and off he goes.

Taking a deep breath, I have to accept that this is as good as this marriage will ever get, especially now that my parents need financial support and I'm the only one who can help.

After a morning of staring at the wall and contemplating how to rewrite my life, I open the door for the first interview of the day.

The home-help agency has sent three women.

The first candidate is barely out of high school and spends the entire twenty minutes glued to her phone. She's an immediate no.

The next woman is in her thirties and comes with excellent references. She is an obvious choice, and I almost offer her the job on the spot. But then, a knock comes at the door, and the third candidate arrives much earlier than expected.

"Oh, I see you're still interviewing," she says.

"One more, but I'm impressed with your references, and you seem perfect. Just give me a few hours. Is that okay? This is just a formality."

"Good. Sure. I'd love to work here," she replies as I walk her to the door.

"I'll be in touch," I say.

As the two women cross paths, the contrast between them is striking—like comparing a beauty queen to a plain Jane.

And yes, plain Jane is where one should place their bets. However, as the young, dark-haired beauty—the third candidate—steps through the door, I change my mind.

SIX

EMILY, MY NEIGHBOR, IS always the first to arrive. Tonight, she's wearing one of her mother's hand-me-downs, I imagine. I'm told her mother was a B-grade actress who passed down her clothes to her one and only daughter.

Emily steps into the hallway wearing a blinding smile as though we haven't seen each other for a while, which isn't the case since it was only a day ago that we chatted while collecting the mail.

A couple of years on, the book club consists of six of my neighbors.

I love my books. I'm not sure if all the participants are as keen, though, judging by the fact that book talk lasts about five minutes before we launch into a night of drinking, snacking, and endless gossip. If I were being completely honest, this little regular get-together is more of a sex-in-the-suburbs symposium than an actual book club, but none of us care to admit that.

Since moving to LA three years ago, I've tried to embrace suburban life as a normal housewife who blends in with the roses and pretty façades.

Emily pecks me on the cheek, leaving behind a ghastly cheap scent.

"Money does not equate to taste," my mom used to say. And since moving here from New York, I've noticed how this area is awash with tacky, overpriced statements. But I always smile. That's all it takes. A smile. Say nice things, and everything rolls along smoothly. On the face of it, that is. Behind one's back, well, I can only imagine. And I'm not exactly that sweet, all-accepting housewife I've been parading around as these past few years.

Tonight is all about fun and showing my gal pals how good my life is. Power comes from putting your best foot forward and showing your best face.

People hate whining. And while a problem shared might be a problem solved, no amount of discussion can slow down the ticking clock. In my case, I'm staring down the barrel at our four-year marriage mark. Only one year to go.

"I'm the first, as always," Emily says with a giggle. Her nose scrunches sweetly. She is the picture of a small-town girl—at least on the outside. Like me, she's hiding things about her so-called perfect marriage.

"Then you're the first to try my latest batch of cupcakes. I'm trying out a new recipe," I say, directing her into the front room, freshly painted in a pretty salmon shade. The room is only used for visitors and book club nights.

Her face lights up. Emily is quite a sugar addict. But then, I think we all are, except for Sophia, who avoids sugar. Denying herself one of the finer culinary pleasures, all because she wants to live well and into old age. That's my husband too. In his case, just the mere whiff of sugar makes him nearly have a panic attack, fearing his cells are turning cancerous just from being in the same room. A slight exaggeration, but he is a serious health freak. There are always two meals prepared at night—one with carbs and one without to observe his strict keto diet. That's whenever he is home for the evening meal, which is rare. His 'Never Say Die' company keeps him out and about in the evenings. Doing what, I can't exactly say.

He wasn't a health fanatic in New York, though.

He once admitted, while wooing me, that I was part of his fresh start—chosen for both my mind and looks. I wouldn't describe myself as pretty, more that I possess regular white features, the type of looks he wants for his children. Racist, for sure. But I keep that close to my flattish chest.

The doorbell rings, and Ana, our new maid, ushers in Sophia, who lives across the road in an impeccably restored American colonial. Possessing exotic Italian looks and curves in all the right places on a firm yoga body, she's stylish and loves exploiting her assets in figure-hugging clothes.

"Hey, y'all," her voice booms as she moves around the room to give hugs.

Before long, the others arrive, and the room is alive with laughter, chatter, and exuberance.

We meet once a month to talk about some book that most pretend to read. But hey, I don't mind. I'm not pushy when it comes to people's habits.

In addition to our monthly get-together, I see each of the women quite regularly. They often drop in for a coffee or something stronger.

Whoever said life in the suburbs is dull has not lived on Marigold Boulevard—a tree-lined strip of prime American colonials and flourishing gardens maintained by eye-candy gardeners. The wives do the employing, I'm told, just as I did when I employed our equally hot gardener. I've become rather partial to relaxing by the pool, watching the shirtless gardener prune the roses, or offering him my freshly baked cupcakes, which he is always eager to savor.

In reality, people's lives can be quite fascinating—once you filter out the overblown talk about their kids' academic successes. I mean, who wants to learn that Marly got an A for writing a short story about an alien who looks like Mickey Mouse or that little Alexis can sing Taylor Swift under the table?

Yes, I know, maybe I'm a little upset that my ovaries are not responding to Dorian's seed and producing an equally astounding little human. But I do love a good chat and always have a fresh batch of cupcakes ready to please. Apart from Isabella, who feels the need to go to confession after weakening at the sight of a cupcake, and Sophia's monk-like discipline at abstaining from sweets, the others gush madly over my little sugary treats, and the tray is always empty by the time they leave.

While some might feel pride at being praised for writing a great book or performing a song in perfect pitch, for me, it comes from people appreciating my baking.

Sophia hands over a bottle of Prosecco to Ana, who helps pour for everyone. Our new maid is a godsend. I don't even have to ask, and she's always there—efficient beyond expectation. The best maid we've had by far.

Sophia smiles at Ana. "You're new. I don't remember seeing you here last month."

The maid returns a faint smile and then leaves us to it as the women all turn and watch her go.

I know exactly what they're thinking, and of course, Olivia, who recently divorced and reminds me of Julia Roberts on a bad day, asks, "She's your new maid?"

The surprise in her voice makes me want to laugh.

I gesture for her to keep it down.

She bites her lip. "Sorry, me and my big mouth."

Yep, she's got that right.

Olivia's story is kind of sad. Her ex-husband is a Hollywood scriptwriter with a penchant for younger women. And believe me, I hear about it nonstop. I just wear a 'you poor thing' frown and feed her enough endorphin-stimulating cupcakes to have her leave in a happier mood.

Ana returns with the refreshments, and again the room's attention follows her out.

After she leaves, Emily looks at Claire, who lives two doors down and is one of only two in our group who aren't married. Not that she's looking. If anything, like Natalie, the rebellious one among us, she doesn't believe in it.

They keep things fresh. I mean, who likes clones?

"Should she be dressed like that?" Emily asks about the maid's very skimpy outfit.

Claire just shrugs like it's not that big a deal.

Olivia nods in agreement with Emily. "Yeah, I mean, Linley, you should get her to dress appropriately."

I open my hands. "What do you mean?"

Olivia shakes her head in disbelief. "Hello, tits hanging out. I mean, she's got great tits. I'd kill for breasts like that, but still. And a short skirt."

Emily nods. "I know I'd hate it."

Natalie shakes her head and opens her palms in protest. "Hello, this is LA. Have you seen what they're wearing in the supermarkets?"

"You're not married, darling. Imagine if your husband came home to someone like her, bending over and serving a nice big eyeful of young, firm skin," Isabella says.

The women all nod, except Natalie, who has never even lived with a boyfriend, so I suspect she hasn't watched the man she's meant to spend her life with going soft in the head over some pretty, young, and curvaceous thing.

"I'd get her to cover up at least a little," says Sophia. "I know I can trust Tony; he's so devoted." She giggles. "But she's gorgeous, Lin."

I shrug. "Good help is hard to find. I've had a few come and go. And Dorian is hardly ever home at night, so he doesn't see her that often."

That's not true. I think about last weekend. It was hot, and I allowed Ana to have a swim before leaving for the day. Her bikini barely held her in. And I noticed Dorian getting a little flushed.

Ana arrives, and we all smile and zip it up on time as she carries in a tray of freshly baked cupcakes. The sugary vanilla aroma sends the room into a symphony of moans.

Claire, who's the easiest among the women regarding diet, takes a bite of one and says, "Oh my God, this is better than sex."

Everyone giggles. Claire is gay, and rumor has it that one champagne-fueled night, she hooked up with someone in our little group. Apparently, the woman in question had her first-ever orgasm, and well, maybe they're still at it. I'm sure it will come out soon. It always does.

"So, any news on Harris and what's her name?" Sophia asks Olivia.

We're all ears. Olivia's is the bitterest of divorces, and now that her ex has moved in with his twenty-eight-year-old former student, Olivia's already substantial alcohol intake has grown considerably. I always have to restock on vodka or gin after one of her impromptu afternoon visits.

Olivia gulps down her Prosecco like she's dying of thirst. "Well, you know how they're living in Venice in her rundown apartment?"

We all nod in unison.

"Jemma, that's her name..." She pours another drink. "I heard she's three months pregnant."

Sophia's jaw drops. "You're kidding. Oh, God."

Olivia drains her drink. "Harris called yesterday to say he couldn't pick up the boys from school. It was supposed to be his night with them. He was calling from the hospital."

We're all hanging on to her words as she pours another glass. She must have some Irish genes because she always seems sober to me—only her speech deteriorates, and she can get a bit dramatic.

"Jemma had a miscarriage while doing sweat yoga. What's that called again?"

"Torture yoga," Claire says in a droll tone.

"Bikram," Sophia corrects. "Oh, that's terrible."

Frowning in unison, we look at Olivia searching for an appropriate response, but Olivia's not showing anything but actual, dare I say, delight. What I'd call unabashed schadenfreude.

Maybe a slight exaggeration, but I'm good at reading people, and I don't see a hint of sympathy on her face.

"How long have you known that she was pregnant?" Natalie asks, brushing her blue-streaked hair away from her face.

Olivia taps her glass with long red nails. "Only a few days."

"How do you feel about that?" Claire asks.

"I'm relieved. I'm not ready for that whole extended family thing. Neither are the kids. They hate Jemma."

The room remains quiet for a moment while Claire and Natalie exchange a disapproving look. As vehement supporters of human rights, they're the ones who often correct us when we dip our manicured toes into the immoral complexity of bitter divorces, generally ending the discussion with a lecture on ethics. That's why serious bitching is reserved for individual afternoon drop-ins.

"It's still sad, though," Natalie says. "How's Harris taking it?"

Not one to fake emotion, unlike myself, Olivia pulls a satisfied smile at the mention of her ex, whom she is still madly in love with. Now that is what I call sad.

Divorce when couples are bored is annoying but necessary, and once the lawyer's feeding frenzy is over, it's all about a fresh new start. However, it's tragic when one partner is still in love.

"I haven't seen him. He only just called on the phone." She knits her fingers.

"Then maybe you should send her some flowers," Natalie suggests.

I swear I can hear a chorus of necks cracking as everyone turns to our youngish, unmarried neighbor, who shares her wealthy dead parents' home with a brother who's a crack addict.

"Are you mad?" Olivia says. "I can't stand her. This is the girl who came into my home and seduced my husband. They even slept in our bed." Her voice has gone up a register.

"That's awful. And yes, schadenfreude is well and truly justified in this situation," I say, rising to collect the book that we're meant to be discussing.

The sound of the front door opening catches my attention just as Emma admits with an apologetic smile that she couldn't get past chapter one of the romance novel selected for this month's discussion.

I wasn't expecting Dorian back so soon. At least this gives me a chance to parade my ideal husband a little. The women always ask after him but rarely see him.

My heart skips a beat, not so much from seeing him, like it once did, but in fear that the façade I've carefully crafted around my neighbors might reveal cracks. It is exhausting maintaining a happy, everything's-tickety-boo face all the time. But here goes.

"This is a surprise, darling. I thought you had a work function."

Dorian is immaculate in a crisp white shirt and slacks that fit him like a glove. All those hours spent in the gym, playing tennis, swimming, and going for jogs have paid off. His shirt strains against his well-defined chest. He's like one of those actors in soap operas—almost too handsome to be real. His light brown hair is perfectly coiffed, not a single strand out of place.

As he strides in, his calculating dark eyes scan the room. Vain to a fault, he thrives on the attention he attracts wherever he goes. I often catch him staring at himself in the mirror or a window.

The women turn, swooning a little as they smile back with admiration. He seems to have that effect on women, I've noticed.

"Hello, ladies," he says with a hint of charm as he walks confidently toward me. "Just popping in for a document I left in my study."

I return a saccharine smile, working overtime to maintain my doting wife façade.

"How was your day?" I ask.

"Productive."

He glances at the cupcakes on the coffee table stained with watery rings. Is that his jaw tensing?

Oops, I forgot to lay out the coasters. I sense it gnawing at him like an ingrown toenail. Normally, he points out little stains as though we're about to be invaded by flesh-eating microbes. Tonight, however, his unease is so subtle, I'm sure no one else notices.

The women are too busy admiring him, seeing how gushy they've become. Except for Claire and Natalie, of course.

I smooth down my hair as I produce the brightest smile from my happy-wife toolbox—one of many masks I've honed over the years. Playing my role to perfection, I allow affection to shine in my eyes.

He leans in, brushing his lips against my cheek, and to my female friends, it's a tender moment. To me, it's cold and rehearsed. I can feel the distance between us, the chasm growing wider every time we play out this charade.

He pulls away and glances at his watch. "I'll just be upstairs."

Five minutes later, he descends the stairs and kisses me on the cheek again. The damp mark from the earlier kiss is barely dry. "Back in a couple of hours."

In the beginning, I hated how little time we spent together, but now I find ways to amuse myself. To Dorian's way of thinking, the only way to make money is to work around the clock. It's paying off because every time he breathes, our bank balance rises exponentially.

"I'll leave you ladies to it," he says, flashing them one last perfect smile before he struts off.

The door closes behind him, and I take a deep breath. I'm getting good at pretending things are great when they're anything but.

SEVEN

The following morning, I'm up early, and like most mornings, I'm in the kitchen baking and humming along to Beyoncé in the background. There's nothing I enjoy more than pottering around the kitchen. As it is, I've already whipped up a batch of keto muffins for Dorian. He seemed to enjoy the last batch I made, so I've started to explore new recipes.

I remove the tray of muffins from the oven and fan the steam toward my nose, breathing in the enticing coconut-rich aroma. The recipe also includes blueberries and white keto-friendly chocolate chips.

A batch of regular chocolate cupcakes sits cooling on a tray, ready for icing. I grab a saucepan and pour in the ingredients. Icing is such an art form. My mother always said it can turn a basic cake mix into a masterpiece. I tend to agree.

Jarrad is always delighted to have one or three, and now there's Ana, who is more than welcome to them. She almost cried yesterday after I suggested she take some home to her partner.

Whether that emotional response is related to my generosity or the fact she lives with a brute, who deserves, in my humble opinion, poisoning and not spoiling, I'm not sure. I don't know if he's bad, but I've noticed bruises on Ana's arm now and then. I even asked if she had injured herself, and her face turned red.

"I must have knocked it somewhere," she had said after a long pause. Hmm... a little unconvincing in my book.

Dorian strides into the room.

I smile. "Morning, darling." Pointing at the tray of plump little muffins, so perfectly matched in proportion, I'm brimming with pride. "I just whipped these up for you, knowing how much you enjoyed the last batch."

He stares at the tray sitting on the gleaming stainless-steel kitchen bench that resembles a mirror after Ana brought out an unopened bottle of polish and put it to work.

He inspects the muffins just as Ana walks in.

Yes, I've noticed how Dorian looks at her. And no, I'm not daft for hiring her. I just need to have that awkward chat with our new maid about her workwear.

"Are they completely keto?" He leans over and analyzes the muffins like they're something rare to behold.

"They sure are." I smile brightly. "Millet, tapioca, almond, and macadamia flour. I also added blueberries and coconut, and I sweetened them with monk fruit."

"Pure monk fruit?" he asks, studying me closely.

"Of course."

He takes a sniff. "They look good. Wrap them up and I'll take them to my morning meeting."

Off he goes. I suppose a "thank you" is too much to ask.

I pour myself a coffee and put my feet up on the floral divan I've just had delivered. The large open-plan space that extends from the kitchen is my favorite part of the house. It's where I'm found most days. The French doors open out onto the patio by the pool, giving the room an expansive reach.

I've only just recently had the walls painted teal, and I must say, I'm pleased with the result. It took some time to convince Dorian, who favors the unfussiness of white and beige. It wasn't until I showed him a chart of colors and their impact on our moods, with teal being linked to success, that he agreed.

I pick up a book by George Eliot. I love the classics. There is something so elegant about the prose, which by today's standards might be viewed as unnecessarily ornate and wordy. That's why I like reading those stories. It's like I'm sharing a cup of tea with a triple great-aunt or a company of women whose observations of life aren't so different from ours; only they use antiquated words that are like rare gems.

Engrossed in the serene bucolic charm of a mid-1800s English village, I'm jolted back to the present as my husband returns from his run, wiping sweat from his face. His wet T-shirt clings to his chest.

On cue, Ana has his juice ready. She's been designated the task of making his morning drink, consisting of a whole Amazonian rainforest of plants promising to keep Dorian alive years longer than the less disciplined of our species, of which I am one.

She hands him the green juice, and his gaze wanders from her pretty face to those spectacular, plump breasts bursting out of a fitted blouse. I wonder if my smallish boobs are to blame for my husband's inability to achieve full arousal. Squeamish when it comes to needles and hospitals, I'm not about to arrange implants.

It's that time of the month too. Ovulation week is a major thing around here. Being unable to conceive is stressful, and Dorian's obvious lack of attraction isn't helping much either.

I sense his porn addiction has desensitized him. I read about that somewhere. I'm not sure if it's an addiction, but it would explain his spending an inordinate amount of time in his study at night. The videos Dorian favors show a violent form of sex. Or is that passion? I suppose if I had such a large penis ramming into me, I'd be squealing from pain too. I've never experienced that kind of athletic sex before Dorian. Ash, the only boy I ever loved, was always gentle, and it felt like lovemaking. I was young when I lost my virginity to him, believing he was the one. But then we lost touch once I moved to New York.

I wonder if I should see a lawyer about my husband cheating on me by using porn. Do I want out?

Lately, I do.

But if Dorian and his legion of attorneys can find a cogent argument against it, then I'm sunk.

As I'm sitting at the island bench that separates the kitchen from the living space, Dorian enters the room dressed like a man about to take over the world in a gray fitted suit and crisp white shirt. He has a fabulous tailor.

I notice him watching Ana, who is bent over, and, well, I think it's time we have that talk about appropriate work clothes. Not that I like to boss people around. It's not my thing. That's why the push and shove of the New York publishing game didn't suit me. I was too nice, they kept saying.

If only they knew.

"So," Dorian says. "The Spitzes are in town. Hayden's running his wellness workshops this weekend."

Hayden Spitz, Dorian's lifestyle guru and now business partner, is responsible for my husband's growing interest in the wellness industry. Dorian is one of those rare beings who can operate on four hours of sleep. He swears by some super powder—one of many supplements his new company promotes to stressed-out business execs. And by that, I don't mean cocaine. That happened back in Dorian's excessive days in New York when he was playing the money market and winning.

Dorian always wins.

Or at least, he sees to it that he wins.

He must have things his way, or else the vein in his temple throbs just like it was doing a moment ago after Ana bent over to sweep up a speck of dust.

He gulps down his green juice. "I thought a dinner on Saturday."

My temperature rises. That's three days away. Can I find a vegan, gluten-free caterer in time?

"Sure. I'll search for a caterer who can organize the right menu."

He holds my eyes. Yes, I know what he's thinking. He wants me to do the cooking so that I can parade around as that perfect housewife. And I want that too. Cooking is something I do well. Only this whole restrictive ingredient thing is challenging for someone brought up on a classic diet of meat, vegetables, and lots of carbs.

Who would have thought carbs are threatening the very fabric of society in the same way communism was thought to in the fifties?

"Or I'll study some recipes and get cracking." I smile.

He gives me a scrutinizing gaze.

Is he thinking what I'm thinking? That he got us wrong? Me wrong?

I can't help but feel guilty for not getting pregnant.

Nowadays, it's not just me who moans over the monthly visit. Except Dorian doesn't have to deal with painful cramps and mood swings.

I kiss his cheek. "Have a nice day. And I'll be sure to be ready tonight." I raise an eyebrow, which is about as sexy as it gets between us these days.

Once it was sexier. But that was during our first three months of marriage. After that, he kept asking me about my periods and the whole ovulation thing, and well, from there it became a little regimented. I've even got an app telling me when I'm at my most fertile.

After Dorian leaves, I call Ana in.

"Take a seat." I point at the sofa.

Her flawless brow creases slightly.

"I just want a chat," I reassure her.

Ana nods, sits down, and crosses her very well-toned legs. I've since learned that she's a budding dancer.

She looks at me expectantly as I pace. Having to tell someone how to dress sucks. I'm reminded of the time I was instructed to ditch the power suit and adopt arty chic while working in the publishing industry back in New York. And here I was thinking the power suit was all the rage for women flying up the corporate ladder. Not that I was keen on climbing anything. I'm a bit jittery when it comes to heights.

"So, Ana," I say, pushing out my chest and adopting that confident boss persona. "It's about the way you dress. You're doing a great job, by the way. You are on top of everything."

Her large dark eyes stare up at me without blinking. "You want me to wear a uniform?"

"Maybe not a uniform. I'm thinking of a white shirt and black knee-length skirts or slacks."

She nods slowly.

I want to suggest something that doesn't show off her curves, but that's taking it too far at this stage. I have to at least show that she is a regular maid. Isn't that why I hired her?

I leave the room to get my checkbook and then return.

After signing a check, I pass it to her. "This is for the clothes."

Looking a little stunned, she stares down at the check. "Thank you, Mrs. Gunn."

"Call me Linley." I smile. "You're a great help, Ana. You do more than you're asked. You work long hours. I appreciate that. Tell you what—have the day off so you can shop. Then tomorrow I might need some help in the kitchen preparing a dinner that Dorian is hosting. Okay?"

Rising from the sofa, Ana straightens out her tight skirt. "More than okay. And I'm sorry. I guess I'm used to dressing like this. We all kinda do these days."

Don't I know it. And if I had her body, I might too.

Pushing aside appropriate dress codes, I'm more concerned about the Saturday night dinner. I need to design a menu that will not only satisfy a vegan but also Dorian, who is not a vegan but is on a strict keto diet.

After Ana leaves, I remove the cupcakes from the oven, place them carefully on a tray, and head outside.

Who says only husbands can ogle the staff?

Jarrad is out there chopping away at a dead tree, fallen after the last big storm. Sad to see the beautiful old oak go; I had one just like it growing up with a treehouse my dad built.

But the weather is so terrifying these days; one minute the place is on fire, and the next, there's torrential rain and wild winds.

Speaking of wild, that's how my hormones are reacting to seeing Jarrad shirtless. He's a Channing Tatum lookalike, according to Olivia, who couldn't stop fanning her face after seeing him in the garden.

Dorian hasn't met Jarrad yet. I wonder if he'd approve. After all, I sense that the gardener has the kind of physique Dorian sweats profusely to achieve. Only Jarrad is far more muscular.

He places the axe down and wipes his brow. It's going to be another scorcher. It's barely midday and the sun's already burning my pale skin. As a redhead, I have this unfortunate tendency to burn. But I do like the sun's radiance, so I tend to sunbathe early in the morning.

Jarrad captures my eye and waves.

"Hey there," I say. "Must be time for a coffee break. You've been hard at it all morning."

He nods and puts on his T-shirt, which is so ripped and faded I'm questioning whether to gift him a new one. But then it could be that hobo-style clothing that men are favoring today—rips in all the right places. Something tells me that Jarrad's not into fashion statements.

Sitting at the table by the pool, I pour Jarrad a coffee. "Can I get you a juice with that? Or water?"

He shakes his head. "Coffee's good. Thanks. You don't have to go to all this trouble, though."

"It's my pleasure." I smile, and he holds my eyes for a moment. His warm hazel eyes have this wonderful calming effect.

I point at the chocolate cupcakes with hazelnut cream icing. "I just made this batch. You're not allergic to nuts, are you?"

"Only of the human variety," he says, with a contagious guttural chuckle.

He takes one from the tray. "These look delicious. You're quite the baker, Mrs. Gunn."

"Call me Linley, please." I stretch out my arms and embrace the day. All it took was sunshine and a smile from this lovely man for all my earlier stress to vanish.

I take a cupcake and savor the fluffy chocolate nut-encrusted cake.

He devours one, making it almost seem sexual.

Stop it. You're objectifying the poor guy.

"Mm... spectacular," he says.

I push the tray toward him. "That's nice to hear. I love having my efforts appreciated."

"I love my food." He taps his stomach.

"I can't tell. There's not an ounce of fat on you."

"I work it off," he says. "Your husband's one lucky man."

I study him for a minute. Are we talking about cooking here? "If you're implying he's lucky that he's married to someone who loves to bake, then I'm afraid that's not the case. He's into keto."

Wiping his mouth with a paper napkin, he looks up at me mystified. "What is that exactly? I know it has something to do with food, but it sounds like a martial art."

I laugh. "It's a carb-free diet."

He winces as if I've just described a heavy-handed acupuncturist threatening to poke needles into the side of the eye. "You mean no bread, cakes, or potatoes, that kind of thing?"

"Yep." I pull a tight smile. Jarrad's reminding me just how difficult it's been catering to my husband's very particular needs.

He opens out his hands. "Why?"

"Dorian is part of this Never Die movement. He even set up a company called 'Never Say Die,' selling supplements that promise to reverse the effects of aging."

Jarrad holds my stare. "Let me guess—he's into cryogenics too?"

"I've heard Dorian talking about that. It's kind of morbid. I mean, when we die, we die. I'd like to live a good old age and have grand..." I stop myself.

"Grandchildren, you mean?" His brow creases.

"Let's start with a child first, I think." My nervous giggle is not lost on him because I notice a glint of sympathy.

Jarrad's very attentive in that natural way that makes me want to tell him everything. So far, I've told him how Dorian married me because he thought we'd make nice-looking, intelligent children and how he'd read somewhere that redheads are stronger than most. Still, I didn't mention that I preferred my husband to see me as attractive and not physically tough. Maybe that was too much to hope for since I've always seen myself as rather plain. But that's the mirror for you—it never shows you the person others see. Or maybe it's that we don't see ourselves with our eyes but with something less tangible—like how we're feeling in that moment.

I'm not sure why I told Jarrad that, but it was following my first Prosecco for the day after Olivia popped in for a quick visit. Though I don't normally drink during the day, I was rather tipsy when I embarked on a deep and meaningful conversation with my gardener.

Back to the present, and here I am pushing the tray toward him, looking for any excuse to prolong this pleasant catch-up.

He takes another cake, and as I top up his coffee, he returns a smile.

"Do you have siblings?" he asks.

"No. I wasn't brought up by my biological parents."

Oops again. More information. What is it about Jarrad that makes me want to reveal things about myself that even Dorian doesn't know?

If my perfect husband knew that I was adopted and that my birth mother was an eighteen-year-old who was more interested in drugs than being a mom, then I wouldn't be here.

Besides, it's okay to have a few secrets, isn't it?

"Well, I'm sure you'll start a family soon." He smiles tightly like he's apologizing for discussing something private.

He munches on the cake and wipes his perfectly sculpted lips. Even that gesture has my hormones singing.

"I hope I don't need to go down the IVF road. I hate needles," I say.

"A friend's wife went through it. She got there in the end. She had a healthy baby."

"Are you from LA?" I ask.

He shakes his head. "New York. And you?"

"I'm from Greenwich, Connecticut. What brings you to LA?"

"The weather. I like the ocean. All the regular cliché reasons."

"The beach is nice here. But it's hot." I wipe my brow. "I might swim later." I smile. "Feel free to take a dip anytime, by the way."

"I'd like that. I'm more of an ocean person, but I'm not smelling chemicals here."

"It's a salt pool. I hate the idea of swimming in chlorine." I laugh.

He rises and stretches his arms. He must be at least six-foot-two. "I'd best get back to work. But hey, I might take you up on that swim later. And thanks for the cupcakes. They sure are delicious. You should be selling them."

"That's such a nice compliment."

His eyes meet mine and we share a smile.

Energized after a sugar hit and quality time spent with a warm soul, I head off to design a menu for Saturday night.

EIGHT

It's Saturday evening, and I'm a little nervous about how my three-course meal will be received. So far, over the first course, I've sat quietly, listening to our guests speak endlessly about their health and how they feel twenty years younger. When did this obsession with well-being start? I reflect on topics shared at dinner parties I used to attend. Back then, it was gossip, the latest trends, politics, and poking fun at something or someone. Tonight, however, it's about liver cleansing, fiber intake, and the microbiome.

"I'm on about eighty at last count," Hayden Spitz says as if he's bragging about some fine achievement. That's if one counts popping supplements as an Olympic sport.

Shelby, his wife, nods. "It's quite a process. I'm not on as many, but the amino acids are important for us."

Dorian nods in agreement. The whole conversation revolves around natural supplements, given that they are business partners in Never Say Die.

"I've signed a contract with the blood drawers," Hayden says.

Now that makes my skin crawl a little.

"You look a little disapproving," Shelby says to me.

"You got that right. She can't even go near a needle without fainting," Dorian says in such a disparaging way that it makes me feel inadequate.

While they've been prattling on about enemas and the like, I've been entertaining myself with a glass of wine. Dropping the whole shrinking-violet act, I can't help but return an eye roll. Dorian's passive-aggressive jibes I can almost stomach privately, but humiliating me before this odious, narcissistic couple is something else.

"You're exaggerating," I challenge. "Lots of people are squeamish about needles."

Dorian shoots me an icy look. He's not used to me pushing back—especially in front of his favorite people. Can't have them witness our flawless marriage splintering. That would never do.

Sheldon turns to me with a look of sympathy. "Oh, you don't like needles? I guess none of us do. But hey, they use super-fine needles these days."

"It's not that," I appeal. "It's just a little strange having the blood of some stranger pumped into me."

"If you're in an accident, a blood transfusion saves your life," Hayden adds.

"Yes, I know, and that's fine, but for a healthy person to take blood from a younger person—that's kind of Frankensteinish, isn't it?"

"She's talking nonsense," Dorian adds without even a hint of a smile.

This time I return a sickly-sweet grin to his obvious putdown.

This whole discussion about needles brings up the IVF treatments Dorian is pushing me toward as a last resort. And it might have to be, as I keep reminding myself, even if Dorian extracts more pleasure from a computer screen than from me.

What other options do I have?

The thought of returning to the push and shove of the corporate world makes me break out in hives. Living in this gilded cage of pretense has softened me somewhat, despite the lack of love.

In the meantime, I'm keeping my parents afloat thanks to the allowance Dorian gives me for personal needs, but lately, he has been asking about those large withdrawals. So far, I've given him the usual excuses—splurging on my mom's birthday, things for the house, and designer clothes for me. I even hit the shopping malls to economize, but he wasn't thrilled about a recent twenty-thousand-dollar withdrawal. I've only just discovered my parents had to mortgage their home, and so now I'm making repayments.

I can't exactly tell him about their financial predicament because if Dorian learns how my parents are struggling financially, he'll be mad. He thought they were rich. And they were when we met.

An hour into the dinner party with the Spitzes, Ana arrives with more wine and tops up everyone's drinks.

Her skirt is knee-length, though virtually sewn on.

Dorian can't take his eyes off her. Hayden also has a nice long ogle. Shelby looks at me and rolls her eyes.

Yes, we know when our husbands are perving. They can't hide it. I'm not so fussed.

I return my attention to Shelby, with her sleek silvery-blonde hair, flawless skin, and attentive blue eyes, dabbing her mouth with a napkin. "This pasta dish is delicious."

"Heart of palm. Low-carb 'pasta,'" I say, feeling a little proud of myself for finding that keto shop where, not only did I fill a cart with items I'd never heard of before, but thanks to the keen guidance of a very helpful assistant, I planned the three-course dinner right then and there.

"You'll have to give me the recipe," she says. "So I can pass it on to our chef."

Hayden, with his tanned, wrinkle-free face, salt-and-pepper waves, and a seemingly permanent self-satisfied smirk, says, "Quentin's a godsend. He's a gourmet keto chef."

"So that must be tricky being vegan and not eating carbs," I say, relieved that at least Dorian's a carnivore.

"Yes, we made that decision last year when Shelby had that cancer scare and decided to maintain it. I feel like a million dollars. It works for us."

And so it goes on, this discussion about foods, lifestyle, amino acid supplements, and blood transfusions from the young.

It's like I'm on another planet.

My mind wanders to Jarrad and how his taut, muscular body shimmers under the sun. I know for a fact he likes his burgers and sweets, and he looks like a billion dollars. He's gone for a few days, and I'm already trying to come up with excuses to get him to work a few extra days. He's my antidote to a soulless marriage. I don't need a supplement to make me feel good—a conversation with Jarrad seems to give me the boost I need.

Is fantasizing cheating? I guess I'm almost as bad as my husband, who can't stop ogling the maid. What does this mean for us going forward?

I know that if my parents weren't in such a terrible predicament, I'd be considering something healthier for my life. The only affection I get from Dorian, if one can call it that, is hard and fast sex.

I sense Dorian's lack of affection stems from a difficult childhood. From what I can glean, his mom, Jenny, drank morning, noon, and night. That can't have been easy for him. Personally, I think my husband could do with some therapy, as I'm sure many of us can, but in Dorian's case, there is something broken for sure. My heart cries at times. I wish I could do more.

But then other days, I feel like wringing his neck for being so goddamn fussy and, well, outright insensitive.

My mother, the only person who knows about this cold marriage, recently asked why I married Dorian. The simple answer, one which makes me hate myself that much more, is that I was so dazzled by the prospect of being a housewife that I forgot to ask the hard questions, like can we make this marriage work on a deeper level?

Over the first few months of dating, we talked about life and aspirations, and I popped on my rose-colored glasses and only saw the nice bits, like how driven Dorian was to succeed and how good he looked. He wasn't hooked on restrictive diets or obsessed with his health back then. He changed when we moved to LA.

Now I extract my affection from my loving parents, and I wish I could have a dog that I could cuddle and love. If only Dorian weren't such a germaphobe, I'd bring one home, but after I suggested a dog, he shook his head. "No way. Think of all the harmful microbes."

After we see the Spitzes out, I go and change into something a little more comfortable, only to find Ana blushing and smiling at Dorian.

She turns to me wearing an innocent—or is that apologetic?—smile. "I'm finished in the kitchen. Will that be all for tonight?"

I nod. "Great work today. Thanks for the help."

Ana did help a lot with the preparation, and I push aside the fact that Dorian, who has had too much to drink, is close to salivating.

After she leaves, he pushes me against the wall, and I feel him go hard.

He is in a hurry. I know why he's all steamy.

He runs his hand over my butt, lowers my leggings, and then bends me over the table and penetrates me in one sharp thrust.

"This time, yes," he breathes into my ear.

I bite my lip and nod. It isn't painful, but the fact that I'm dry doesn't help. Foreplay has its uses. Normally, at this time of the month, I get myself warmed up with my vibrator before Dorian jumps into bed. But tonight, he's all hot and raring to go, thanks to Ana.

As he pumps into me, I can only wonder what is going on in his mind as I summon up images of Jarrad—shirtless under the sun—in the hopes of firing up my libido.

Yep, this mutual lack of desire between me and my husband is becoming messed up.

NINE

It is Saturday morning, and Dorian, who doesn't sleep in, rises early. Always waking me, he starts off the day with a jog followed by a workout. I think he feels it is important that I get up with him. I prefer to sleep and often return to bed once he leaves the house. Nine o'clock is my sweet spot for getting out of bed.

"About that money you're sending to your parents," he says while drying his hair with a towel.

I sit up and rub my eyes.

"Can't we talk about this later?" I ask. My head is pounding after what was a night of heavy drinking. For me, at least. I'm one of those sneaky drinkers. Apart from being tipsy last night, Dorian hardly drinks anymore. Another one of the habits he kicked.

I preferred him when he was that wild party boy. At least he'd laugh and joke around a little. Not now. He is so darn serious all the time.

"No." He glares at me, and I reach for the water at the side of my bed. "I know you're sending your folks money regularly. Why? They're fucking loaded. It's my hard-earned cash."

So you keep saying. One billion dollars in the bank from the last count.

"They've fallen on difficult times." I gulp some water, which is making me nauseous. Dorian's hard stare isn't helping either.

He drops the towel and rubs his well-defined muscular legs. Most women find him hot. I can see how they look at him. I once might have felt jealous, but now, I feel nothing. My emotions are so tangled where this marriage is concerned that the only thing that keeps me going is the need to save my parents from a disastrous fall.

"What happened to their millions?" he asks.

"Dad made some pretty bad investment decisions, and well…" How do I tell him that my parents are close to bankruptcy thanks to his buddy's dishonesty?

"And we're now supporting them?" He frowns.

The doorbell echoes through the house, jolting me away from my thoughts. Grateful for the interruption, I scramble for the right explanation.

"That must be Ana. I asked her to come early because I need the curtains cleaned."

He wraps the towel around his waist. "I'll let her in." He stops. "This discussion isn't over."

Dorian is horrible when he's angry. Everyone is. And why is he going to the door in a bath towel?

As I stand at the door, I hear Ana giggling along with a rare chuckle from Dorian.

Tears sting as I struggle to keep from breaking down. The weight of every poor decision I've ever made comes flooding back to haunt me. Yes, I know, regret is brutal and unfixable.

The day's warm, and I'm lounging by the pool when I get a text from Emily asking if she can come over.

Responding with a thumbs up, I welcome the distraction.

Five minutes later, Ana lets her in.

"Ana, you can have a break if you like," I say.

The maid nods, wearing what looks like an awkward smile—or is that guilt for flirting with my husband?

As we watch Ana leave, Emily shakes her head while frowning.

"What?" I ask, rubbing sunscreen onto my face.

"Is she that good?"

"Ana's thorough and doesn't need me to tell her what to do," I say.

"But that's you, Lin. You're a soft touch."

"I don't like causing scenes. And there are more than enough kick-ass females getting around. The world doesn't need another."

Emily's head lurches back. "Are you kidding? We all need to be kick-ass after the centuries we've had."

I laugh. "You're not about to bring up the witch burnings, are you?"

"No. But we can't let our men walk all over us. I don't take shit from Mark."

"Same here." Oops, a small fib. But one must keep up appearances.

I think back to Dorian's passive-aggressive jabs, saying things like, "Why would I expect you to remember something I've said a hundred times?" I can't even recall what he was complaining about that time. There are so many barbs; I just bite my tongue, despite the pain becoming unbearable. My self-esteem is already in bad shape, thanks to how much I beat myself up.

Emily is right: I am a soft touch. But what choice do I have? My parents come first. No, I'm stuck in this marriage until the bitter end, which could be sooner than I hope if I don't conceive by year-end.

"Your husband strikes me as respectful, so I can't imagine you having to assert yourself."

Emily nods pensively as she sips coffee. "Mark is a sweetheart. We just haven't had sex in like a year."

I sigh. "We broke the monthly drought last night." Too much information. But I'm human, and Emily is not the type who would think anything of it.

Her eyes light up as if I just announced I won a grand prize in a cake competition. "Your cheeks do look a little rosier than usual."

"That's my new makeup." My dry tone makes her chuckle. "It was more of a groping session over the table."

Her jaw drops. "How passionate."

"Mm... Not sure if I'd call it that. Let's just say he was a little more aroused than usual."

Something to do with the maid.

I keep that to myself. I can't have Emily pointing the finger at me and saying, 'I told you so.'

"He watches porn," I reveal with a sigh. I need to talk to someone about it.

"Oh, you've caught him?" She shakes her head. "They're so silly, aren't they? They think we're all blind to their little indiscretions."

Emily goes a little dark for a moment. I might have stirred something. She once found homosexual porn on her husband's computer, but he swore black and blue that someone at work had sent it to him as a joke.

Good story.

I saw how Mark checked out Dorian's butt at a dinner party we had recently. I kept that to myself. Well, okay, I might have mentioned it to Olivia after she told me she saw Mark flirting with some young guy somewhere.

"Hey, you want to hear the latest?" she asks, lowering her voice, despite there being no one within earshot.

Even if I didn't, I'm about to. In any case, I don't mind being lulled out of my own complicated life into another's.

"I went out for a drink with a couple of college friends last night, and we ended up at this bar, and who should I see tucked away in a corner looking all loved up?"

I shrug.

"Isabella. She was there with Max, the yoga instructor. Remember we went to that one class that time? The hot young one?"

I nod. "He liked to get a little touchy-feely, didn't he?"

She giggles. "Yeah, and he hovered behind us while we performed the downward-facing dog."

Isabella, who claims to be happily married to Jackson, a Hollywood producer whom she married in the hope of landing acting roles, hasn't hidden her attraction for the younger yoga instructor.

"Anyway, they were all over each other."

"That's not very wise, is it? I mean, this is a small town."

"I think Jackson's having the odd fling too. You know all those young pretty actresses."

I shake my head at how twisted this whole marriage game has become. Whatever happened to marrying for love?

"Isabella called me this morning and begged me not to tell anyone."

I laugh. "And so here you are."

She pulls a guilty face. "I'm bad, aren't I?"

"Not really. We all like to know that not everyone's squeaky clean and having a perfect marriage."

"But you are, aren't you? Apart from the porn, I mean. Many do it these days anyway. It's almost the norm."

I sigh. "Maybe. It still doesn't feel good, though, does it?"

She shakes her head. "No. It sucks." Her face brightens. "Regardless, you and Dorian looked happy together the other night. That was sweet."

I return a smile. Maybe I missed my calling in Hollywood after all.

"And talking about happy marriages, Sophia's got it right."

"She married below her. Look at her, she's a goddess and Tony, well, he's a lovely man, but she could do better," I say.

Emily nods. "It's all about that, isn't it? Finding the right balance. That's why I chose Mark. There was Brad at the practice where I worked, who did look like Brad Pitt." She giggles. "But he had roaming eyes and women throwing themselves at him. He liked me, though, and we did have a few months together." She sounds wistful. "But I couldn't see him as remaining faithful. At least, Mark..." She knits her fingers. "Doesn't look at other women."

No, he looks at other men.

She twirls a strand of hair around her finger, looking sad.

I touch her hand. "Sex and intimacy aren't always easy to sustain in long marriages. At least he's affectionate, right?"

She nods. Her face brightens slightly. "Maybe I should get a lover, too. It's all the rage."

I laugh. Then I think about Jarrad, and that warm, tingly feeling returns.

"Why not? Men have been doing it to us forever." I utter that almost to myself because I am wondering about whether Dorian is cheating with escorts. Perhaps I need to hire a PI, thinking of that cheating clause since his porn habit might be challenged and thrown out of court only to blow up in my face and land me on my butt, penniless.

"But it's crazy. Why are we all vowing to be faithful? It seems so wrong."

"It's all about keeping the family unit tight. For your children," I say. My voice falters at 'children' as a sinking feeling returns.

Emily returns a sad smile. "I'm sure you'll get there soon. It can take a while."

I frown. "Late September I'll turn thirty-six."

I've marked the calendar. I have a little under a year left to get pregnant.

"I'm wondering if passion returns." She shrugs. "You know Mark never made my knees go weak. But he was so nice to me. And funny. He makes me laugh. And he's such a great father."

Dorian has arrived. We can see him chatting with Ana. They're oblivious to us, it would seem, and it doesn't look like a 'how's your day' kind of chat, going by Ana's growing smile.

Emily notices, of course, and I imagine that within two hours, half of Marigold Boulevard will also know.

TEN

IF THINGS WEREN'T ALREADY bad, they have just gotten worse. My dear father has suffered a heart attack, and after a frantic rush to the airport, I traveled back home to Greenwich. Following a restless night, I'm now in the backyard with my mom.

The two-story white American colonial I grew up in stands proud among towering oaks. My treehouse is still there. As I look up at it, nostalgia warms my veins. Across the road, an overgrown garden smothers a derelict gabled two-story house that wouldn't look out of place in a scary movie.

I sit at a cast-iron table in the garden, surrounded by pots of lavender, gardenias, and roses. A herbaceous and floral scent fills the air, and as the sun warms my skin, I feel a sense of serenity. A gentle breeze adds to the relaxation. The day is comfortable, not scorching hot like in LA.

I remove my jacket and stretch out my legs. As I breathe in a familiar earthy scent, warm memories of sitting at that table during my childhood flood back to me, reminding me of a time when the only complication I faced was deciding what to wear to prom.

With her silvery blonde hair shimmering in the sunlight, dressed in denim jeans and a pink cotton shirt, my mother carries a tray of coffee and donuts, setting it down on the white filigree table.

My attention wanders through the garden to the tennis court my father had built for my mom, a keen tennis player. Memories of our neighborhood tournaments flash before me. I smile thinking of the fun we had: the homemade lemonade, the dogs running around chasing balls, Ash playing opposite me, and how I struggled to return his serve.

Wistful reflections sweep me away as I sigh. If only I could rewind and start from that point again. I could have remained in Connecticut and opened a cake shop or café instead of trying to find myself in New

York. If anything, I lost myself in that bustling metropolis where standing still meant being knocked over by the push and shove of those racing to succeed.

My mother points to the plate of homemade donuts. "They're still warm."

The delectable spongy treats waft their jam-infused aroma up my nose and rouse my appetite. To hell with my latest resolve to make use of that gym membership I keep renewing and eat less sweets.

I sink my teeth into warm doughy bliss, and pleasure rumbles in my stomach. When I was growing up, Ash and the neighborhood kids would find any excuse to visit. My mom's donuts were legendary. As the sweet, welcoming aroma filled the house, nothing else mattered. We were carefree and wild, driven by simple desires—like homemade donuts dripping with hot raspberry jam that always burned our tongues and had us pleading for more.

"Yum," I sing, wiping my sticky lips with a napkin.

She wears a thin smile. "I thought I'd whip up some for the nurses at the hospital. They're doing such a fine job."

The mention of the hospital and my father's recent heart attack brings me tumbling back down to reality and the grim reason for my visit. "How's he doing today? When can we visit?"

"He's doing well. Visiting hours are in a couple of hours. We'll go then." She smiles tightly.

My dad's health shock has impacted her badly. The dark rings around her eyes are telling. "It was such a good idea having the defibrillator installed and taking that course when I did."

"You saved Dad's life, Mom." I lean over and hug her. "I'm sorry I couldn't get here sooner."

She pats my hand. "You're here now. That's all that counts. And you've got a life too. We understand."

"You're not lonely in this big house?" I ask.

"I've polished the silver, made enough jam to last two years, and I'm about to whip up some new curtains. I'm keeping myself busy. You know me; I'm not good at standing still."

I smile. That's where we differ. While I couldn't stop reading books, my mom was always moving around and keeping herself busy.

"Jilly from next door keeps coming over with casseroles. I've got a fridge full of them." She chuckles. "Guess what we're having for dinner tonight?"

"I don't mind. As long as it's real food and not some strange purple stuff."

"Dorian's still on his health kick?" she asks.

I nod. "He's determined to live forever."

She chuckles before turning serious. "Jilly's a widow now, as you know. We keep each other company."

"Neighbors are so important, aren't they?"

She sips coffee and nods. "Is Dorian fine with you coming here for the whole week? You've got help, haven't you?"

I think of Ana, who has agreed to stay.

Sophia's shocked response comes to mind. When I told her I was leaving for a week and that the maid would be staying over, she shook her head in disbelief. "You can't leave her with your husband. Alone."

I just shrugged it off. "I trust him."

Sophia's head lurched back, grimacing as though I'd lost my mind.

My mother studies me for a moment. "Is this maid pretty?"

"She is. But hey, I'm not worried." I sip water to wash away the bitterness in my mouth. Little to do with coffee, but more to do with stress, because I know how this looks—like I've lost control of my life. And in many ways, I have. But for the sake of my mother's well-being, since she's having to deal with so much right now, I keep my marriage issues to myself.

"Darling, I can't tell you how much we appreciate what you've been doing for us. We wanted to thank Dorian too. Your father called him just before he became ill."

My brow furrows. "Oh? Dorian didn't tell me."

Looking worried, she asks, "Is something the matter? Did your father do the wrong thing?"

"No." I sigh. "Just that Dorian never mentioned Dad calling."

"I'm sensing something in your voice. Is there a problem?" Her frown deepens.

Maintaining stoicism around my mother is close to impossible. The anxiety in her eyes is unmistakable. Ironically, she wore the same worried expression the day Dorian first visited our home, during the whirlwind of our engagement.

Afterward, she intimated how he struck her as controlling. There was a moment when I showed my mother a dress I'd picked out for an important dinner hosted by Dorian's firm. Dorian was there and asked to see the options. I showed him the dress I had in mind—a silk floral knee-length dress with ruffles—and he immediately dismissed it. He then scrolled through my saved options and picked a bland beige sheath that my mother hadn't liked. Nor had I, for that matter.

She winced at his sharp, commanding tone, and the following morning, I questioned her about that reaction. She admitted to worrying about him being a little on the controlling side. Sensing Dorian was hiding something, she also felt unsettled by his smooth, calculated charm. When she asked him about his background, he gave vague responses before changing the subject.

Returning to the present and the sensitive topic of helping my parents with their bills, I stare down at my hands, suppressing tears. "He didn't know I was sending the checks."

"Oh." She frowns. "Is this creating waves at home? We don't want to do that. And we've got that trailer…" Her voice cracks.

"There's no way you're moving from your home. Not while I'm breathing."

There's a tough note in my voice that I haven't used for a while. It's time to roll out that version of me. Everyone, including my husband, thinks I'm a pushover. Well, they're in for a surprise.

I'm never going to allow my family to be on the streets. Ever.

"It was that Wall Street guru that Dorian introduced us to. Remember that dinner you hosted in New York a few months before leaving for LA?"

How could I forget? Dorian turned what was a traditional family dinner into a business opportunity by inviting some colleagues.

"Your father was looking for a way to make some interest on our savings. The banks weren't offering much, and Brendon Crib had this scheme."

More like a scam.

I exhale. "You should have run it past me. He's locked up now. A ton of people lost their savings."

"Yes, we know." She wrings her hands. "Wasn't he working closely with Dorian?"

I nod. That was just before we hurried off to LA. I recall dropping into his New York office and seeing shredding machines in use.

I knew then that Dorian was hiding something, but I decided to turn a blind eye because I wanted this marriage.

Silly me.

"Are you happy, love?" she asks. The change of subject brings me back to the present.

I fidget with my shirt sleeve. "My happiness is no longer the issue here, Mom." I sigh. "I just wish Dad hadn't called Dorian. I was trying to keep that a secret. He's not into sharing money."

"Not even with you?"

"I've got my expense account. And I don't need anything, so I send it to you instead. Dorian is loaded. He made ten million dollars this month alone."

She whistles and then her face goes dark. "He's not selling those shady investment schemes, is he?"

I shake my head. "No, he's making a killing from the wellness industry. Supplements mainly. Powders that promise eternal youth." I chuckle at how ridiculous that sounds.

"And people are buying it?"

"Well, yes, you know everyone's taking supplements these days," I say. "Dorian takes about eighty at last count."

"My lord." She shakes her head. "Oh well, I suppose it's a money earner. As good as any. In my day, only hippies took that kind of stuff. They did yoga and promoted natural products. Vegetarianism was linked to people dropping LSD and living in communes."

I giggle. "You grew up during a very colorful period."

"It was colorful. And a little less complicated." She sighs.

I stroke her hand. "Don't worry, Mom. I'll make sure you don't lose this house. You'll be looked after as long as I'm alive."

Tears well up in her eyes. "You're a good daughter."

I'm a better daughter than a wife. But she doesn't need to know that.

That's if being unable to conceive makes me a bad wife.

Or a failed woman.

Brushing aside pessimism, I pick up another donut and discuss the hospital's opening hours for visiting Dad.

ELEVEN

I cut my visit short to Greenwich and am back home after three days instead of seven. My father is doing well, and my mother has returned to her old self despite their ongoing money issues.

As I step through the white picket fence, I take a moment to admire the grand elegance of the luxurious colonial house I call home. The entrance, flanked by columns, has a Corfu blue door with a brass knocker that gleams in the sun, making one feel welcomed.

The front lawn is pristine, thanks to Jarrad's tireless efforts, and a flourishing magnolia bush sits proudly in the center, filling the air with a sweet, elevating scent.

The first time Dorian brought me here, we'd just married. Squealing with delight, I visualized a perfect life in this sprawling two-story home. The house reminded me of the kind you see in movies, where merry families enjoy endless celebrations, and kids play ball with their charming dads.

Crushed by reality, I know that dream is long gone. But the house still shines brightly in my eyes, and for the first time in three days, I smile. It's time to take control of my life and this marriage. IVF, here we come. No more wallowing in 'poor me' crap. Squaring my shoulders, I push open the front door and step inside my castle.

The gleaming house is quiet, and an uplifting herbal fragrance creates a tranquil vibe as Ana meets me in the sunny front room, wearing a big smile. "Welcome back, Mrs. Gunn."

"Please call me Linley." I've never liked that surname.

Trust Dorian to invent such a name for himself. I would have preferred his birth name, Eden, but he hates his childhood. He doesn't know his father, despite hunting high and low. Not that he admits that. He always gets a bit snippy whenever I ask. Something tells me that's why he married me—a white, regular girl next door who'd only ever had one other boyfriend.

I send his mother, Jenny, gifts on her birthday. Dorian doesn't know, despite sending her regular checks, which have little to do with filial affection but are devised to keep her out of his hair.

I enter our sparkling kitchen. "The place is so clean. And it smells heavenly," I say.

Ana looks proud. "I've made a fresh pot of coffee. And there are some gluten-free keto cookies I whipped up."

For a minute, I question whether Ana's the woman of the house. And aren't I meant to be the baker around here? Not that Dorian can go anywhere near my cupcakes. The first time I cooked some, I may as well have shown him a batch of tarantulas, such was the horror on his face.

His business colleagues, however, loved them, so that put me in his good graces. After all, my role is to make him look good. "Behind a successful man is a great woman," as they say.

Am I that great?

The dinner I created for the Spritzes was a success, so I've proven I can step it up.

"Did everything go well?" I study the maid closely. She's dressed modestly in slacks and a loose white shirt for a change.

But when I notice a bruise around her wrist, I ask, "How did you get that?"

She tugs down her shirt sleeves. "Oh, it's nothing."

I catch a hint of anxiety as she looks down at her feet.

"Has someone been hurting you? You can tell me."

She pours a cup of coffee and holds the pot for me, but I decline. I refuse to let this subject slide. "Well?"

"It's Hector, my boyfriend. He doesn't like me staying here." Her almond eyes catch mine for a moment and then dart away. It's like she's hiding something. Whether it's the grim reality of a violent home life or something else entirely, I can't exactly tell.

This is the first time we've talked about her life. In the interview, she mentioned how her parents came here from Mexico and that she lives with her boyfriend in East LA.

"You need to go to the police if he's hurting you."

Yes, I know it's not an easy conversation, but I can't let it go. Too many women struggle to open up about abusive partners. That's why I'm not backing down. If nothing else, I need Ana to know she's not alone. That I'm here for her.

Shaking her head, she looks terrified, like I'm suggesting she take a dip in a river frequented by alligators. Ana frowns. "No way. I can't do that." She plays with her fingers. "He's just seriously jealous. Maybe a bit too much at times." That last statement she murmurs to herself.

I leave it at that, but I get the narrative: controlling boyfriend, a beautiful girl staying at a billionaire's home, alone.

Since when can't wives leave their husbands with their housemaids?

Forever, silly girl.

It is all too much. What with my father being in the hospital and my parents' precarious financial situation, I need to put them first and not worry about my husband's potential infidelities.

Entering my makeshift office filled with books and childhood things—a contrast to our clutter-free home—I go to my desk overlooking a vibrant, flourishing garden. I often sit and daydream here.

IVF pamphlets describing the procedure stare back at me. Paperwork I haven't been able to bring myself to read. But now is the time. With ten months until my thirty-sixth birthday and that four-year clause arriving as a nice birthday gift, I can no longer rely on natural processes to deliver a little bundle of joy.

We made a deal. Or were those wedding vows?

With this constant reminder weighing me down, I'm back to feeling more like Quasimodo than some blithe housewife living the dream.

Setting down the pamphlet, I head back to my favorite part of the house, looking out onto the terrace and turquoise pool, and pour myself a coffee.

Ana is cleaning the bathroom, and I'm alone, which is fine. At least I don't have to make small talk or show a friendly face. That can get tiring, especially now that my mood has dampened again.

Plopping down on the sofa with coffee in hand, I promise myself I'll make my first appointment tomorrow as trepidation over medical procedures settles over me like a dark cloud.

A rap on the glass door snaps me out of this sudden depressing thought. Saving me from drifting deeper into a rabbit hole of gloom, Jarrad gives me a half-smile. His way of asking, "Is this a good time?"

"Any time is a good time," I feel like saying.

He's looking drop-dead gorgeous as always.

My day has turned technicolor. All those pesky problems evaporate from just one of his dimple-producing smiles.

"Hey, stranger," he says, looking from me to over my shoulder.

Ana's back in the kitchen washing her cup from earlier. That girl can't see one dirty dish.

I turn to her. "You can have the afternoon and night off. I've got this. Have the weekend off."

She lingers, appearing uncertain. "But, Dor... I mean, Mr. Gunn, asked me to cook for tomorrow night. He has some friends coming over for dinner."

I nod slowly. He did, did he?

"He hasn't mentioned that to me."

I hardly spoke to Dorian while away—just one call when I arrived in Greenwich. And while I expected him to discuss the payments to my family, he didn't. I'm now hoping he leaves that tetchy subject alone. I even cooked up a way to make the withdrawals less discoverable by taking out cash for those numerous discretionary purchases a wife married to a wealthy man might make.

I return my attention to Ana and the dinner she's been called on to arrange. "Okay then, see you tomorrow, since it seems like you've got this whole keto thing down pat."

Should I be worried?

Maybe.

But all I feel is numb. Probably due to my period arriving.

Won't Dorian be pleased?

I wait for her to leave and then go to the fridge and grab two Coronas. Jarrad's always up for a beer break and a chat. And I could use cheering up.

We sit outside and, not one to miss much, Jarrad says, "What was that in there?"

I sip on my beer first and wipe my lips before answering. "Am I that transparent?"

He shakes his head. "Sorry. I don't mean to pry."

My hand trembles slightly. Sensing I'm about to burst an emotional artery, I swig on the beer to quell the knot in my chest.

Now is not the time to confide in my gardener. The mayhem turning my life upside down might just pour out in an endless rant, and Dorian is due home soon. He sent me a text message earlier, in response to the one I sent, telling him—or was that alerting him?—that I would be home sooner than planned.

What was I expecting to find had I kept my early return a surprise?

"Life's a bit challenging right now," I say at last with a forced chuckle—my attempt at keeping things upbeat despite a welling of emotion. "But hey, let's not talk about me. How are things with you?"

He shrugs and then tells me about a contract he recently signed for a bigger apartment. As I listen to his deep, comforting drawl—like a favorite song—I sit back and soak in his charismatic presence, allowing it to take me on a holiday somewhere warm and sunny.

For now, I do what I do best: send my problems packing.

TWELVE

It's five in the afternoon, and after a calming chat with Jarrad, I'm feeling a little more relaxed about the all-important conversation with my husband. There is one major topic to discuss: my parents' situation and how imperative it is that we help them, even if it means a loan rather than a handout. He might find that more palatable.

I can't sit back and let Ana take over the kitchen, so I flip through the keto cookbook and make a plan for the dinner we're meant to be hosting when Dorian walks in and nods.

No hug or "Nice to see you."

In sharp contrast, I give him a dazzling smile. "Hello, darling."

Looking a little tired, he returns a thin smile.

I close the book and point to it. "I thought I'd study a menu. Ana tells me you're entertaining a group of friends tomorrow night."

Setting down his laptop, he says, "I've decided to make it a boys' night instead."

"Oh?" I wonder who these boys are. Dorian doesn't have that many friends. "Anyone I know?"

He goes to the fridge, removes a bottle of Perrier, unscrews the top, and takes a deep swig. "Just a couple of buddies from New York and some of their friends."

"Then no keto food?" I ask.

He shakes his head. "No need. Maybe look up a caterer who can do pizzas."

"Like pizza delivery?" I can't hide my surprise.

"No. Gourmet pizzas, I think, and order some keto versions."

"Oh? You just said no keto. But isn't keto carb-free?"

"Whatever." His distracted manner intensifies when Ana enters the room, clutching her bag.

Our maid glances from me to Dorian, and her cheeks flush.

Why is she blushing?

Dorian ignores her entirely, as though he's trying to avoid looking at her, and there's a sudden tension that even a chainsaw wouldn't be able to cut through.

Or am I reading too much into this?

I turn to Ana. "My husband tells me that tomorrow night isn't happening after all. You won't be needed."

"Okay, then." Appearing nervous, she fumbles with her bag.

"Have the weekend off," I say. "I'll be fine. We'll see you on Monday."

She responds with a slight nod, her eyes shifting from me to Dorian before she leaves. Dorian, meanwhile, is distracted, lost in his thoughts.

"Why am I sensing tension here? Did something happen between you and Ana while I was gone?"

Raking through his hair, Dorian walks from the kitchen into the living room and sits down on the sofa. Even his light brown hair, normally impeccably styled, is a little tousled as he brushes a strand away from his temple.

"Is there something the matter?" I ask again.

He shakes his head.

"Just that..." I knit my fingers. "I saw how you were flirting with Ana the other night after the Spritzes left."

He rolls his eyes. "Paranoia does not become you, Linley."

"It's not paranoia, Dorian. It looked like flirting from where I was standing."

"I was tipsy, and you're imagining things."

I take a deep breath and play with my shirt sleeve. "My mother told me Dad called you about the money."

"He did. I would have preferred it coming from you."

"They're close to bankruptcy, Dorian. They need our help."

He gulps down some more water and stares out into space for a moment. "I'll pay off their mortgage. But the house will be transferred into my name so they can't draw on it again."

My father will hate that the house is no longer in their name, but at least this arrangement will stop the bank from foreclosing. "But how will they live? They still need to be supported."

"Okay, then set up a monthly stipend and run it by me." He pulls out his phone and scrolls through it.

"Do you have to be somewhere?" I ask.

"There's a meeting in an hour. I thought I'd drop in for a shower."

"Is there an issue?"

He shakes his head. "No. Hayden's heading to India to source a supplier, and one of the suppliers has lost his accreditation."

"Oh. For a new supplement?" I rarely show interest in his company, but as the sticky subject of my parents' support has been broached and resolved for now, I want to make an effort to bring harmony into this marriage.

I can't help but wonder why he switched topics so quickly and didn't even quibble about the handouts going forward.

If only that pregnancy would arrive, then all would be good—loveless but good. Because as long as we remain husband and wife, my family will be cared for. That is all that matters to me. My personal happiness can wait.

He is staring down at his phone and doesn't hear my question. He lifts a finger. "I just have to make a call." He rises and goes into the other room.

As I sit there staring out into the beautifully manicured garden, I sense that something's happening with Dorian. There are more questions than answers. But at least I'm breathing a little easier knowing I can support my parents openly without having to hide large cash withdrawals.

But then, do my parents lose their home to Dorian if I don't get pregnant and he decides to walk? I'm close to hyperventilating again.

When he returns to the room, I say, "I'm about to make an appointment for IVF."

He nods. "Good."

Noticing the same concerned look return to his face, I ask, "So, is there an issue with a particular herb?"

I've lost him again to his phone. He looks up and says, "No. I mean, maybe. Hayden is going over to sort it. I'm sure it will be all right." He picks up his water and drains the bottle in one thirsty gulp. "I'm just going to shower and change. I'll be late tonight."

Off he goes, always in a hurry to leave, it seems.

I know he is hiding something, but for now, at least, one secret is out in the open.

Returning to the living room, I go to my laptop and Google "keto pizzas."

I wonder if Olivia might be up for a girls' night out. I know I could use one. There is no way I'm hanging around, and I can't imagine Dorian wants me there, hovering about.

THIRTEEN

It's Saturday night, and Olivia's excited as we bounce along the Sunset Strip to one of Isabella's favorite bars. Dorian has been so nice and compliant about everything. His agreeing to send regular checks to my parents without even a fight has me scratching my head. It's a nice welcome, nevertheless. Maybe one of the many supplements he's taking has softened him at last.

My veins tighten at the thought of all those needles, but I'm prepared to go through IVF if it means helping my parents.

What if I'm not able to conceive?

Do I really want to stay in this cold marriage if I do conceive?

Don't I want love? Everyone deserves a shot at love.

Could I broker a deal to extend the four years by a year or so? Or even remove it? How good would that be? Not having to count the days. Maybe it's time we discuss the prenup. He's never brought it up once in our marriage.

Could he have forgotten about it?

In many ways, his buying my parents' mortgage is a double-edged sword because if Dorian decides to uphold that arrangement and I'm childless, then my parents become homeless.

I file that thought away in the too-hard basket and think about our night out instead. Dorian gave me an approving look as I kissed him goodbye just as a couple of his New York buddies arrived. One must keep up appearances, and Dorian likes the world to know he's living in domestic harmony.

I'm more than happy to play the 'ideal wife' role. For now.

It's a struggle keeping up with Olivia, who, along with an also wired Isabella, must have taken something. They're almost bouncing along the street.

"Hey, you two, slow down," I say, tottering in my new nude stilettos, which I have yet to break in and are digging into my ankles.

"Here we are," Isabella says. Done up to the nines, she's wearing a shimmering purple body-hugging dress that barely covers her pert butt.

Olivia is also wearing a bodycon that reveals her slim frame. She's been on a diet since Harris left home and has dropped two dress sizes. It is amazing what sadness will do to one's waistline. In my case, it adds inches, given my tendency to binge on sugar when I'm feeling down.

All hyped up, Olivia's determined to get laid tonight, or she'll howl at the moon, as she threatened while we rode a cab downtown. Strange thing to say, I know, but it's no secret that Olivia's rather fond of THC gummies. According to her, they helped her cope after Harris left.

Classic tunes greet us as we step into the dimly lit retro bar. The women are mostly in sparkly tube dresses. They have tight, smooth skin, curves galore, and enough collagen implants, I imagine, to float a ship.

"Woo hoo," Isabella screams. "Let's do tequila shots."

I shake my head and laugh. "No way. I'll last an hour at most. I'll stick to beer, I think."

Shot glasses are lined up on the bar along with my Corona.

I've always preferred beer to wine, but Dorian hates me drinking beer. He thinks a woman looks too masculine with beer, especially when drinking from a bottle. He is so 1950s with those 'his and hers' views. I'm amazed we don't have a set of his and hers towels.

We take our drinks and settle into a quieter part of the venue, which I appreciate. I don't like to yell.

"Harris had the nerve to bring Jemma over today," Olivia says, throwing back her shot and chasing it with a sip of her margarita.

"Ew." Isabella pulls a face.

"It's his weekend with the kids, and he dragged her along. Can you believe it?"

"Did she stay in the car or come in?" I ask, relieved that I'm not dealing with such awkward family arrangements.

"He brought her in. Harris thinks it's a good idea for everyone to become friendly since they're gonna get married." She shakes her head and drains her margarita. "And you should have seen what she was wearing. Holy shit. Hardly anything. Like tiny shorts and no bra. I'm sure she's had her boobs done. And her lips get puffier each time I see her."

We give her sympathetic smiles. What can one say to a bitter divorcee?

"Hey, you want to hear some juicy gossip?" Isabella asks.

I welcome the break from Olivia's divorce.

"Well." She leans forward. "Remember how Natalie told me, after drinking half a bottle of wine, that Claire fooled around with one of the wives on our street one drunken night?"

We both nod. This should be good. We've all been curious about this little story for a while now.

"Well, I ran into her yesterday and invited her in for wine, and she ended up nearly polishing off the whole bottle. Poor Natalie's dealing with her brother who's back. You know how he's into meth and all of that?"

We both nod mournfully for poor Natalie and her loser twin brother who looks like he's stepped out of an episode of *Breaking Bad*. He even talks like Jesse Pinkman.

"Anyway, we spoke about sexuality and how she's not really into either men or women and that being asexual is sadly underrated."

"So, who was it?" Olivia asks.

Isabella signals the server, and we order some more drinks. Once the server is gone, Olivia says, "Tell us, for god's sake."

"Emily." Isabella grins, looking from me to Olivia.

"No. You're shitting me," Olivia says.

My jaw drops. "Girl-next-door Emily? The same Emily who blushes whenever sex is mentioned?"

"Apparently, Emily dropped into Claire's one night a little upset after Mark hadn't come home. They started drinking, and one thing led to another. And then Claire opened up to Natalie about it, telling her how Emily admitted to never having orgasmed before that night. And there's more."

While processing that, I think about my sexual pleasure and how Dorian hasn't a clue where my clit might be. The one night I tried moving his hand down there, he flinched.

"Wow. Didn't see that coming," Olivia says. "To be honest, Harris never went down on me."

"It's a deal breaker for me. If Jackson wants me to blow him, then he must reciprocate," Isabella says.

Are we doing this; talking about fellatio?

The book club continues to descend into a symposium for sex in the suburbs, which I find rather entertaining when it's about other people's lives. Just like now. This latest piece of gossip has our fascination bubbling away like Isabella's Prosecco.

"Emily and Claire. Who would have thought?" I say.

I'm not in the mood to talk about my beige sex life. The first couple of years, Dorian made me blow him. I hated it. He isn't circumcised, and well, I just hated doing it. He knows that. So he no longer demands it. He just watches porn instead.

That sinking feeling returns. When did my marriage get so toxic?

How did I let it get this bad? Maybe I should watch some of his porn and emulate the women. But I'd need to change my look. Like wear a dark wig, get big fake breasts, and dance around in lingerie.

I amuse myself thinking about that before a dark cloud drifts over me again.

Yep, I'm a failed wife. The whole sex kitten act is just not me. Maybe if I were with someone who makes me all hot and steamy, I might be tempted to get around without panties and do a Margot Robbie in *The Wolf of Wall Street*, but not with Dorian. Now with Jarrad...

Don't go there.

"Anyway," Isabella continues, "Emily's been spotted visiting Claire late at night a few times."

"Mark's hardly ever home. And there's that gay thing with him too."

"Then maybe they can admit to being bisexual and have one of those open marriages," Olivia says.

Isabella's phone vibrates. She reads the message, and her face lights up.

"What?" Olivia asks.

"It's Max," Isabella says, turning into a teenager and getting all giggly. "Talking about hot sex. Oh my god. He's got such a big dick."

Olivia looks at me, and we laugh.

I do feel a bite of envy, though.

Is this my life for now—sex with a man who sees me only as a baby-making machine?

Dorian's a provider, I remind myself again. My life is so comfortable. I have everything but love and affection.

My heart sighs at that stalemate because my soul needs more than material comforts to shine. If only I'd discovered that about myself before signing my life away into this marriage. A marriage I would have walked away from by now were it not for my parents' precarious situation.

Isabella rises. "I have to love and leave you."

She hugs us both. "Not a word to anyone. Promise?" She tilts her heavily made-up face. Her purple sparkly eyeshadow matches her dress. With those dark eyes and olive skin, she can get away with anything, I imagine.

"You don't hate me, do you? For cheating?" Isabella forces a smile.

"Men do it," Olivia says dryly. "Go, girl."

After Isabella leaves, Olivia shakes her head. "She's besotted. I mean, Max is pretty hot, to be sure. But she'll get caught."

"I won't tell Jackson."

Olivia's head lurches back. "Don't look at me. There's no way I would. I mean, I'm a victim of a cheating husband. And I hate cheating, but Isabella's one of us, and I'm not about to rat her out."

She looks over my shoulder. "Hey, isn't that your hottie gardener?"

I turn around, and sure enough, Jarrad is sitting at the bar chatting to a friend. "It is." I'm suddenly all smiles.

As someone who doesn't miss much, Olivia narrows her eyes. "You've got a soft spot for him."

"You've seen him without a shirt, haven't you?" I cock my head.

She chuckles. "Hey, his buddy's hot. Why don't we go and talk to them? I could do with some flirting. And who knows?" She moves her eyebrows up and down.

I gulp down my drink and rise. "I'll see what he's up to. They could be waiting for girls to show up. If not, I'll invite them over for a drink."

"Yay." She's like a happy penguin all of a sudden.

I take a deep breath and walk with slightly wobbly legs to the bar. I've only had two drinks. Or am I swooning? Like in those steamy romance novels I've been reading of late. It's like I'm living my sex life vicariously through those books. And when it comes to leading-man material, Jarrad Hunter's well cast.

I stand behind them, and Jarrad's friend sees me first before my gardener turns and gives me a bright, stress-busting smile.

"Hey, what brings you here?" he asks.

"It's a girls' night out."

His eyes linger, and my knees turn even weaker. Those hypnotic hazel eyes, warm and welcoming, steal my tongue.

"Linley, this is Tommy." He turns to his friend. "Linley's my boss."

I laugh. I am his boss, given that Dorian has nothing to do with Jarrad; he doesn't even notice him.

After some small talk, I say, "I've got my friend over there; do you care to join us?"

Jarrad nods without a moment's thought, which is nice.

Olivia is all smiles as we join her, looking on as the men collect a couple of chairs and settle in.

After the standard introductions are over, Tommy and Olivia are off in their own world.

Olivia's not hiding her attraction, and Tommy, who looks a little younger, appears happy to flirt back.

Feeling tipsy after a couple of drinks, I tell Jarrad about my father and mother's predicament, and things get a little serious.

"Oh, that's terrible. I'm sorry."

"I'm sorry for bringing up such a dark topic," I say.

He looks down at his fingers and shakes his head. "Don't be." He exhales. "My dad went bankrupt."

"Is he okay now?" I ask.

"He's dead. He took his life."

He glances down at his hands, then lifts his eyes to meet mine. His face is tight with tension. I have this sudden urge to take him into my arms and console him.

"I'm so sorry," I say at last. "Your mother?"

"She's still alive, but you know, she never got over Dad's passing. My sister's there. She helps where she can, and so do I."

"Have you got much work?" I ask. Suddenly, I want to give him money. Not that I'd make that obvious. Jarrad strikes me as too proud for handouts.

"I'm working close to seven days. I'm doing fine." He shrugs. "Enough about me. Feel like a dance?" He tilts his head toward the dance floor. "I love this song."

Olivia and Tommy are already on the floor dancing, virtually on top of each other.

"I'm not great at slow dances," I say, blushing.

Blushing? Am I eighteen again?

He crooks his finger. "I'll lead."

Up I get. Who can resist this man?

And as we glide to Ain't No Sunshine, I feel his hard body close to mine, and my heart is beating like mad. Or is that his heart?

He smells divine too.

I don't even think my feet are touching the ground.

"You're so good at this," I say.

"My mom was a ballroom dance teacher," he says. "She used to make me dance with her students when I was a teenager."

"No way. That's out of left field."

He laughs. "Ain't it? Oh well, we've probably all got silly little stories about our lives."

He's got me thinking for a moment. "I've had a pretty boring life, to be honest."

His head lurches back. "You don't strike me as boring. I enjoy talking to you. You're easy to listen to. You've got a lovely voice. It's soft but also deep and comforting."

My heart skips a beat. What a nice thing to say.

"I like talking to you too. And I also like the sound of your voice."

Until now, I've never given much thought to people's voices—how some draw us in while others have us tune out. I think about Dorian's voice, which is deep and confident, but there's so little emotion in his words. They sound almost hollow.

Our eyes lock in a lingering gaze as we share a warm smile. It's like we're alone in space. The heartfelt, bordering on sad, song sinks deeply into my pores, making me yearn for something deeper, like a nurturing soul connection.

Emotion swells in my chest like an ocean before a storm. The empty void that shrouds my life has never felt as visceral as this moment.

I never want this dance to end.

It does, and as we separate, we share a lingering gaze that sends a hot flush through me.

While moving back to the table, I notice Olivia's almost on top of Tommy.

"They're looking close," Jarrad says with a subtle head tilt directed at the randy couple. He turns to face me. "How about a walk down the beach?"

Caught off guard, I take a moment to answer.

The idea grows on me, though, especially seeing how Tommy and Olivia are virtually tongue-kissing.

"It's such a nice night, and it's getting a bit too loud for me. Hip hop's not my thing."

Feeling dreamy after that magical moment on the dance floor, I respond with a slow nod. "I'm not a big fan either."

His eyes trap mine as though he is trying to decipher me. "I hope you don't think I'm being too forward. It's just that it's still early. Does your husband expect you home at a certain time?"

I think of Dorian and his buddies, who are probably playing pool or doing adolescent things like seeing who can hold their breath the longest underwater. The one time he had his New York friends over, they were so drunk I found them crashed out on the floor. Even Dorian dropped his guard and drank heavily.

"No. He won't even notice me gone, probably."

Jarrad's brow creases.

Yes, it's a loaded comment. I don't share my home life with anyone. Not even the girls. It's in poor taste to complain when I have everything.

So why am I crushing on my gardener? And going for a midnight beach stroll?

That's looking for trouble, isn't it?

Pushing aside the moral implications of hanging out with another man late at night, I go with my heart for a change. After all, there's no harm in going for a walk along the beach.

"I'll just let Olivia know."

"I should say goodbye to Tommy too," Jarrad says, following me.

Hating to intrude on Olivia's little romantic moment, I stand close, hoping she'll see me there, but she is too far gone.

She deserves a nice night. I just hope she doesn't get too attached. Tommy, with his surfer-boy looks, doesn't strike me as the loyal type.

"Hey." I tap her on the arm, and she turns and throws me a big cheesy smile.

"There you are," she says.

"Are you okay to stay without me? I'm heading off."

"I'm good. I'll just catch a cab later. Or who knows?" She sounds excited.

Tommy seems like a nice guy at least, and Jarrad endorsed him after I asked if he could be trusted with a fragile divorcee.

"If she's not looking for a relationship, he's a good guy, but if she hopes he'll stay, well…" He gave me a 'don't say I didn't warn you' smile.

I shrugged it off. "She's a grown-up. I meant more in the sociopathic sense."

"I haven't met any of those so far. Not as buddies, at least."

I nodded reflectively at that comment.

Had I met any sociopaths, other than Brendan Crib? Maybe.

FOURTEEN

We ride a cab to the beach, and with Jarrad sitting so close, I can feel his shoulder touching mine. Butterflies invade my stomach as though we're about to do something forbidden, which is both exciting and frightening. Definitely wrong for someone married. Okay, unhappily married, but still, these guilty pangs of desire are making me jittery.

I check my phone just in case Dorian has called. There are no notifications, which isn't unusual—he never calls during the day, let alone at midnight.

As though reading my thoughts, Jarrad asks, "Are you sure your husband won't mind?"

"No, it's fine. He's having a boys' night. I told him we'd be clubbing until the early hours. You're doing me a favor. I would've been in the way with Olivia and Tommy, and my other friend left earlier for a pressing matter. Which would've meant me going home to a bunch of men. Dorian wouldn't have wanted me there. It's a big house, but when you get six males channeling their worst inner toddlers, it can turn ugly."

He chuckles. "I can imagine."

I tuck my phone into my bag. "You don't have those kinds of male bonding sessions?"

"We don't get drunk and behave like kids. No. Not that I'm judging anyone here." His mouth curls at one end. "I've made a few friends since moving here from New York, but I mainly keep to myself. Tommy's landscaping one of the neighboring gardens I'm working at, and that's how we've gotten to know each other."

"I forgot you're from New York. What part?"

"Queens."

"Oh wow, that's where Dorian's from."

He nods. "This place is full of New Yorkers."

I knit my fingers. "Don't tell him I told you that."

"Oh?" He frowns.

"It's meant to be a secret. Dorian hates people knowing. He likes people to think he's from Manhattan. So we tend to run with that."

"But it's bullshit. What's his problem? And anyhow, rags-to-riches stories are all the rage."

"Maybe. Not in Dorian's case."

"What about your in-laws?" he asks. "Are they still in the picture?"

"He was brought up by a single mother. Dorian doesn't have much to do with her."

Jarrad shakes his head. "I'm sorry. I know he's your husband, but he doesn't sound like a good person."

"He has his good points," I mutter.

"Those being?"

Blame it on alcohol, but my tongue has loosened. For some reason, Jarrad makes me want to be real for a change and remove that 'happy in the suburbs' wife charade I've been playing for three years.

"He gives me the freedom to do this, for instance."

"Do you talk at least?" he asks.

"I talk to him, but I'm not sure he hears me."

"He doesn't listen?" he asks, frowning.

The cab pulls up at the beach before I have a chance to answer that somewhat loaded question.

Jarrad goes to pay, but I gently push in and hand my card to the driver. "I insist."

He rolls his eyes.

"I'm the one married to a billionaire here."

The cab driver looks at me, and I bite my lip. Oops, too much information.

We step out of the taxi, and I take in the endless horizon, where a beam of moonlight reflects silvery ripples over the ink-blue sea. Perfect for a nocturnal stroll, the night is balmy and still.

As we move along the path, I point out the calm, shimmering ocean and the pearly orb above it. "What a perfect night. I never do this."

He turns to me. "Oh? You live within walking distance."

"I know. During the day, I come down for a walk, but not at this hour. Walking alone at midnight strikes me as inviting danger. It's so sad that women can't enjoy the same freedoms as men."

"I think it's dangerous for most, but sure, a woman alone at this hour isn't safe. And I agree it's unfair that women can't be free to enjoy nature whenever they want. The night is like poetry and full of surprises." He points up to the sky. "And the moon is full."

I smile, feeling more alive than I have in ages. If only I didn't feel guilty because I'm so drawn to Jarrad, I could easily let myself do something wrong.

My heart and head are battling because my instincts are screaming for me to surrender to the moment as a breeze caresses my naked arms and face like it's stroking my soul.

I'll remember this moment forever, despite the tightness in my chest.

Though Jarrad is so easy to be around, it's this sudden bout of guilt colliding with desire that's turning me upside down.

Can I control the urge to kiss him? Or allow him to make that first move?

There's Dorian's porn habit, and lately, having smelled perfume on his shirt, I sense he's cheating on me. I've even considered hiring a PI, but it's all too tacky, and I would hate for my life to descend into a shitshow. I don't have the stomach for it. It's easier to do nothing and let destiny do her thing. Like right now. I mean, how did I get here? Walking under the moonlight with a man who takes my breath away.

Weed smoke blows my way as a couple sharing a joint laughs loudly. One of many couples on the sand, embracing and running their hands all over each other's bodies, virtually having sex.

The night is alive with lust.

"I think I should take off my shoes," I say, almost stumbling on the cracked pavement.

Jarrad points to a bench. "Sit here, and I'll take them off for you."

I lower myself down and stretch out my leg as he removes my shoes. His hand slides up to my ankle, and I feel a sizzle of heat slide all the way up my thigh. It's probably the most erotic thing I've experienced in years. If ever. We both stand up.

"Are you always such a gentleman?" I ask.

"I try. You don't mind?" His eyes meet mine.

"Oh, there's always room for chivalry in my life. I'm a little old-fashioned like that."

"Old-fashioned's good," he says.

We continue, walking in companionable silence for a while.

"This is so lovely. I should do this more often," I say. "Only I don't have anyone to do this with. Maybe I can ask one of the neighbors."

"You strike me as lonely. If you don't mind me saying."

I stop walking. "I miss my family and my life in Connecticut. I'm still that person."

"And who's that?" he asks.

"Do you want to know?" I smile tentatively.

He shrugs. "That's just how we are as humans. We try to understand each other, and in so doing, we understand ourselves a little better."

"You're a deep man, aren't you?" I say.

He smiles tightly. "Maybe. Sometimes too deep. I feel things. I let things get to me."

I nod pensively. "I try to avoid dwelling on the depressing stuff myself. But sometimes it's easier said than done."

"Why are you married to such a jerk-off?"

I turn to face him square on. That was so unexpected.

"Sorry. I shouldn't have asked that."

"No, you're right. Dorian is a jerk, all right. He was my way out, you could say. And, well, I was a little smitten too. I mean, he's quite the catch."

"And did you catch him with just one hand or both?"

I arch my eyebrows. "Interesting metaphor. Um, I suppose if by two hands you mean his entire devotion, then I'd say it was more a fluke one-hander." I sniff. "He asked me where I saw myself in five years, and I replied, 'As a housewife with two kids.' He liked that response and asked me to marry him."

"I'm sensing disappointment."

I sigh. "I just agreed to start IVF."

He turns to look at me. "You don't look too happy about that."

"No. But it's either that or my parents being on the street."

"You've done a plea bargain?" He shakes his head. "Marriages."

"You've never been married?" I brush a strand of hair away from my face.

"No. I've been too much of a drifter up to now, I guess. Fell in with a bad crowd back in New York. That's why I came here to start again. Anyway,

I need to make good before I can think about marrying and starting a family."

"Do you want that? I know you're still young. You're in your mid-thirties, aren't you?"

He smiles. "I'm forty-two."

"Oh, wow, you don't look it."

"You didn't read my papers? You got all those, didn't you?"

"I probably popped them in a drawer somewhere. I'm a little trusting like that. You struck me as an honest man."

"As much as I'm touched by your belief in me, it's not a good practice, Linley. And what about the maid? Have you seen her boyfriend? Or is that her husband?"

"What about her?" I ask. "And no…" I stammer. "I don't know him."

"The other day, while you were out, he arrived, jumped over the fence, and I dealt with him. He was out of his mind on meth, I'd say. The maid came running just as I was about to toss him out."

"I didn't know that. Why didn't you tell me?" I ask.

"I promised her not to."

"So he came to see Ana?"

"More like to heap abuse on her. She gave him some money, and he left. She then begged me not to tell you."

I nod slowly. "Okay."

"So, you might want to check on that arrangement. She seems a nice enough girl, but with that kind of arsehole for a boyfriend, you might find a few things missing."

"Good help's hard to find, and she's thorough and respectful."

"And is flirting with your husband," he adds.

I have to smile. "My, you have been keeping an eye on things."

"I'm not spying, if that's what you're implying."

I stand still and touch his hand. His eyes trap mine. I'm lost for words, and though I'm shaking my head at that suggestion, I lose track of what we were talking about because I see his tongue running over his lips. That's all that captures my attention.

And before I know what's happening, I fall into his strong arms, and our lips crush. A deep, passionate kiss that I've dreamed about.

It was like this moment was always going to happen. From the moment I laid eyes on Jarrad, my heart was leaning toward him.

Instead of pulling away, I almost push him along until we come to a palm tree, and our bodies come together like magnets. I can feel all of him. His desire. Hard. And real.

FIFTEEN

Ana

Hector's slumped on the couch, watching some loud, violent crap on television. There are beer cans, cigarette butts on a plate, and his meth pipe spread out on the table. I want to scream and throw him out. But I can't because he'll hurt me, and his cartel family in Mexico will kill my dad.

It's all so messed up.

He smells of smoke, sweat, and that chemical stink he gets from his drugs, like he's sweating the toxic crap out of his skin. When he holds me, it's like I'm holding someone who's been in a chemical waste bin.

It's awful.

He's awful.

He was never this bad. That teenager I fell hard for—large brown eyes and wavy black hair, tall and muscly—has become a skinny rake with lifeless eyes. Like a monster has taken possession of him. Every time he sucks on that glass pipe, that monster grows stronger.

His feet are up on the coffee table like he's a kept man. He is. Cabrón.

I look at him with hate in my eyes before he notices me there.

He sits up. "You're late. Again."

I take a deep breath and ask myself how my life turned into this shitshow. The contrast between our rundown apartment and the Gunns' home is like comparing a shithole to a palace.

I love my job and being in a house that seems to sparkle under the sun. But then I have to come back to this slum at the end of the day.

He gets up off the couch, looking even skinnier in a loose singlet. His once muscly arms are thin and wasted, and his rib cage is poking out. Even his tattoos look sad.

He used to be hot. The love of my life. Meth happened, and it all went to shit.

Then Mrs. Gunn employed me, and I met her husband, with the roaming eyes and hands that I'm getting addicted to.

He's becoming the man of my dreams. Except he's married, and he wants to stay that way, he says.

"Got any money? Weren't you supposed to get paid today?" Hector asks, fumbling through my bag.

"Hey." I tug away the Prada bag that Linley generously gave me. Can't have him finding my torn underwear.

It was a fiery session with Dorian today. We've begun meeting at a hotel. At least I showered.

I remove a fifty-dollar bill from my bag and hand it over. It's one of the ten fifties Dorian gave me. Yes, I'm bad. He's paying me. But hey, I want to be there. I just have to work out how to win him from her.

Linley's nice. Too nice. I wish she was a bitch. It would be easier to screw her husband and not care. But I do care.

It all started a week ago. She was away for a few days visiting her folks and asked me to sleep over. I have to say, Linley doesn't know her husband well because it didn't take long before one thing led to another.

I'd seen how Dorian looked at me from the get-go. And yes, I was always sure to unbutton my shirt a little or bend over at the right times. I've decided that the only way out of this horrible life is to marry a rich man.

Hector threatens to kill me if I leave. All because he loves me. Love? I'm more like his prisoner.

I go to change quickly before he discovers I'm not wearing panties. Hector's insatiable. I used to love that. Now I've got to be careful that he doesn't find out about Dorian. He'll kill him for sure.

That can't happen because I want to be the next Mrs. Gunn. I know they hardly have sex. Dorian tells me she's a cold fish and doesn't turn him on.

I do, though.

I see how his eyes burn whenever I'm there cleaning the kitchen or making his green juice.

Two hours after his wife left, I was in his bed. It didn't take much. He just pushed me against the wall and rubbed my tits. I surrendered to him. It wasn't something I'd planned, but seeing how they live and all the comforts of wealth, I decided I wanted in. And he's crazy about me, going off body language.

Only there's my boyfriend. And if I leave him, my father will be murdered.

But that's another story. It relates to drugs. I hate them. They've been around me all my life.

I change into my sweats, and hearing the door shut, I flop onto the couch and put my legs up. Hector's no doubt gone to buy drugs. I don't care; I'm glad to be left alone. There's a lot to think about. I have to figure out a way into Dorian's world. Make it permanent somehow. But first, Hector's got to go.

That won't be easy. Not with my father being threatened by Hector's drug-dealing family.

Can I have sex with two men? I'm already sore from Dorian, who was so horny I barely made it through the door of the hotel room before he started tearing off my clothes.

Dorian keeps saying it's only sex for him. Like he's trying to warn me not to expect more. That's why I accepted his cash. Why not? I've got to live somehow, especially with a vampire boyfriend who sucks my earnings dry.

Unlike my loser boyfriend, I've always worked. I like to stay busy. I can't just sit around and do nothing. Escorting or dancing at clubs is not my thing either, and anyway, Hector's too jealous.

He's killed before. Hector saved my father's life when he shot a man from behind who was holding a gun to my dad's head. That's part of the reason we're still together.

Hector will never let me go.

But now I've got a plan. I've just got to work out how to get my prize and somehow save my dad in the process.

SIXTEEN

Ana

LIKE EVERY DAY, I arrive early. I love my job. It's so much more than just the anticipation of catching Dorian eye-fucking me. It's being in that beautiful house and dreaming of it being mine. One day I can hire my own maid. Not a pretty one, though. Can't have that. I don't get why Mrs. Gunn even continues to hire me, but I'm not giving her any reason to complain. I'm thorough.

After I get out of my car, I pause to admire the beautiful house. Instead of stinky leaking sewage and overflowing garbage like around my shitty apartment, this place smells of flowers and fresh grass.

It should be in a movie, like those films where everyone is hugging all the time. When I was a girl, I dreamed of that being me one day—living on a tree-lined street with large houses that look like wedding cakes. And now here I am, screwing the rich guy starring in that same dream.

Smoothing out my shirt, I button it up so that Mrs. Gunn doesn't get the wrong idea. I push open the picket gate, and my daydream carries me along like it does every time I come through the gate. The grass is so green and smooth like carpet. I'd love to walk barefoot on it. There isn't a single weed anywhere, just flowers of every color and butterflies fluttering about like I've walked into a fairy tale.

When I live here, I won't change a thing. I can see myself hosting pool parties with Dorian's arm draped around me. He looks like one of those rich guys you see in magazines, dressed in a white linen shirt and knee-length shorts. I'm wearing a breezy designer dress with just a hint of cleavage, not some trashy bodycon or anything like that, but something stylish that says I don't need to dress all slutty to win the man of my dreams.

Snapping out of that fantasy, I knock on the brass hand knocker, excited at the thought of seeing Dorian.

Mrs. Gunn answers the door with a smile. "Good morning, Ana."

She steps away from the door and lets me in. "Good morning, Mrs.—I mean, Linley." I smile, despite a knot in my stomach. I feel bad for wanting what she has. But guilt won't stop me. It's all about survival.

She's pretty in that boring, non-descript kind of way, so she'll find someone else. Dorian tells me they hardly ever do it. That's a loveless marriage in my eyes. She's nice, though, and deserves more. If anything, I'm doing her a favor.

I set my bag down and roll up my sleeves, ready for a day of cleaning, polishing, and making Dorian's favorite juices. He says he prefers mine to Linley's. Personally, I don't know how he can drink that green shit, but hey, he could drink mud for all I care.

She points at the dark mark on my wrist. "Is everything okay at home?"

Linley looks worried, which kinda freaks me out. I mean, why does she give a shit? Why can't she be a bitch? I wouldn't feel so bad about taking her husband. "No. I'm good."

"Just that you've got some bruising."

I shrug. "My boyfriend can get a little rough sometimes."

Ha, that's putting it nicely. When Hector came back from scoring, he demanded I blow him. I said I was tired, and he squeezed my wrists until I dropped to the ground.

I bruise easily—that's an excuse I give most people.

Her brow scrunches. Even my mother, when she was alive, didn't look that worried when I'd come home hurt. Often from rough play at school—falling over while chasing a ball or something innocent. Not like now, living with a boyfriend from hell with a drug problem.

Hector insists he's only like this because he loves me. That I'm his soulmate. He only says that when he's drugged and in a good mood and not chasing a hit. Being imprisoned is not how I'd describe true love, and it is not how I want to spend my life.

He is not my happily ever after. Dorian is.

Only, as I look at the concern shining in his wife's eyes, I start to question whether I should find another house to clean with a bitchy wife and a hot, rich husband to seduce. That would help me sleep easier at night. I have a conscience, you know. But I also need saving, and Dorian has gotten under my skin. I like the way he smells and how he feels. We're a perfect fit. He even said that to me last night, even if he seemed a bit jumpy as he checked his messages.

I know it can't be easy losing half your fortune to a wife who doesn't make you happy, but hey, he's a money magnet.

"Is he hurting you? Do you need somewhere to stay?" Linley asks.

Yes, here, in your bedroom.

"Um. No, I'm good. And hey, thanks for offering. I'll be okay."

"It's just that I need to go away for a few days to visit my parents. Again." She taps her long fingernails together.

I'm already popping a champagne cork in my head at that thought, but I make a sad face like she is right now.

"I was hoping you might stay over. Dorian has requested it. And he likes his early morning shakes."

He likes more than that in the mornings.

I think of Dorian's hands all over my tits. He can't stop touching me.

I have to control the urge not to smile and just nod, wearing a serious face. "Sure."

"Will your boyfriend be okay?" she asks.

"He'll understand. We can always use the extra."

She studies me for a minute, and I hope she can't see how bad I'm suddenly feeling. I mean, why does she have to be so nice? And then there are those gifts like the red velvet Dior jacket and Prada bag she no longer wants, which I love swinging around like I'm someone special.

Dorian enters through the front door. He's puffing and sweaty after his run. I get a whiff of his cologne, and my body heats up. His eyes capture mine, and if his wife wasn't so close, I swear he'd have his hands all over me.

Linley's either half asleep or something else. I mean, can't she see how he looks at me?

Weird. But I must play my cards right because I need this job, and any minute she might wake up. Dorian mentioned something about losing money if she finds out about us.

I get that he's happy paying me, but I don't want to be some desperate nobody selling her body.

Linley turns to him. "I'm just heading out. Will you be back late tonight?"

Dorian stares at her with cold eyes. There's no love there for sure. It's like they're strangers to each other. Linley kisses him sometimes and calls him 'darling,' but I think that's just for show. I've seen how she smiles around the gardener. She's never like that around Dorian.

"Not sure when I'll be back," he says.

He's avoiding me, I can tell, and I move away before I give something away.

"There's a meeting at six. We might take it to a bar afterward. I'll let you know."

Linley collects her bag and leaves us there. Alone.

I head to the kitchen to make his juice and prepare his fruit. Dorian's very particular and likes things done a certain way.

I like to be seen as useful and am a quick learner.

As I'm peeling the apples, he enters and rubs himself up on me.

"I've got something I need you to do first." He signals for me to follow him up the stairs.

Once we're there, he lowers his sweats and briefs, and then, placing his hand on my shoulder, he gets me to kneel. He loves my mouth.

"Aah. You're good. Too good," he says with a moan as I blow him.

He then withdraws, lifts me, and bends me over the bed, rubbing my tits and taking me from behind. He comes quickly.

"God, I can't get enough of you," he says, panting like it's a problem. Like I'm a problem.

"I like it. I like you," I say, smiling.

He doesn't say anything as usual. He doesn't like to say nice things. That's okay. I don't see him kissing his wife or showing affection, so I get that he's not a touchy-feely type of guy.

Whichever way, I want him. I want this.

SEVENTEEN

Linley

It's morning, and I have a plane to catch. Dorian arrives just as I'm packing. He enters the bedroom. "So you're off again in the morning? How did your IVF appointment go?"

His eyes wander to the skimpy new bra hanging from my hand. I'm not sure what compelled me to go shopping for lingerie.

I'm glad that I'm getting away for a few days just to clear my head, even if this isn't exactly a fun trip. My parents need me.

All I can think of right now is that kiss. I don't know what came over me or who initiated it. It was like I'd been in a dream—the kind a teenager might have about that gorgeous boy she's been crushing on for a whole summer. Long mental foreplay that builds up to an eruption just from lips melting together. That's how it felt.

"I attended the first consult." A tight swallow follows.

I have yet to share that I just received the results from that first consultation. During the second visit, the conversation with the doctor went something like this: "The problem is you don't have many quality eggs." He leaned back in his chair without a hint of sympathy. It was like he was telling me that my credit card was overdrawn.

"It went well," I lie. "I've got another appointment in a week, and we should be good to go." Yep. I'm stalling for time rather than facing this situation head-on.

His scrutinizing gaze makes me wonder if he can read my lie. I suppose I'm crushing the T-shirt in my hand instead of folding it. Bad body language.

"My mother needs me right now." I shake my head at how things have gone from bad to worse. "She's been diagnosed with breast cancer."

I reflect on that gut-wrenching phone call from my dad, his voice breaking from suppressed emotion. "Darling, I have some bad news."

Thinking it had to do with money problems, I squared my shoulders.

"They've found a lump in your mother's breast."

It was like a force of wind pushed me down onto the ground as I fell onto the chair. My heart clenched. My mother was not just a mother but my best friend, my everything person. I couldn't lose her. "How bad?" I asked at last.

Taking a moment, he said, "They'll have to operate. They say she will lose the breast, and then there'll be chemo."

"I'll jump on the next flight, Dad." I gulped back a sob. "She'll get through this. I'll make sure she does."

Right now, I could use a hug, but Dorian is looking distant, as though he doesn't know how to respond to such heavy news.

He nods slowly. "Oh, right."

No sympathetic, 'how awful, I'm so sorry' response. Just that empty expression he has when topics go somewhere dark.

Dorian doesn't do emotion. I get that. Though he's good at anger. I'm even wondering if he's on the spectrum. The little I've read about autism seems to correlate with my husband's cool response to emotion like he doesn't quite get why anyone would cry or laugh.

"I hope it doesn't run in the family. I'd hate for our daughter to inherit some bad gene."

Some bad gene? My brows gather.

Is he for real?

Talk about twisting the knife in a little deeper. If it's not bad enough learning about my mom's diagnosis, I've also got a husband worried about our elusive offspring falling victim to cancer.

"Well, no. I mean…" I want to scream at him, but I'm emotionally constipated.

Just like him.

Funny about that.

Maybe it's contagious—a pair who don't know how to express deeper emotion.

My emotions are there on the surface, ready to break into a show and tell for Jarrad. What is it about him that brings it all out? I'm almost emotionally naked around him.

This 'happy housewife' role has become second nature. I've almost convinced myself of that. But then along comes Jarrad, and it's like he's helping me be myself—the real me. That person I left behind years ago. I miss her. I'd prefer to be that woman minus the fairytale aspirations that blurred my reality—aspirations that led me into a marriage wearing a blindfold. And by that, I don't mean some fifty shades of kinky.

"My mom's not my biological mother," I say quietly.

Dorian looks stunned as if I've just told him I'm the offspring of some psycho.

I go to move off.

"Wait." He holds up his palm. "I haven't finished. Why didn't you tell me they weren't your parents? Or was your dad married to your biological mother, and this is your stepmother?"

I go to bite a nail and stop myself. I ended that ugly habit years ago, but this is as tense as it gets. "I don't know my real mother and father." My voice cracks.

Strange how this awkward topic came out naturally with Jarrad.

The sympathetic look in his eyes made me want to cry. In sad contrast, Dorian's look is anything but sympathetic. I guess that's my bad. I should have told him, but he wasn't exactly sharing details of his family tree either.

The frown on his face has deepened. "Have you looked for them?"

I shake my head. "Why are you so interested all of a sudden?"

"You of all people know that all I want is healthy, intelligent children who'll make me proud. Genes play into that."

I roll my eyes. "Some of the world's most successful people have come from peasants, like Leonardo da Vinci, who was illegitimate and one of the greatest geniuses of all time."

He looks at me as if I've lost my mind.

Rubbing his jaw, he says, "You should have told me."

"You refused to talk to me about your parents. You kept changing the subject and closing me down. How is that any different?" I appeal.

"It is fucking different. You should have told me." He's now pacing, something Dorian does when he's challenged.

I swallow back the buildup of anger that started from the moment he forgot to support me in this latest struggle.

"I'm sorry for not telling you." As the knot in my chest tightens, I force a steady breath and slip back into the obedient wife role. Now's not the time to stir the pot.

He returns a contemptuous grunt and is about to move away when I add, "I'll be back in a couple of days. And I promise I'll get a blood test and have a genealogist go over it with a fine-toothed comb if you like."

"Whatever. Let's just focus on the IVF treatment." Dorian huffs as though he's tired of this discussion. Once again, I'm having to take the blame.

I lean in and kiss him—something I've forgotten to do lately.

My only ambition right now is to protect my mom and dad and sleep well at night.

That kiss has rattled me.

I want Jarrad like I'd love to devour a slice of Black Forest cake, which, of course, I never deny myself. But an affair to remedy this empty marriage? How could that be helpful?

As Dorian strides off, I wonder why he doesn't just divorce me and move on to someone young and fertile, with a perfect gene profile. The answer arrives quickly: it's all about money.

I think back to New York and that dinner party where he first met my parents. I almost frothed at the mouth with joy as he sat in my shoebox Village apartment, asking my parents questions about the kind of diet they prescribe, the books they like to read, and so on.

I was too in love to even question that interview masked as a social get-together. With the benefit of hindsight, it was blatantly obvious even then that this marriage was merely a business transaction. That prenup surely read like one. I didn't even read it properly. I wasn't about to cheat, and, as far as babies went, well, I told myself it would be fine. Though at the time, that ticking-clock approach to baby-making did seem rather heavy-handed. I was smitten then.

Snapping my carry-on shut, I say, "I'll be back in a few days."

He doesn't even offer to carry my luggage down the stairs.

Tears burn at the back of my eyes as I gulp back bitterness and force a plastic smile when his cool gaze meets mine.

As I descend the stairs carrying my case, Ana looks up at me, puts down the duster, and runs up the stairs. "Here, Mrs. Gunn, let me take that for you."

I hand it to her and swallow back tears. It's all a bit too crazy. I just want to go somewhere and howl.

EIGHTEEN

Ana

Hector points at the overnight bag I've just set down on the table. "I don't like you staying there." He runs his eyes up and down my body. At least I'm wearing my latest loose black slacks and a blouse fit for a nun. I want to downplay the whole sexy kitten look that Dorian seems to be crazy about. I can't let Linley see what's happening, and this way Hector doesn't get all shitty about me dressing like a whore, which are his words, not mine.

He thinks Linley's going to be there and that they've asked me to be around for a late-night party. It's the best excuse I could come up with. I can't believe she's even asked me to stay. I mean, I wouldn't if the roles were reversed.

"You like the double-time pay I get," I say, removing my phone from the charger.

"How long for?" he asks, watching me closely.

"A few days. They entertain a lot," I lie. "I'm needed to prepare an early breakfast and to make sure the place is sparkling clean. It's a huge house. A mansion. And he's a clean freak and seriously fussy about his food."

"So how much are you getting?" He scratches his balls, and I swear I want to scream. He's a fucking Neanderthal.

I shrug. "Not sure. I haven't worked it out. But it's like forty an hour, I think."

He whistles. "What, over three days?"

I lied about that too. It's more like fifty dollars an hour. But I need to keep some for me.

Hector's always going through my bag like everything I own is his. It's not just my body and soul but all my cash too. Not for long. I've got it all planned out. Dorian's hooked, and Linley's making it easier than ever for me to take her husband away.

He returns to the new game console I bought him just to shut him up. He's seriously into console and computer games, and if that keeps him out of my way, then it's a good investment. Though he did ask me how I could afford it after I said I couldn't pay the electricity bill. I mumbled something about getting a bonus and then left the room in a hurry. Hector's good at reading my face.

I lean in and kiss his cheek. He hasn't showered, and I feel like puking. I can't believe that I sleep with this creep. Dorian has spoiled me. He smells so good. Billionaire cologne's sexy.

I shut the door behind me and take a deep breath as I walk to the elevator. Of course, it's not working again. It hardly ever does.

One day soon, I will leave this dump, I remind myself. I just have to play my cards carefully.

I open the graffitied door to the stairs. Everyone's so angry around here, like they're owed a good life without having to do anything. I can't stand their whining voices and sad 'little old me' stories. We all make our opportunities, and I'm making mine. Enough of this bullshit about destiny dealing out a bad set of cards.

Growing up in Mexico with a father who didn't bother to find work wasn't a great start for me, but I'm not going to sit around and feel sorry for myself. Work doesn't scare me. I love it. Especially when there's a hot billionaire who can't take his hands off me.

I walk down the stairs and, sure enough, there's some loser slumped over. The needle is still stuck in his arm. I want to ignore him, but there's some good left in me, so I check to make sure he's breathing before hurrying off. Junkies are like zombies sucking out brains for that next hit.

I cover my nose with my hand. The smell has become unbearable, and the cracks on the walls look like the apartment tower's about to crumble.

I'm about to jump in my car when a call comes from my dad.

"Papa." I slide onto the seat.

"Bonita, I might have found a way out. There's a friend who can take me to Chile. For a price, of course."

"Chile? What will you do there?"

"I'll have a new identity. You'll be free to leave that hijo de puta."

I take a deep breath. "How much?"

"Fifty thousand dollars. That buys me a new passport, ID, everything. They won't be able to find me."

If my father can escape the cartel that my wasted boyfriend is affiliated with, I'm free to go.

While I'm with Hector, my daddy's safe. Only it's becoming more dangerous. Hector's becoming crazier. He's already tried to strangle me that time I wouldn't give him cash for his drugs.

But I need to get out ASAP, because what will I do when Hector discovers I'm pregnant?

I only just found out.

Fifty thousand dollars is like a day's wage for Dorian. I know, because he likes to brag about how much he makes.

I've even packed in lacy lingerie. Whoever said you can't win a man through his dick hasn't met Dorian Gunn.

"Okay, Papa, I'll see what I can do."

"I don't want you doing something wrong, though."

Too late.

"I might be able to borrow it."

"Is that hijo de puta still hurting you?" he asks.

"If I give him money for meth, he's not so bad."

"I am so sorry, cariña. I should never have gotten mixed up with this lot. But I had to for your mother. You know that, don't you?"

I think about my mother, who died from ovarian cancer when I was fifteen. To pay for the hospital bills, my dad joined a cartel. He ended up working for one of Hector's brothers. Jose is the ruthless one in that family. He helped set us up in LA in return for Hector running a few errands. I think it was to get him out of the way before he screwed things up for the family.

It's all just a freaking mess.

And now I'm expecting.

I missed my period, and I did the math.

I know it's Dorian's because I've been without contraception forever and Hector's the only man I've ever been with other than Dorian. That's eight years of sex and not getting pregnant.

I might have found a way in.

I know how much Dorian wants kids. I've heard him talking to his wife. She's even agreed to do IVF. It's not nice to snoop, but I hear everything.

I just have to convince Dorian to leave Linley. What better way than being the mother of his baby?

But for now, I have to play my cards carefully. I don't want to bring up a fatherless child, and if Hector gets wind of Dorian, then that's what will happen.

The first thing, though, is to get cash to free my dad.

NINETEEN

Linley

Lush green lawns and manicured gardens flash past me as we drive down Magnolia Boulevard and arrive at my sprawling home. The sun shines brightly, and I pray that's a good omen as I pay the driver.

Just as I step out of the cab, Jarrad arrives in his old Chevy pickup.

We haven't spoken since that midnight stroll down the beach, which was only two weeks ago, even though it feels like months.

Invaded by disturbed thoughts, I hardly slept these past three nights in Greenwich. My mother's health preyed on me, as did the doctor's doubts about IVF working.

What the hell am I to do? I know Dorian will just bide his time, and then I'm out on my butt, almost penniless.

Maybe hire a PI?

I push that messy thought aside again. For now.

Jarrad steps out of his car and strides over. My heart flutters like a teenager with a ridiculous crush on some out-of-reach guy.

I take a deep breath, and my cheeks fire up.

Stop it. This can't happen.

It certainly can't, not after seeing my parents. My dad asked if he could put the house on the market. I had to remind him that the house was now in Dorian's name after he'd paid off the mortgage.

My father went pale. "Why didn't you tell me?"

"Because you'd just been released from the hospital, and Mom, having power of attorney, agreed to it. There was little else she could do."

Looking like he'd aged ten years, my father clutched his wrinkled hands and nodded. He bit his lip, as though trying to push back tears, which made me want to find somewhere to hide and sob, but I kept things cool, if only for his sake. The last thing the poor thing needed was for me to erupt in tears.

"Mom made me promise not to worry you." I touched his hand. "She knew you wouldn't agree. But at least this way, the bank is no longer threatening to foreclose on the house, and you'll be able to stay here forever."

I gulp at that promise because once I'm out of this marriage, Dorian will toss my parents out. He's not the most compassionate person I've ever met.

Looking defeated, Dad said, "I can try and get some work."

"No way. Your health comes first. I need you here for years to come. And so does Mom." Tears sprang out of me without warning, and my dad hugged me like I was the one in need of support.

Now I'm home, and all I want to do is fall into Jarrad's arms and cry some more.

I suck it back and wait for a healthy dose of composure to kick in before speaking.

He beats me to it. "How was your trip?"

I smile sweetly like it's any normal day. "It was fine, thanks."

He isn't buying it. As our eyes meet, tears burn at the back of my eyes. Swallowing back emotion, I'm still raw from the past few days.

The concern shining in his eyes, like he knows I'm hurting, is triggering a flood of emotion. Any minute now, I'm going to lose it.

I move on quickly.

"How are your folks?" he asks as we walk along the path to the entrance.

"That's a big story." My mouth quivers slightly. And no, I'm not having a stroke, but I might as well be because, overwhelmed with emotion, the part of my brain that's well-rehearsed at glossing things over seems to be malfunctioning.

I'm the queen of cool. Or was, until I met Jarrad.

We're now at the door, and he's dying to say something, but just as he's about to speak, Ana opens the door, and her welcoming expression morphs into a curious smile on seeing Jarrad.

Can she see our attraction? Or is there something else?

I don't think I can handle anything else right now. But she does look different. Not as sweet. Like her smile is fake. Maybe it's always been like that, and I'm only just seeing it.

It's amazing how razor-sharp one's attention to detail becomes when faced with crises, fueling paranoia.

"We'll talk about the garden later," I say to him.

He nods and walks away.

We never talk about the garden. I just leave him to it, and he's doing a fine job. The garden's thriving.

Once we're inside, Ana returns to her chores in the kitchen, chopping up fruit for Dorian's endless juices. She certainly knows how to keep busy, and the house is sparkling as always.

I lay my bag down on the sofa and then pass her by the bench to make myself a coffee.

"Can I make you something?" she asks, wearing a caring smile.

"A coffee would be nice." I return to the sofa and flop down.

I can see Jarrad, who has removed his shirt, trimming branches with the sun gleaming on his tanned, muscular body.

I sigh. It's all too much. Can I rewrite my life? With a few million dollars thrown in to help my parents?

Help that they wouldn't have needed if they hadn't met Brendon Crib. I noticed how quickly Dorian changed the subject and swiftly paid off my parents' mortgage. Funny about that. Though putting the house in his name soured things.

Ana brings me coffee and sets it down on the side table.

I take a sip. "Mm... that's good. Thanks."

She returns to wiping down the bench and placing the chopped fruit and veggies in separate containers for the fridge.

"Was everything okay while I was gone? Dorian wasn't too demanding?" I ask.

"No, he wasn't here very often."

"Oh?" I scrutinize her because she strikes me as jumpy.

A cup smashes, having slipped from her hand, and she covers her mouth. Her eyes fill with terror as though it's something more catastrophic than just broken crockery.

"Don't worry, it's only a cup," I say.

She's on the ground, sweeping the shattered bits into a dustpan. Her nerves seem more on edge than mine.

She stands up and says, "Sorry" again, and then wiping her hands with a cloth, she asks, "Is there anything else, Mrs. Gunn? I've got an appointment with a doctor."

"There's nothing I need. You're doing a great job. The house looks so clean and smells heavenly."

Ana has put on weight. In all the right places. "Nothing the matter, I hope?"

She bites her lip and then starts to sob.

I point at the armchair. "Why don't you sit for a minute?"

Ana falls into the seat and buries her face in her hands.

I pass her a tissue from a box by the table. "I hope your boyfriend isn't hurting you again." I scan her bare arms for marks.

She shakes her head. "No. It's just that I'm pregnant."

Noticing her hands shaking slightly, I take a moment to respond. "Oh, you're not happy about that?"

Ana stares down at her hands. "I wasn't expecting to be a mother so soon. I have plans."

"How's the father taking it?"

I notice her flinch. "He still doesn't know." She releases a breath and then stands, smoothing down her knee-length skirt. "I'm sorry. I've taken up your time."

"It's okay. I'm good."

"I can still work here, I hope?" Her question is more of a plea, and my heart goes out to her.

"Of course you can. And if you need time off, just ask."

"I can't afford that."

"I'll cover you for those hours."

Dorian won't be happy, but he doesn't need to know.

She wipes her eyes. "Thank you. You're too nice."

I watch her leave and then put my feet up and think about how unfair life is. A woman wanting to get pregnant can't, while another as much as looks at a man and conceives.

On that sobering note, I decide to speak to Jarrad about that kiss and to quiz him about the odd look Ana gave him because I noticed a change in him too. Like they knew something.

A knock comes at the front door just as I rise.

Peeking through the window, I spy Olivia standing there, shifting from one leg to another. Here we go, another overwrought person. Must be in the stars.

I open the door to find Olivia wearing one of her 'Sorry if I'm interrupting something, but I'm going crazy' expressions. She says, "Hope you don't mind me dropping in like this."

Stepping out of the way, I let her in and she follows me into the front room.

I hope she doesn't ask me about what happened after leaving the bar with Jarrad. I'd love to talk to someone, but not Olivia or anyone from our little group for that matter. The rumor mill would spin out of control and before you know it, I'm on with the gardener and, "My, how cliché is that? A rich, bored housewife jumping her hunky, shirtless gardener's bones."

Jarrad is more than that, I appeal to my jaded mind.

"What can I get you?" I ask.

She peers down at her phone and then puts it away. "Is it too early for a drink?"

It's never too early for Olivia. I smile. "What will it be?"

"Um, whatever you've got."

"Oh, it's like that?" I go over to the trolley and lift the bottle of bourbon, and she nods.

I pour some out and pass it over.

Taking the glass, she says, "Thanks. You're not having anything?"

I shake my head.

She sips her drink and then her face starts to relax a little.

"So what's up?" I ask.

"I've been seeing Tommy."

"Like more than just that one night, you mean?"

"Uh-huh." She gulps back her drink. "We've spent every night together." She shakes her head. "My. God. He makes my toes curl. He's hot and so good in bed."

"That sounds nice." Her euphoric afterglow proves contagious, as I visualize Jarrad in my bed and welcome that warm swell of desire. Whichever way, Olivia's excitement shines a spotlight on the sad lack of pleasure in my life.

"It's more than nice. Only…" She huffs. "I'm falling hard for him. And he told me last night, after I introduced him to the twins, that it's all a bit too much and that it's been nice but he isn't looking for anything serious."

"Wait. You introduced him to the twins?" I fail to mask the shock in my voice.

"He dropped in, and the boys were there. What was I supposed to do?"

"Okay. I guess that's on him."

She rises and pours herself another bourbon. "I'm crazy about him."

"Sweetheart, it's only been two weeks, and he is young. Maybe just enjoy the experience you've had."

Olivia gulps the liquor down. "I'm going crazy. My life's so dull. Shit." She starts to pace.

I'm about to respond when another knock comes at the door, and this time it's Sophia.

Olivia wipes her eyes. "Hey, don't say anything."

I shake my head. "Between us."

I go to let Sophia in, welcoming the distraction—I'm not in the mood to help tackle Olivia's marriage dramas.

In sharp contrast, Sophia is the poster child for what a happy marriage looks like as she steps through the door, glowing as always.

Whether she is dressed up or wearing athleisure like she is now—leggings with hearts and an oversized orange crop top—Sophia looks flawless. I wouldn't be seen dead in what she's wearing, but the bright outfit suits her vibe. At least it's nowhere near as garish as some of the flashy, exorbitantly priced activewear going around these days. It's astounding how expensive polyester seems to look better than the cheap stuff. It's still plastic, though, and I prefer natural fabrics myself. I read somewhere about how synthetics can be hormone disruptors.

The only hormone disruptor in my life is a crap marriage, but I keep that little gripe buried. After all, these women think I'm the success story within our little privileged enclave.

"Hey, Olivia, you're here too," Sophia says. "How are you both? I'm reading Nine Perfect Strangers, and it's brilliant. It's my favorite so far."

I haven't even had time to pick up that book. The book club is next week, and while finding time to read has never been an issue, given my love of books, I'm finding myself too distracted to read. At the last meeting, I wasn't dealing with ailing parents threatened with bankruptcy; a nail-biting medical procedure involving injections in goodness knows where; and a husband who looks at me like I'm an unwelcome houseguest.

Carrying a dish that wafts cheesy, tomato-rich deliciousness through the room, Sophia hands it to me. "I made a whole lot of lasagna, some to freeze for those 'can't be bothered cooking' nights." She giggles.

"You don't have too many of those. You love cooking," says Olivia, almost as an accusation. I sense that Olivia resents Sophia's perennial domestic bliss.

I take the dish from Sophia's perfectly manicured hands. I can't help but wonder how she manages all that cooking without breaking those talon-like nails.

"This is so kind of you," I say.

"I thought of you and Dorian."

Olivia scoffs, and Sophia tilts her head with a look of curiosity.

"Dorian has a carb phobia," I say.

"Oh, that's right." Her lips curl, stifling a giggle. "You say it like it's a medical issue."

"More psychological," Olivia adds, with a hint of scorn.

In defense of Dorian, I add, "He insists carbs make him feel bad. And I've heard it bloats some people."

Sophia nods, wearing the kind of sympathetic pout one would give a child denied sweets at a party of sugar-intoxicated kids. "I wouldn't know how to cook without carbs."

Olivia chuckles. "Join the club. Poor Linley turned herself inside out organizing a dinner for some of his Never Say Die colleagues."

I nod solemnly. "Next time, I'm getting it catered. Only Dorian loves to parade me around as that hands-on wife." I arch an eyebrow, and I sense they read something salacious into that comment, going by their smiles.

"How did the dinner go?" Sophia asks, still standing.

I point at a chair. "Take a seat. Can I offer you a drink?"

She shakes her head, settling down onto the settee by the window. "Oh, that's better. It's the first time I've sat in hours."

"You work too hard," I say, grateful for the break from Olivia's issues, who's glancing down at her phone every two seconds. I imagine she is waiting for that elusive text.

Ah, the days of dating. I don't miss those. I do miss heart-racing anticipation, however. Something I'm getting just thinking about Jarrad being there now, so close, working in the garden.

Suddenly, I want to be left alone. My stomach is rumbling, and I can't think of anything I'd love more than to stuff my mouth with some of this delicious lasagna.

Twenty minutes of small talk later, my neighbors leave, and I head outside in search of Jarrad. I find him on his knees weeding.

"Hey, can I interest you in some freshly baked lasagna and a beer?"

He looks up, and a smile forms on his handsome face. "You sure can."

Jarrad rises, dusts off his jeans, and follows me before pausing at the door.

He goes to remove his boots when I stop him. "No need."

"It's not a problem, Linley."

I love that he's using my first name at last.

He had his tongue nearly down my throat, so the whole boss-and-staff dynamic makes no sense at this stage.

"Can I help at all?" he asks, standing on the other side of the kitchen island.

I dish out a large serving onto one plate and a smaller portion for me. "No need. It's under control." Sauce slops onto the marble benchtop, which contradicts that comment. I smile. "Oops."

I point at the terrace. "Why don't we eat outside by the pool? It's such a lovely day."

I pass him two bottles of beer. "Here, take these out, and I'll bring the food."

"Sure." He hovers, appearing a little awkward despite the easygoing vibe I'm giving out like a seasoned performer.

He strides over to the pool barefoot, looking more like the man of the house than the gardener.

I wish.

After setting the plates down, I sit across from him. "Go on, dig in."

He swallows a forkful of food and then nods. "This is delicious. Your recipe?"

"No. Sophia, my Italian neighbor, makes the best pasta."

"Send her my compliments. It's sensational. And I really could use a good hit of carbs. I've had a big week."

Oh heaven. A man who loves his carbs. Is there anything about this man I dislike?

I dab my mouth with a napkin, take a sip of beer, and then regard him for a moment, searching for the right words. "About the other night."

He peers up at me and wipes his lips—which I'm trying to avoid ogling—while searching for the right thing to say.

"Yes, well... It was a nice kiss. One that I've thought about. A lot."

"Oh?" I ask, feeling warm all over.

He plays with the bottle. "It's not my thing to kiss married women. I'd had a few drinks, and well..." He takes another swig.

He's clearly uncomfortable.

My heart sinks. What am I wanting to hear: that he can't stop thinking about me, just like I can't stop thinking about him?

I nod slowly. "You're right. We'd been drinking."

We leave it at that. He's right. This can't become anything. Unsatisfying as that is, I have to accept it. I'm unavailable. And it speaks volumes of his morals because one flirtatious smile from him, and I'd be on the phone arranging a hotel room somewhere.

"Hey, don't get me wrong. You're a very desirable woman, and if you weren't already with someone, then..." He wears a lopsided shy smile. Intimate subjects are obviously not his thing.

"It's okay, Jarrad." I swallow the cool, bitter liquid, and my heart reverts to sleep mode.

Yep. Suck it up. Pleasure is for those who haven't got sick parents who are close to bankruptcy.

Just as that somewhat bleak thought washes over me, Ana arrives. I thought she had a doctor's appointment. She sees us and gives us a quick wave before leaving the room.

I return my attention to Jarrad, who's just given our maid a weird look again.

Curious about that mood shift, I ask, "Is something the matter?"

He's lost in thought and doesn't answer me at first before snapping out of whatever's stolen his attention. "What was that?"

"I asked if something was wrong. I just saw how you looked at Ana. Has something happened?"

What am I asking here?

"Huh? What?" He grimaces. "God, no. I'm not interested if that's what you mean."

"That wasn't what I meant." Was it? Ana does not strike me as Jarrad's type. I quickly push that silly idea aside, given that Ana's probably every hot-blooded man's type.

But I can't shake off the feeling that something's going on.

He drains the bottle and then takes a deep breath. "I'm not sure how to tell you this..." He wipes his lips, and all I can think of is how nice they felt massaging mine.

Lust has hijacked my senses again, and I'm trying to remember what we were saying.

He rotates his bottle on the table pensively. "The other day when I was repotting"—he points at the palm in a large ceramic pot—"I wasn't trying to snoop or anything, but through the door, I saw Dorian squeezing Ana's butt. She giggled, and he led her away by the hand."

I forget to breathe for a moment, which isn't due to a stab in the heart or anything. If anything, I'm not surprised. More humiliated that Dorian's inability to control his sexual urges away from the marital bed has become so blatant.

I'm also annoyed at myself for turning a blind eye. And while I've been able to live with Dorian getting off on some big-breasted porn star via the internet, the thought of others knowing about this shambolic marriage makes me want to pop a Xanax. Though I'm masking my anxiety well, judging by Jarrad's bemused expression.

"Doesn't that worry you?" he asks.

"Of course, it does. But Dorian's been cheating on me for ages."

His frown deepens, and the look of shock on his handsome face almost makes me laugh.

"And you stay with him?" he asks.

I sigh. "Let's just say it's out of necessity right now."

I explain my situation with the prenup.

"So it's about money?" he asks.

How do I tell him I stopped loving my husband the moment I saw him at his computer playing with himself? After that, he made me feel sick, but then my parents' diabolical financial situation became apparent, and well, here I am, learning about my husband and the maid. It's all so cliché I don't know whether to laugh or cry. Especially now that I've fallen hard for my gardener.

Even if Jarrad wore a paper bag on his head, the chemistry between us would still sizzle. It feels so effortless with him. The way he listens, the way he gets me, it's like he is nourishing a part of me that has been neglected for years. Starved of someone I can truly trust, I've let my walls down with him.

"If my parents weren't going through what they're going through, I would have left ages ago," I admit.

Locking eyes, he remains silent, like he's searching for the right thing to say again.

We're so lost in our own little bubble that we both jump when Emily calls out to me, stepping through the glass door to join us by the pool.

Jarrad springs up, probably a little too hastily. I'm sure Emily notices.

"Better get back to it." He smiles at my neighbor and then gives me a nod, and off he goes.

Watching him walk off, Emily shoots me a knowing smirk.

Cringing a little, I take a deep breath before pasting on my brightest smile.

"I'm sorry to crash on whatever that was," she says.

"It's nothing, Emily, just Jarrad having a break. He's a nice person, and we enjoy our chats."

"I'm sure you do." She glances at him.

"It's not like that at all. He's just a good guy."

"I'm just playing with you." She sighs and then turns serious as she shifts the chair closer and looks around like she's about to tell me a secret.

I imagine this has something to do with the rumor about her and Claire hooking up.

My, oh my, what a neighborhood. And why do they all come running to me? Am I giving off some Dr. Phil vibe?

Just as she's about to speak, her phone sounds. She rolls her eyes. "Sorry, I've got to take this."

She holds the phone to her ear. "Oh? Okay. I'm coming now."

She rises. "This will have to wait. Sorry to intrude, but now I've got to run. Whittaker just threw up. He's on a playdate." She shakes her head. "You're so lucky you don't have kids."

On that rather loaded statement, I escort her to the front door. "What were you going to tell me anyway?"

"It's about Claire," she says almost in a whisper, looking around again as though she's about to share top secrets that could spell the end of civilization. The poor woman is clearly stressed.

"Oh?" I play dumb.

"Just that, well, we're thinking of making it official."

My eyes widen. "Oh? And Mark?"

"He knows." Her mouth wobbles, and she starts to cry. "I'm so confused."

"How do you feel about Claire?"

"I think I love her." Her eyes pool with tears. "Isn't that insane? I mean, I've never had a thing for women before. And my parents. Oh my God."

I hug her at the door. "Don't worry, I won't tell anyone until you're ready. And look, come over anytime and talk it through with me. I'm here for you."

She kisses me on the cheek. "You're such a good person. The best. You're the only one, other than Claire, that I feel like I can trust. You're so kind and, well... authentic."

A thin smile lands on my lips. If only she knew.

After I wave her off, I return to the kitchen and decide on a second helping of lasagna.

Dorian arrives home to find me sitting at the kitchen island just as I'm about to shovel in a forkful of pasta.

He sets down his laptop bag on the table in the living room and then enters the kitchen.

He points at the dish. "What's that you're eating?"

No "Hello, how are you?" or any other greeting. His entrances are always so jarring.

"Sophia dropped by with a lasagna. It's divine." I push the plate toward him. "Here, try some."

He almost jumps back like I'm offering him a plate of dead frogs. I have to bite my lips so as not to laugh.

"You've been stacking on the weight lately," he says, going to the fridge and removing a container of swampy juice.

"And you're losing weight," I say, digging at him, knowing how hard he works to get that muscular look that Jarrad makes seem so easy.

"You never told me about the visit to the doctor. You raced off to your folks. When's the first treatment?"

I push the plate away. My appetite is suddenly gone. "In a few days, I think."

He holds my stare. I don't blink. Show nothing. Just like him. He is great at that.

"You think?" He frowns, and his face barely moves. He is partial to Botox, I've discovered. "You don't seem that interested."

"Oh, I'm interested, all right. I'll check my schedule and get back to you." I soften my tone. Now is not the time to fight with Dorian. I need a check for my mother's hospital bill.

I hate asking for money. It's so stressful. "I need to send some money to my parents."

Now that Jarrad has witnessed something happening between my husband and the maid, I can file for divorce based on infidelity.

I squirm.

It's too much to deal with.

Do I want to roll out this clown parade for all to see? That's what will happen. Nothing but humiliation.

Dorian will fight it for sure. That will make matters worse. His word against mine, and do I want to drag Jarrad into this shitshow? Have him testify on my behalf?

The lasagna suddenly feels like a heavy rock in my stomach.

"How much money this time?" he asks, snapping me out of my disturbing inner dialogue.

His irritation isn't lost on me, and I feel like screaming at him, but I take a moment to cool down. "Fifty thousand should do it."

A line forms between his brows. "That much?"

"My father asked me if he should see an attorney regarding Brendan Crib's Ponzi scheme, thinly masked as a property investment portfolio, and sue the company he worked for, which I believe you still have some shares in."

He turns away, goes to his satchel, pulls out a checkbook, and pops it on the counter.

No more questions. Good. I'm tired. And at last, I've found his Achilles' heel. Could that be enough to rescind that prenuptial?

Then there's that disturbing insight into Dorian and the maid.

I know I should let her go. But I also feel sorry for her. She's with an abusive partner, and she's pregnant.

But by whom?

Afraid of falling into a black hole of speculation, I head upstairs for some downtime.

TWENTY

Ana

Surrounded by five-star luxury, I wait for Dorian as I move around the nice-smelling room—all white with artwork streaked in blues, pinks, and reds.

We meet here at least four times a week. I could almost move in. I wish. I'd love nothing more than to live here or in some slick apartment right in the heart of the city, close to trendy cafés and designer shops, where I could shop till I drop. I sigh, pushing that dream away. There are bigger issues right now.

My legs are shaking. I'm that nervous.

How is Dorian going to take what I'm about to tell him?

Standing at the floor-to-ceiling window, I stare down at the city. The roads are choked with cars, and the sidewalks are filled with people from everywhere. And in seven months, I'll add another human to the world.

I love this city. I love America.

I can't ever imagine returning to Mexico. I don't miss that noisy, stinky shithole I grew up in.

Returning to the king-size bed where we've made love all these weeks, I run my hands over the silky cotton sheets that we'll soon mess up. I'm flexible, according to Dorian, and going by how ferocious our lovemaking gets, I know I please him.

I change into a lacy corset and stockings and slip into my new pair of red Jimmy Choos. A present from Dorian. He has a thing for red heels. And so do I. I peppered him with kisses when he handed me the box along with a bag of super skimpy lingerie.

Staring into the mirror by the bed—that Dorian loves to gawk at as he's fucking me—I run my hands over my tummy. I won't be able to fit into corsets soon. Will he still want me when I start to show?

I push up my cleavage. My boobs have gone up a size, which should make him happy. Dorian loves my body.

A knock comes at the door, and I answer it with a smile. He steps in. No greeting or anything. Just silence as he removes his jacket, undoes his Italian leather belt, and lowers his slacks and briefs like he can't wait to fuck.

He sits in the chair and pushes me down on my knees. He's my master, and I'm his servant. I don't mind. I like giving him pleasure, and he can't get enough of my mouth.

Just as he's all hot and hard, he lifts me off the ground and takes me to the bed where we fuck like tigers.

I orgasm loudly. I'm not faking like I do with Hector, who gets pissed if I don't moan and groan while he's ramming into me. He hurts me. They're groans of pain, not pleasure. With Dorian, I feel hot.

We stay like that, me in his arms, my ear pressed to his chest where I can hear his heart racing.

After a few minutes, I take a deep breath and say, "I've got something to tell you."

He rises and heads for the bathroom. "I've got a meeting in half an hour. You better be quick."

"I'm pregnant," I say.

He stops at the door and turns to face me. He's not easy to read. The only time I see anything is when he's turned on.

He pushes back his hair with his hands. "Whose is it?"

"Yours," I say, sitting up against the padded bedhead.

His eyes narrow. "How far are you?"

"The doctor says around six weeks."

"But we haven't been fucking that long."

"Two months ago," I say. "The week Lin... I mean Mrs. Gunn went to visit her parents."

"Mm," he grunts and starts to pace.

I wish I wasn't so attracted to him. It's not just his money. I want him. We're electric together.

"But how do you know it's mine?" he asks at last.

"Because I haven't had sex with Hector for a few months."

That's a lie. But I'm convinced it's Dorian's, and he doesn't need to know about my sex life with that creep.

"I thought you were on the pill."

"I never said that. The pill makes me sick. I mentioned condoms, but you didn't want to." I give him a flirty smile, hoping he'll loosen up a bit. Dorian is making me feel guilty, like it's my fault I'm knocked up.

"I didn't plan this, you know," I say, opening a bottle of water by the bed and taking a sip. My mouth is so dry from stress. He's not making this easy.

"Didn't you?" His eyes burn into mine, and now he's pissing me off. "It may not even be mine," he adds, walking around with a towel wrapped around his waist.

The fact that we've fucked like rabbits for the past two months seems to have escaped Dorian. So damn hypocritical. They're happy to fuck us without contraception, but when we get pregnant, the finger-pointing starts.

He goes to his satchel and pulls out a checkbook. "How much?"

"I don't understand," I say.

"How much do you need to terminate it?"

What?

My eyes pop wide open. Abortion hadn't even entered my thoughts.

"It's our baby," I protest.

"Abort it," he says, like he's asking me to toss something away in the rubbish.

Fire burns in my stomach. I want to yell and scream. Instead, I breathe deeply to calm myself down. "That's wrong. It's murder."

"I won't father a Latino baby. Never." He stares at me like I'm a piece of trash.

"Then maybe you should stop fucking Latinas," I bite back.

His eyes darken. I can't tell if he hates me or wants to fuck me.

He sets down the checkbook and is back to pacing. "What a fucked-up situation. I have a frigid wife who can't conceive, while you get pregnant just from having your tits fondled."

"That's because she's sterile," I say.

His head turns sharply. "How do you know that?"

I can't exactly admit to being a snoop. Something I do when Mrs. Gunn leaves the house. She shouldn't leave her laptop lying around. It doesn't even need a pin to open it.

I can't tell him how I read an email with the doctor's report, so I lie instead. "I just overheard her saying something like that to one of the neighbors."

"She told one of the neighbors but not me?"

He is about to explode. I haven't seen him this emotional before. Only when he's turned on and talking dirty.

I prefer that. Not this racist douche version.

He sits down and picks up the checkbook again. He looks at me. "How much do you want to terminate it?"

I'm about to tell him to stick the check up his ass when the conversation earlier with my dad replays in my head. If I can help him escape, then I'll be free to leave Hector. Or at least run away, knowing that no harm will come to my dad.

"Fifty thousand should do it," I say, staring him down, because I hate how he's talking to me.

I'm Catholic. I don't believe in terminating anything but bad relationships. And that's about to happen. Only I have to be careful. Hector's a psycho. He's not going to let go that easily.

There's also what happened while Linley was away recently when the gardener saw Dorian run his hands all over my tits. Dorian didn't see him. I kept quiet about that. I hoped that the gardener would tell the wife. They're pretty chummy, those two.

I'll lose my job, but at least Mrs. Gunn will divorce Dorian, and we can then be together, properly.

Stop!

It's a fantasy. The man's a fucking racist.

I take the check. And then instead of leaving me cold to have his shower, he pushes me down and fucks me again.

"I thought you had a meeting," I say.

"Did I?" His mouth turns up at one end, the closest to a smile he ever gets.

He's such a liar. A sexy liar, who will pay big time.

If he won't marry me, then he'll just see what I'm capable of.

This time, I close my heart while opening my legs.

Whatever it takes to give my child a better life.

A life I was denied.

Until now.

TWENTY-ONE

Ana

Three months later.

Linley is packing. She's leaving for a few days, and how am I going to explain the bump that's starting to show to Dorian? He still doesn't know I'm keeping the baby and only just commented on how I'd put on weight when he visited me in the apartment he bought. It's now my home that I'm meant to be renting, but so far, the only rent has come from me pleasuring him.

I'm determined to become the new Mrs. Gunn. They don't even hide their dislike for each other, and Dorian confessed that he didn't see it lasting beyond the year because Linley hadn't started IVF treatment as she promised.

What a weird world. Here I am carrying his child and giving him everything he ever wanted, but he is still married to a woman he doesn't like.

Though Linley is always respectful and nice to me, I'm starting to hate her for being in my way. Especially now that I'm having to think about not just myself but my baby too.

I will do anything to give my child a good life.

At least she doesn't hide her unhappiness anymore. Not like in the beginning, when Linley was such a happy domestic goddess, baking cakes and always smiling.

I can't understand why she stays with a cheating husband.

I'm in love with a cheater. What does that say about me? When I become the next Mrs. Gunn, I'll make sure he doesn't need to stray. I'll give him everything. And I know what he likes.

He wants me. I know that, even though his cruel words sit somewhere deep, and when I'm alone, they return to hurt me. I'm proud of who I am and hate how Mexicans are seen as bad people when we're like anyone else, just trying to survive. And who would do their cleaning and serving for such little money? Even if Linley is more than generous. They need us as much as we need them. It's a mutually beneficial arrangement, as my father, who's now free and living in Chile thanks to Dorian's money, keeps telling me.

I finish chopping apples and place them in a large bowl of fruit and veggies so I can make Dorian's favorite juice. My phone keeps pinging. Of course, it's Hector.

I've got a restraining order on him. It was a midnight escape. While he snored, I packed and left with that golden key warming my palm. A key to a new apartment. One from a building that Dorian owns. It is gleaming clean and modern with wall-to-ceiling windows that look out to the sea. I love having my coffee on the balcony and spying on the cute guy next door who does his yoga stretches on the balcony.

Life is great, except for two big problems: Hector and Linley.

At least Hector doesn't know where I live. Yet. It's a matter of time. I even sensed him following me the other night.

Linley enters the kitchen. "Right, well…" She stares at me for a moment. I sense that she knows that once she leaves, I'll be in her bed, giving her husband what she can't: a good time. How can she not know? I've seen how she studies me when she thinks I'm not looking.

"I should be back in a few days." She points at my stomach. "I see you're starting to show a little."

I take a deep breath. Any minute now, Dorian will have to know.

"Have you managed to move?" she asks.

I nod. "He's still following me, though."

The concern on her face is almost moving. Why does she have to be so damn nice? It makes me feel like shit.

"I have a restraining order on him."

Dorian arrives, and the cup in my hand trembles slightly, and Linley notices. She notices everything but how Dorian looks at me.

Or does she see that too?

I've seen the way her eyes travel from him to me like she knows something, but then she smiles at me and treats me respectfully.

It's all a bit screwy, but I can only think of myself right now and the baby. All I care about is getting away from my loser ex and my old life back in Mexico where good and bad crossed over. One minute, I'd see someone at church helping their elderly mother kneel for prayer, and then the next, the same guy was pimping kids and selling drugs.

That life is no longer mine. This is my life. And if it means stealing this decent woman's husband, well, so be it. Linley could do better, and I've caught the vibe between her and Jarrad. They're crushing on each other for sure. I'll be doing her a favor. Everyone deserves a shot at happiness.

Dorian fills his shaker bottle with juice. "Restraining order on whom?" he asks, obviously having overheard our conversation.

He still doesn't know about Hector. Dorian never asks about my life. He's only interested in one thing, and that's getting me naked and having fun.

"It's nothing." I leave them and head to the lounge room and pick up the dusting cloth.

Now that he has set me up in his apartment, I know Dorian doesn't want me working there, but as I told him, I need the money. He's even offered to find me another job. I rolled my eyes at that offer and said, "I'll find my own job, thanks."

I even hinted at telling Linley about us if he forced me to leave. He hasn't brought it up since. It's only a matter of time before she confronts him. How can she not suspect something?

I hear them talking but can't quite make out what they're saying. Then I hear Dorian's steps as he leaves, and a few minutes later, Linley waves goodbye.

Feeling tired, I kick back on the leather couch and turn on the television. I love being here alone, imagining the changes I'd make around the place. I like color, and it's all a little too white and beige for me.

TWENTY-TWO

Ana

Eight months later

Javier is sleeping in the new crib Dorian just delivered. A real little angel, he even sleeps at night. He's so beautiful I can't stop smiling. Sometimes I cry, overcome with joy, while holding him. He wiggles in my arms, and I smother his chubby little body with kisses. I could stare at him all night. I've never felt anything like this before—the way my heart swells around him, like a warmth that fills every part of me.

If only I weren't so stressed.

Hector has discovered my apartment. He thinks Javier is his.

He stopped me on the street the other day and pointed down at the stroller, saying, "That's my son."

I couldn't say anything because he'd kill me if he knew it was someone else's.

It ended with me saying, "Don't make a scene or I'll scream." Luckily, there were cops close by.

And now he knows where I live. He stood outside and yelled my name during the night. I had to call the cops. Justin, my neighbor, who I've gotten to know from our balcony chats, offered to wait with me until the police arrived.

Dorian visits nearly every day. It's his apartment, I guess, and I'm living there rent-free. For now.

How can I have what I want when he's a serious racist? My skin isn't dark. If anything, I'm on the paler side, and why should I even worry?

The door opens, and Dorian enters carrying gifts for Javier.

It didn't take long for him to fall in love with his son.

It's been tough, though. Dorian was pissed off that I hadn't terminated our baby. He refused to talk to me. But I wore a tight shirt half unbuttoned, and with Linley visiting her parents, he devoured me, and we haven't stopped.

He even came to the hospital, which I thought was sweet.

Not to watch the birth of his son. I suppose he couldn't tell them he was my lover, but after I'd given birth, he arrived with flowers. That brought tears to my eyes. It wasn't so much for me, though. It was so he could see his son.

His face lit up when I told him it was a boy, and when he saw Javier and held him, he didn't want to let go.

I am one step closer to achieving my dream. Only I wonder why he hasn't left his wife. I asked him if it was about money because he admitted one night he didn't love her.

He said, "I've got a prenup, and if there isn't a child soon, I owe her very little."

"Then why stay together?" I asked.

"It's not exactly four years," he responded after a long pause.

"Is that soon?" I asked while he tore at my shirt, hungry for my body.

"I'm not here to talk about Linley."

That was the only time he spoke about his marriage.

I'm still working there. Dorian demanded I resign, but I like the money. And Linley is still so nice. I hate that she's making it difficult for me to find a way of getting rid of her.

Dorian sets down a bag of baby supplements and more practical stuff like cute baby clothes.

"Are these safe for a newborn?" I lift a vial of liquid vitamins.

"Never too soon to give him that boost for good health."

He goes to his son and takes him in his arms. It's quite moving to see father and son together. Though I can't help but wonder how Dorian would have reacted if Javier were darker.

I can see the resemblance. That's why Dorian has fallen for him. Javier is a beautiful baby.

"He's put on a bit of weight," he says with pride in his voice.

I giggle. "You only saw him yesterday."

He lowers Javier into his crib and then gives me a serious look while rubbing his jaw. "I'm going to tell Linley about the baby," he says.

I nod slowly. "Okay. And then what?"

He scratches his jaw. "I've got something I'd like to propose."

I sit up, feeling excited. "Oh?"

Dorian paces around the room, which puts me back on edge. "I'm prepared to transfer this apartment into your name, and I'll deposit ten thousand dollars a month into your account until the boy turns eighteen. You won't even have to work."

My brows tighten. "What are you suggesting here?"

"I want to adopt Javier."

"Like take him away from me?" My voice cracks.

He puffs. "You know how Linley can't conceive and my need to become a father, and this seems a perfect solution."

"And me?" It feels like someone's choking me; I can barely talk.

"You'll be well looked after, and you're still young."

"And us?"

He looks at me as though I've lost my mind, like I'm some child expecting a fairy castle to be built with nothing but dust.

"It's time I think about my son's future."

"Our son's future, you mean." My voice is trembling, and I'm finding it hard to think straight.

He joins me on the sofa and takes my hand. It's the most affectionate he has ever been—more like turning it on to get me on his side. Dorian's idea of affection is tipping me over a table and ripping off my panties.

"Think about his future. He'll have the best of everything."

I pick up one of the glass vials and smash it against the wall, which makes Javier cry.

"Hey, calm down," he says.

"The best of everything? Like feed him all this crap when breast milk has everything he needs? And then when he's older, feed him eighty supplements of god-knows-what."

Dorian rises. "It's understandable that you're a little upset. Sleep on it."

"You're leaving now before we've had a chance to discuss this properly?"

"I'm supposed to be somewhere." He walks to the door and then turns. "I don't want you working at the house anymore."

"Tough. Linley likes me there."

He rolls his eyes and leaves.

My father calls, and I take a breath. "Hey, Papa. What's happening?"

"Darling, I hate to ask, but I need some money."

Here we go again.

"But I sent you a thousand dollars a week ago."

"I've gotten myself into a bit of trouble."

"What kind of trouble?"

"I owe some pretty bad guys."

"Bad guys? Like you've been there a minute, and you're already caught up in some bullshit?"

"I'm sorry, sweetheart, but this is serious."

"How much are we talking here?" I sigh.

"Twenty thousand for now."

"For now?"

"You're seeing that rich man, and now you've had his son; he owes you, doesn't he?"

I should never have told my dad about Dorian, but I was upset and needed someone to talk to.

"Leave it to me. But this has got to stop."

"I'm sorry. I promise I'll do better."

"So how much do you owe them?"

"A hundred."

"For what?"

"It's a long story."

"Isn't it always?" I'm now seriously pissed. Why are all the men around me determined to drag me into their shit?

I end the call, shake my head, and scream. First Dorian's terrifying suggestion about adopting Javier, and now my father's at it again. I'm sure that's what killed my mother—his bad behavior. Can I sit back and watch him die? Why am I such a good daughter when he's such a bad father?

Sensing my angst, Javier starts to cry, and I pick him up and rock him in my arms. "One day you'll show these losers what a good man looks like."

I kiss my son's warm, chubby little cheek and push all the self-pitying crap aside. I begin to plot instead.

There is no way I'm giving my son up.

TWENTY-THREE

Linley

At least there is some good news; they didn't have to remove my mother's breast after all. The lump is shrinking, though she has lost most of her hair.

I wanted to stay there for her, but she pushed me out the door because she hated my fussing over her.

After a long, exhausting flight where a passenger ran up and down the aisle telling us that Jesus loved us, I'm home at last. For a moment, I thought he might shoot us. How would my parents survive without me? I wasn't ready to die. Already on edge, I reminded myself that smuggling a gun on a plane was close to impossible, but my imagination still ran amok, just like the barefooted bearded man on the plane.

Lounging back with my feet up, I'm in the front room for a change. Jarrad's car wasn't there, I noticed, and though I've been missing our little chats, I need to collect my thoughts. My mother's mounting hospital bill, close to a hundred thousand dollars, needs to be paid now.

The front door sounds, and with that deliberate, pacy stride, Dorian walks in.

I've been away for a week, and instead of a kiss on the cheek or a warm welcome—something that I'm sure happens in most healthy marriages—I get a chin lift as acknowledgment.

"We need to talk," he says, setting down his leather satchel.

My spine stiffens.

Is this it?

I go to the liquor cabinet and pour a shot of bourbon. "Want one?"

He shakes his head. "We have to talk about a delicate matter."

I remain by the sideboard. "Oh?" I swallow the shot and clear my throat. "That sounds serious."

His sharp exhale tells me he's not about to inform me of a dinner party that requires special dishes for guests subsisting on fruit.

"You know how much I want to be a father. We've been married for four years, and still no pregnancy."

His pacing only adds to my anxiety as I stare down at my feet, imagining having to work two or three jobs just to get my family through.

I can handle the thought of leaving LA, though, but never seeing Jarrad again? That would be difficult. Even though we've never really gone beyond that one kiss, I see how he looks at me, and he features in all my fantasies about what a great life might look like. And yes, I know I shouldn't be thinking about him when my life is about to come crashing down. But that's me in escape mode—finding the nicest mound of sand to bury my head in.

The more steps Dorian takes around the room, the stickier my palms get as I clutch my hands. His agitation is contagious.

"I haven't exactly been a model husband."

You think?

He rubs his jaw repeatedly and then clears his throat. "I discovered the other day that I'm a father." His mouth turns up at one end. He's the most apologetic—or is that groveling?—he's ever looked.

"Okay." While I should be shocked, I'm not. "Let me guess, Ana?"

He stops still. His jaw slackens. "You know?"

"I'm not a complete fool." I wring my hands. "Our marriage has never worked. I've seen how you look at Ana. And when she told me she was pregnant, I put two and two together."

"But it could have been..."

"Her boyfriend's?" I interject.

His eyebrows crash, and the shock on his face deepens. "What?"

"She's living with an abusive partner. You don't know that?"

"She's living in my apartment."

That comes as a slap. I shake my head in disbelief. "It's getting more sordid by the minute."

"You knew all this time?" he asks. "And you still had her stay here while you were away?"

I return to the side table and, with a trembling hand, lift the bottle of bourbon. This is hardly the time to remain sober. "I know, that's my bad." I pour another shot and knock it back. "But to be honest, this whole marriage has been a joke for a while now. You know it. I know it. And there's that infidelity clause."

"What about it?" he asks defensively.

"If you cheat, I walk away with half of your fortune."

He shakes his head. "You can't prove a thing. And the fact that you're barren and haven't delivered the child we agreed on would negate that claim."

I roll my eyes. "A good lawyer would argue that you started screwing the maid prior to the four-year cutoff."

"A good lawyer can argue anything. And you won't win."

"What about your porn addiction? That's also cheating in my book. I've done screenshots and dates."

"You can't prove a fucking thing." His brows merge. "A good wife wouldn't spy."

"A good husband wouldn't use porn or screw the maid."

He mutters something and grunts scornfully as though I'm nagging him about not putting down the toilet seat and not something as serious as infidelity.

"If you had talked to me like normal healthy couples do, I would never have needed to enter your office. I heard you getting all hot and bothered one night. What was I meant to do?" I say, choking back a sob. I take a deep breath to regain control. "You refuse to talk to me about the deeper things in life. I even stumbled on counselor notes dating back to when you were expelled from high school for fighting."

His forehead creases. "You what?"

"I found it among some files."

"More fucking snooping around," he says with ice in his voice.

"Call it what you like. I married a stranger."

"I've given you everything." He gesticulates around him. "A beautiful home. A lifestyle that any woman would envy."

"Yes. That's true. You've given me everything but love." My voice trembles as a pool of tears blurs my sight. This is too much. It's like poking at a throbbing boil that refuses to burst.

"You're a dreamer. You live in a fantasy world, Linley." He opens his hands. "If I'm that bad, why did you stay?"

I sigh. "Because of my parents. And after reading those counselor notes, I felt sorry for you."

He stops dead and locks eyes with me, his intense gaze searching—like he's trying to extract more meaning from my words. Dorian hardly ever looks me in the eye. Usually, it's just passing glances, like he's trying to hide, keeping himself closed off. But right now, even with that guard up, there's a flicker of vulnerability slipping through.

"And what conclusion did you arrive at?" he asks.

Searching his face, I brace for sarcasm but catch a hint of uncertainty instead.

"The counselor's notes made it clear why you got into that fight. It said you lashed out after a boy teased you for not having a father at home. That was your excuse at the time. The counselor pointed out that this type of reaction was common among kids from broken homes, especially teenage boys."

"So? We all say and do stupid things when we're growing up," he says, back to putting up walls.

"Isn't it better to get things off your chest? I mean, some days it looks like you're about to erupt. The tension around here is palpable."

"To lose control is to show weakness," he says, like it's some kind of slogan.

"That's not true. I think it's an act of bravery, sharing deeper thoughts and experiences. To show vulnerability."

He pushes his head back like I've suggested he walk the streets naked. "Why would I do that? That's a recipe for failure."

"I suppose that's why you need me and this fake perfect marriage because it reveals to the world that you're normal and not some loser living alone. You chose me because I blend in with the furniture. Unlike your mother, in her outlandish outfits, who likes to talk loudly and doesn't care who hears her."

"That's because she's a fucking alcoholic." The palpable hatred in his voice saddens me.

"She's still your mother." I pause to find the right words. "What I'm saying here is that this is your shot at normality. At creating a family life you missed out on."

Dorian rubs his face. "Spare me the amateur psychology."

He then falls into an armchair and looks out into space. A tense silence follows.

At a loss for words after hitting a wall with my husband again, I circle back to the shocking fact that he has a child with the maid. A cloud drifts over me again. All we've done is open another door to a room full of unprocessed emotion. Hoarding memories that should be scrapped but stare back at us in neat piles, festering away.

"What now?" I ask.

He takes a deep breath. "I want us to adopt my son. He's beautiful. White. Looks like me."

Of course, he does.

It's like I've just crashed into a brick wall. I'm so bewildered that it takes a moment to digest what I've just heard. "Are you serious?"

He half smiles. "I know it sounds out of left field, but it would be like a surrogate child."

"Only the father fucked the maid to make it," I say with a chill in my voice.

"Don't be like that. You're the one who lied to me about your family history."

"That's bullshit, Dorian. You just never asked. Now that I think about it, you were never really that interested in anything I had to say. Let alone my fucking life story."

He flinches. I know he hates women swearing. Bad luck. From here on out, I'm no longer that constipated subservient wife who stifles her farts when in his presence.

"But Ana would never agree to give up her child. Wouldn't she want to marry you?"

He pulls a face and scoffs like I might have suggested he marry a goat. "Are you joking? Marry her? Never!"

The visceral disgust in his voice sends me into shock as words fail me.

He spreads his palms. "Can you imagine the dinner parties? She's uneducated and coarse. I'm not going to marry a commoner. Or a..."

"Latina," I add, staring him in the face. "You didn't seem to mind screwing her. And I saw the porn on your laptop. All dark-haired women with olive skin, the opposite of your perfect white wife. I can't say what hurt the most: the fact they were the physical opposite of me or that you were getting off on porn instead of making love to me." I wring my hands, holding back the tears. "Though, I discovered pretty quickly that you don't know what love is."

He rolls his eyes and groans like I'm missing some vital point in this argument. "Not more fucking amateur psychoanalysis. You don't know me."

"You're right. I don't. You're just a shell of a man whose emotions have been scooped out. All those enemas have done more than just empty your colon."

This is our first proper argument, and it's liberating to drop the tolerant wife act for a change. Like I've unclasped an uncomfortable bra.

He throws me a chilly look. "You didn't satisfy me. I had to use porn to get off."

I'm reluctant to bring up the lack of passion in our marriage because I'm not exactly innocent, considering I never felt that same fire as I do around Jarrad. In the beginning, I'd convinced myself I loved Dorian. But having now met a man who truly makes my heart melt, I'm only just discovering what love really feels like.

He exhales loudly. "Back to the subject of my son."

The sound of breaking glass comes from the kitchen, startling me, and when I turn, a shaken Ana enters the room. I had forgotten she was here.

"You heard?" I ask.

She nods and then points at Dorian. "He forced himself on me, Mrs. Gunn. I never meant for this to happen. I'm going to press charges."

I go to comment when Dorian jumps in. "That's bullshit, Ana, and you know it." He turns to me. "She's the one who walked around the house wearing next to nothing, bending over in front of me."

"Oh, spare me that 'I couldn't control my dick' argument as some moral justification for forcing yourself on a woman." I shake my head.

Ana charges off, and before Dorian can stop her, the door slams.

I'm frozen more by what happens next.

Dorian follows her out and grabs Ana by the arm, and much to my horror, they begin having a lovers' tiff smack dab in the middle of my front yard for all to see.

Oh, and it gets worse, because along comes Emily.

She's having her own Days of Our Lives moment. Her husband has fallen for some young guy, Olivia took great delight in telling me.

At least it's not Sophia or someone having a perfect life watching on.

When did my life become a trash heap?

Resigned to my fate, I open the door for Emily and force a smile. Despite the awkwardness of the moment, a distraction isn't such a bad thing, I suppose.

"What's happening there?" she asks, cocking her head toward the lawn where Dorian is trying to calm Ana, who is howling like a banshee.

I tell her every sordid part except for the baby, of course.

"Oh my god." Her jaw drops. "We did warn you about hiring a sexy maid."

TWENTY-FOUR

Ana

I'M BACK IN MY beautiful apartment. There is no way I'm moving. This is mine, and I'll make it happen.

Dorian is pissed off with me, not just because everything has turned into a shitshow, but because I put Javier into childcare so I could work.

"Where is he?" he demanded while we stood in his front yard. This was after I slapped him just as a pair of neighbors walking their dog passed by. I almost laughed, not so much from the weird look they gave us, but at how the blood drained from Dorian's face.

Good. Let him suck lemons for a change. Hearing him talk about me like I'm some kind of skanky Latina made my blood boil.

I hate him.

I hate myself more, though, because I still love that racist asshole.

"I need to work," I reminded him.

"Can we talk somewhere else?" He led me to the back garden, only to find Jarrad there.

The gardener looked up and nodded, as if me being with Dorian wasn't weird or anything. I suppose he doesn't want to lose his job by sticking his nose into things.

And where was Linley? Was she watching me and her husband fight?

It's all a bit weird. If that were me, I would have gone nuts. But I'm fiery like that, whereas Mrs. Gunn is so cool that I can't help but respect her, even if I resent her too.

As I said, it's all messed up.

Dorian asked, "Where's my son while you're working here?"

"Javier's my son too."

The sound of the door opening snaps me back to the present, and Dorian walks in.

I pass him our son. "Here, hold him for a minute. He needs changing."

He smells bad, and Dorian makes a face and hands Javier back. "I don't want him in childcare."

Taking my son again, I lay him down on the changing table. "I need to work."

"I'll employ a nanny. But he has to live with us."

I remove the dirty diaper and wipe Javier's bottom with a wet wipe. "By us, you mean you and Linley?"

"I'm not going to leave Linley and marry you." He looks down at the mess on the table and then turns away like it's offending him.

"You hate that I'm a Latina. I got that loud and clear. Your son is part Latino."

"He'll be given the best of everything."

I should just tell him to fuck off, but there's the issue of my dad.

He's the only family I have left. I know I shouldn't care after everything he's done, always thinking about himself.

I still couldn't live with myself if something happened to him.

After I change our son, Javier smiles back at me. He's such a happy little thing. If only he knew about the shitstorm going on around him. That's why I'm determined to protect him and give him everything I missed out on.

I notice a rare smile growing on Dorian's face. Having a son has softened him a little. He's still a racist pig, though.

"I don't like that name, by the way. I prefer Xavier."

I shrug. "Whatever. You can Americanize it all you like, but I'm calling him Javier. Javi for short."

"That will only confuse him. I've made you a good offer, Ana. Maybe..." He pauses for a moment. "You could be the nanny."

My jaw drops. "Are you for real? And then what, you can screw me on the side?"

He looks down at his Rolex. "I've got to be somewhere. Let's talk later. For now, don't come to the house. It's tense enough being around Linley."

"Why aren't you divorcing her? I know I'd walk out if I was her."

He takes some time to answer, like I've asked him to try and figure out the solution to some complex mathematics.

Dorian combs his fingers through his hair, pushing it back. "She's my wife."

"No shit." I sigh. "But it's obvious you don't love her." I stare him down. His eyes look empty, cold almost. Or is that just the mask he pulls whenever things get personal?

"You don't know anything about me," he says. "Linley makes me look good. She's educated and well-presented. That's all I've ever wanted in a wife."

"And a wife that will give you a child. What about that?"

He says nothing to that.

"Then if it's love you feel for your wife, why are you fucking me?"

He looks lost for an answer again. "I think it's obvious that what we have is purely sexual. And men and monogamy are not always suited."

I roll my eyes. "Oh? Really? And what about women? Don't they deserve a partner they can trust?"

"Linley wants for nothing." He turns his back and then pulls out a checkbook from his satchel, writes me a check, and hands it to me. "This is at least double your monthly wage. I'll expect an answer soon."

He walks out the door, leaving me to stare at the ten-thousand-dollar check.

I want to scream. Cry. I hate him.

How can I want this man?

What's wrong with me?

It's like when we're together, that's all the communication I need to feel wanted and nourished.

Or am I just sick like the rest of them?

My mom and dad didn't always look that loved up. Is that why I'm fine with crumbs?

Everything is so fucked up. I have Hector, who says he loves me with his whole soul but beats me up. And then Dorian, who hates me for being Mexican but can't take his hands off me. When we fuck, he holds me tight like he's crazy about me.

My phone pings and an image of my dad with a hood over his head comes up.

My heart stops.

I call the number, and a man answers. "One hundred thousand or he dies. You've got two days."

He ends the call before I can speak.
I fall onto the couch, bury my face in my hands, and cry my eyes out.

TWENTY-FIVE

Linley

"Why do you stay?" my mother asks.

I bend down and pluck a weed from the once-pristine garden.

I remind her about the prenup.

"Two million is a fair sum, darling. And you're bright and young enough to start again. That can buy you a nice apartment somewhere."

"And who's going to pay your hospital bills and help with expenses?"

"We'll find a way. It hurts us to know you're with that awful controlling man just for our sake."

When I heard the positive news of my mother's cancer being in remission, I jumped on a plane. Any excuse to escape the turbulence at home.

And now here I am on my knees pulling out weeds as though they symbolize the untidy parts of my life.

"If I leave, Dorian will either sell this place or charge an exorbitant rent," I remind her as I remove dead leaves from the roses.

"Your father and I have been talking. He can take on a few contracts, and then we can rent something affordable."

"Not while I'm breathing. You're staying here. This is your home. Our home. And for some strange reason, Dorian hasn't even mentioned divorce yet." I take a deep breath. I can't understand why he hasn't brought that up.

My heart sinks at the thought of remaining in that loveless marriage, but I'm left with few options.

Jarrad now knows everything, including Ana giving birth to my husband's child. He's the only one I've told. So far.

We shared a drink after Dorian sprung the adoption idea on me. I needed someone to talk to.

"That's pretty weird stuff," Jarrad said. "Expecting you to bring up another woman's child. I saw how they were together."

Wringing my hands, I nodded solemnly. "I guess I could have gone about this better."

"Don't beat yourself up. You're a good soul, Linley. Probably too good."

Despite the crazy situation around me, I felt blessed that a decent man like Jarrad was there to hold my hand.

"Why did you keep Ana on?" he asked.

I took a moment to answer. "She has this psycho boyfriend, and I felt sorry for her."

"Even while she was messing around with your husband?" The shock on Jarrad's face slapped me with a sense of guilty shame.

"Oh, Jarrad, not you too," I appealed. "The girls are giving me shit."

"What? They know about the baby?" he asked, looking shocked.

I sighed. "No way. Promise me, not a whisper."

"You can count on me. Know that." His eyes held mine. He then broke eye contact and stared down at his calloused hands from years of labor. "When it comes to making a mess of things, I've had my share of fuck-ups."

He smiled apologetically, which made his eyes soften. I just wanted to rewrite my life right there on the spot. "Sorry for swearing."

"Swear all you like. I've been known to utter a few f-bombs of late." I sniffed. "The news is making the rounds—it's common knowledge now. I should never have confided in Emily, who must have told Olivia, which means everyone knows about my husband and the maid."

He wore a sympathetic frown. "She's stalking Tommy, you realize."

"Olivia's not at a good stage in her life. Her ex just married his considerably younger girlfriend."

Jarrad's cynical smirk wasn't lost on me. "Is that a snigger?"

"I'm just thinking of how screwy marriages can get."

"You're not the marrying kind?" I couldn't believe I'd asked him that.

"With the right woman, I am."

"You haven't met her yet, I take it?" My chest tightened despite having no right to that emotional reaction, but I wanted to know if he was single and available. For me.

If only.

"Oh, I think I have, only she's married."

Having taken a sip, I broke out into a coughing fit.

"Are you okay?" He looked worried again.

"It's fine. Just went down the wrong pipe." I paused to revisit his comment. "Does she know how you feel?"

"I think so. Not so much in words. But I can't take my eyes off her."

My face burned hot at that, especially as he kept staring at me as if to make a point. For the first time in ages, I became that smitten teenager being told how an out-of-reach boy liked her.

Leaving that warm reflection aside, I return to the moment and regard my mother, watching her pour some tea.

Wiping my soiled hands on my jeans, I stand up. "There's something else I need to discuss."

Her brow furrows. I feel bad for springing my issues on her, especially after what she has been through, but I need her perspective on things because Dorian's baby adoption plans are keeping me awake.

I tell her all about it.

Her mouth opens, but no words follow, so I babble something about how people adopt all the time.

"You're seriously considering this?" she asks at last.

"What other choice have I got? It solves the issue of me not conceiving, and at least this way he can't divorce me. And in a couple of years when I ask for a divorce, then I won't worry about money the same way."

"Oh, darling." Her shoulders slump. "You can't keep making these sacrifices for us."

I hug my mother. "I could never live with myself otherwise."

I'm not about to admit to my frail mother that if it weren't for their predicament, I would agree to live in a tent with Jarrad. I chuckle silently at that silly idea. But money only means one thing now to me, and that is to save my parents from living in some shoebox apartment with plumbing issues.

"You're really about to agree to adopt a baby? And do you know who the mother and father are?"

And there it is, the big question. Should I tell her the dirty truth or a big fat lie?

As that revolves around my busy brain, I reflect on Dorian returning home a little more buoyant than usual with the news that Ana had agreed to allow us to adopt Xavier, as my racist husband insists on naming him.

"He's a great baby." He was all smiles like we were buying the latest designer car. "He sleeps all night."

"And how will this work exactly?" I asked him. "He needs his mother to feed him. I take it she's breastfeeding?"

My voice cracked. Why wasn't that me? Why couldn't I conceive? It was at that moment I felt a chill go through me. Like life would never smile on me again. That I would be stuck in a loveless marriage raising another woman's baby.

Why did I let it go this far?

"We can employ a nanny," he said. "So that there's no real disruption to your routine."

My routine? What was that again? Baking. Ogling Jarrad. Playing de facto counselor to a bunch of neighbors. And now, rearing my husband's love child.

I wanted to laugh and then cry and scream. But I bit my lip, sucked it up, and nodded.

If I brought up the child for a couple of years, then I could divorce him, and my parents would be in the clear.

I return my focus to my mother, who is waiting for some kind of explanation.

"It's Dorian's." I can't bring myself to lie to my mother. I go on to tell her the whole sad story. Well, maybe not the complete story.

My mother hasn't managed to pick her jaw up yet. Her eyes are wide with shock.

"Please don't tell Dad," I plead.

"But he'll want to know, love," she says.

"Tell him how we've checked out the family and are satisfied. It's kind of true. I mean, I know Ana." I sigh.

"Darling, you don't need to do this."

"I do. For now. Don't worry, I have a plan. But that might take a couple of years, and by then, this is all yours again."

"But how?" Her frown deepens.

"I only agreed to the baby adoption after Dorian agreed to transfer the house back to you. In your names." I'm smiling at that little win I was able to broker with my husband. "And your hospital bills will be paid, and then I will go to plan B."

"That being?" she asks.

"Plan B is finding a happy life somewhere."

A sad smile reflects from her tired eyes. "I'm sorry it's turned out this way."

"I'm partly to blame. I married him for all the wrong reasons. And you wouldn't be in this mess if I hadn't introduced him to the family. Dad wouldn't have invested with that scam artist."

She sighs deeply and lifts the teapot. "Another?"

I smile. "Sure."

TWENTY-SIX

Ana

Dorian is at my apartment early. Almost jogging on the spot, he's pumped as he watches me change my little boy.

My eyes are raw from tears. I held Javier all night like it was our last time together. Life is so strange. A year ago, I hated the idea of being pregnant, and now I can't imagine life without my son.

Why am I entangled with all these toxic men? There's my dad, my loser ex, and Dorian, who is just as bad.

But I need him more than ever. Not only for my father's freedom but for mine. I don't want to return to the slums, and I want everything for my son.

Dorian heads over to the balcony to take a call.

It's probably his wife.

I can't believe that Linley is still around after Dorian told her about me and how Javier is his son. Instead of walking out of the marriage, like most people would, she's hanging on like a bad smell.

Tears start to stream again as I rock my baby. He's staring into my eyes and I swear he gets it, because he's got this 'don't worry, Mama, everything will be okay' look shining back at me.

"They can't sue. She could have taken anything. According to the report I just received from my attorney, she was on a ton of supplements," Dorian says while pacing. "All right, call me when you hear anything."

"How's this going to work?" I set my son in his bassinet.

Lost in another world, Dorian takes a moment to respond. "If you want to accept the role of nanny, then you'll get to be with him more than you would otherwise."

"More than I would? Like never see him again? Is that what you mean?" I fire up.

"Hey, keep your voice down," Dorian snaps.

I open my hands. "Then what?"

Javier starts to cry. I lift him into my arms and rock him.

"See, you've made him cry," Dorian says.

"More like *you* made him cry. He wants to stay with me." My tears drop onto Javier's little face. I kiss them away from his soft, warm cheek, and he stops howling. He is so attuned to me.

How can I not watch him grow?

"This will all be yours." He waves his hand around the space. "Ten thousand dollars a month too. And I can throw in a nice car."

"Won't my becoming Javier's nanny piss off Mrs. Gunn?" A black cloud floats in just hearing myself say that.

"She'll come around. I can get Linley to do anything," he says, sounding full of himself.

Yeah, like staying married to a douche like you.

"Let me sleep on it," I say.

TWENTY-SEVEN

Linley

CLAIRE AND EMILY ARRIVE first for a change. It's book club night, and while I probably should have canceled, given the current turmoil in my life, I decided there was no time like the present to announce our adoption of a baby boy.

As always, Dorian is out. He is up to his neck in some legal issue relating to his supplements sending some people to the hospital. His lack of concern for the victims shocked me. That's after Hayden Spritz arrived at our doorstep looking paler than usual. Tempted to ask if he'd forgotten to take one of his eighty supplements that day, I removed my tongue from my cheek and offered Hayden a cup of peppermint tea instead.

Looking stressed, he asked, "Have you got anything stronger?"

As I poured Dorian's business partner a bourbon, my husband suggested, "Pay their hospital bills and send them on a vacation."

That was after he'd learned how the supplement-takers were doubled up in pain with liver complaints.

"We won't even have to do that according to the attorney," Hayden said, downing his drink in one go.

I walked out at that point. Living with a heartless man is one thing, but I refused to be privy to a discussion on how to dodge one's moral obligations. There was no way I would be an accomplice to that. So I found another mound of sand and buried my head in that instead.

And now I'm a stepmom. Break out the champagne.

He is a lovely baby, despite my ambivalence, seeing as I haven't experienced the swelling of love people normally feel around a newborn.

Sophia arrives dressed impeccably in a green silk dress, showing off her tanned figure. She's living her best life, or at least that's her vibe. As is

Isabella in hot-pink activewear. She's probably just back from a yoga class with her lover. I imagine they're still together, going by the glow on her cheeks.

What is it about animal attraction? There's this electricity sending a thrill through your veins. Suddenly you can conquer anything. At least, that's how I felt earlier, after seeing Jarrad wearing a 'don't worry, I'm here for you' smile.

I can get through anything with him around.

Isabella kisses my cheek. "You look lovely."

That's just her attempt to be nice since I'm dressed in the same jeans I've been wearing all week. Who can shop for new clothes when dealing with a cheating husband who doesn't seem to care that some of his supplements are landing people in the hospital?

As the women settle into the living room, Ana arrives with a tray of snacks.

Olivia and Natalie have only just walked in. I haven't had time to catch up with Olivia, but I sense the whole Tommy thing has blown up in her face. Jarrad mentioned something about a restraining order.

The room's attention slides to Ana as she delivers drinks and snacks. I can only imagine what they're thinking.

By now, they know about Dorian screwing the maid, but not about Xavier. That will never happen.

When did my life become a low-budget soap opera?

After Ana leaves the room, Sophia places her hand by the side of her mouth and whispers, "She's still here?"

There goes discussing *Nine Perfect Strangers*.

Who needs books when my trainwreck marriage is on full display like Kanye West's semi-naked wife?

I take a big gulp of Prosecco. It's hardly the time to exercise moderation. My supposed Irish genes have been a little underutilized around my judgmental husband, but now I don't give a damn what he thinks. I'm almost looking forward to a dinner party and offering enough sugary delights to tempt even the most disciplined of that health-obsessed movement.

My nosy neighbors' expectant faces gleam back at me. Even Claire and Natalie, who normally roll their eyes at gossip, are all ears.

Emily, the most sympathetic, gives me an apologetic smile. I notice that she has changed seats and is sitting nice and close to Claire too.

Now why can't we talk about *that* new relationship?

I guess it's second on the agenda, going by how she keeps nervously shifting around in her seat.

"Dorian's reassured me it has stopped. And... Ana's a great help." My voice cracks.

Sophia's dark eyes nearly pop out of her head, while Olivia's jaw drops. Yes, I know. How can I be so liberal?

"Stopped what? Fucking the maid?" Olivia asks, blunt as always.

"It was only once and he was drunk," I lie. "Ana needs this job and she's very reliable."

Looking perplexed, they all nod at the same time.

And to think, I agreed to Ana becoming the new nanny. That opens up a whole new complication.

At least the neighbors don't know Xavier's hers.

I take a deep breath and say, "I've got some news."

They stop chatting about how they wouldn't keep a housekeeper even if she'd turned a new leaf and became Mother Teresa with the haggard features to match.

"We've adopted a baby boy." A smile trembles on my lips as I finish the rest of my Prosecco in one go.

They all look at me as though I've just admitted to adopting a busload of unwashed hippies' kids.

"What? When?" Olivia asks.

"It's been something we've looked into for a while. Didn't want to say anything because, well…"

Isabella says, "I get it. You wanted to make sure everything was just right. It's a huge thing, though."

I throw her a grateful smile, and after a moment, as it's taking some time to sink in, everyone agrees with a collective, if hesitant, nod.

"He's here?" Emily asks.

I nod. "He's sleeping now."

"When can we meet him? And is there a name?" Sophia asks.

"We've named him Xavier. And maybe I'll arrange a little get-together soon. It's just that Dorian's a little preoccupied."

"I bet he is," says Natalie, looking a little dark.

Necks creak all around as the women turn their attention to her.

"Oh?" I ask. "Why would you say that?"

"He poisoned my aunty."

"What?" Everyone's jaws drop.

And while I welcome the shift away from me, I'm also lost for words.

"What do you mean?" Claire asks.

"The supplements his company is peddling put her in the hospital. Do you know about that?" Natalie turns to me.

I bite into a nail, something I haven't done for years. But my alcohol intake is too low at this stage. "No. I haven't heard anything from Dorian. We don't talk business."

I'm so grateful I didn't give my mother some of those purported 'cure-all' pills they've been promoting. I nearly did after Hayden raved on about how they cure cancer.

"So what happened exactly?" Emily asks Natalie.

"My aunt bought into the hype and ended up in the hospital with liver failure. It was touch and go there for a minute."

I want to crawl under a rock. Why are they looking at me as though I had something to do with it? "I am so sorry, Natalie."

"It's not your fault. But I'd say Dorian's company's in for one big lawsuit."

"Let's talk books, shall we?" I say with a trembly smile.

Silence follows as the bewildered women look like they've just learned about an asteroid arriving any second.

"Sure. Yeah," they all say in a chorus of disinterest. I mean, who can talk about books at a time like this?

I go over to the side table, pick up the bottle of Prosecco, and then go about filling everyone's empty glasses before heading into the kitchen to make sure there are a few more bottles in the fridge. Something tells me I'm in for a long night.

TWENTY-EIGHT

Hayden Spritz waves his hands around like he's suffering from some neurological disorder. "They can't prove a thing."

"You sure about that?" Dorian asks, looking as ruffled as his hair, which he keeps raking with his fingers. "It's all over the website how you visited an Indian village and discussed the herb with a local doctor."

Hayden nods pensively. "They're the healthiest octogenarians in the world. Their livers are healthier than most forty-year-old Americans."

"These people have robust immune systems," I can't help but add. "I mean, they've been bathing and drinking from a river that's so polluted it defies modern science that they're not suffering from cholera. You can't assess the safety of a substance based on that."

Dorian shoots me a dirty look.

I just smile back. It's his mess, not mine. And they crashed my space and reading time by discussing this current supplement fiasco while chugging their murky juices.

Dorian runs his fingers through his hair again. The supplement scandal has him anxious—and I'm right there with him. For different reasons. Those poor people. And one woman is dead.

Only her passing isn't what they're discussing. Unbelievable. The cost seems to preoccupy my husband more than that tragedy.

"It won't cost anything. Kempton has reassured me," Hayden says.

Nodding pensively, Dorian sighs. "That's a big relief."

"You could at least send some money to the woman's family," I say.

The men look at me as though I've lost my mind.

"And admit guilt?" Dorian frowns. "Plenty are taking the supplements and thriving. It says on the container that it's best to consult a doctor before taking them if you have pre-existing conditions."

"But from what I've read, she was a healthy woman," I appeal.

Dorian glares daggers at me again. There've been a few of these tense moments today. His first sneer came the moment his mother wheeled her carry-on through our front door a few hours earlier.

Speaking of the devil, she's just arrived with two handfuls of shopping bags. Though her frazzled son's yet to learn that I handed her a wad of notes and sent her on her merry way to shop to her heart's delight. And that she did. She swapped her stained Walmart jeans and faded T-shirt for a hot pink tracksuit—the type worn by the nouveau riche, often accessorized with gold chains, having missed that lecture on stylish casualwear. But at least she ditched the tattered, body-hugging jeans she arrived in, which had Dorian gagging on his keto muffin.

She greets us with a tipsy grin, while Dorian ignores her and directs his simmering frustration at me as his mother strolls to the fridge, oblivious to her son's unwelcoming vibe. At least Hayden, escaping this heartwarming display of 'happy families,' is glued to his phone by the pool.

I called my mother-in-law, bought her a plane ticket, and invited her to stay so that she could meet her new grandchild.

Knowing how her presence would stir things up a bit, I wanted to get back at Dorian for turning our model marriage into a circus. All my hard work parading as the perfect housewife has degenerated into nothing but gossip fodder. I know I should be concerned about deeper things, like securing my parents' future, but I'm human, and no one likes to be made a fool of.

I can already hear the neighbors saying, "Wow, would you look at that? Linley's picture-perfect marriage crumbling right in front of us."

Incensed by his mother's arrival, Dorian pushed me into the bedroom and sprayed me with, "How could you do this to me?"

I had to bite my lip not to laugh in his face. I mean, this is coming from a man who's just had a baby with our maid.

"She's got a right to know about her grandchild, and my parents have been invited too."

"Why are you turning this into a fucking circus?" he snapped.

"You started it." That sharp, pithy response made him blanch. I walked out. Nothing like having the last word.

I'm now officially stepping into my rebellious era—starting with inviting his mother. It's not easy for someone like me. Confrontation makes me break out in a sweat. I'm that person who usually allows the loudest mouth in the room to win. But it's amazing what a few years married to a cold husband will do. I've learned you either fight back or get walked all over.

TWENTY-NINE

Guests mill around the pool after gushing over Xavier. The sun is bright, and it's a perfect day for a party.

Ana has been given the day off. The party idea didn't sit well with her. I imagine she hated the thought of her baby being paraded around like he's the latest must-have object.

The turquoise pool shimmers in the sunlight, with soft chatter and laughter in the background. It's a typical party gathering, suitably light and breezy. The unfolding drama that brought us here in the first place is now neatly tucked away.

It's like an out-of-body experience as I observe from a distance while clutching my bottle of beer. Dorian shot me a disapproving side-eye glance after I took a swig, which amused me. When we were dating, he made some snide comment about women drinking out of bottles, so I switched to wine.

But I'm no longer that eager-to-please little wife.

Defiance surged through me the moment Dorian sprung the adoption on me, especially once he'd transferred my parents' home back into their name.

I'm finally resurrecting that easygoing bookworm I buried back in New York. It seems that tying the knot ended up tying me in knots. But I'm slowly untangling myself from this complicated marriage.

At the very least, the adoption has won me some breathing space while I bide my time, pay off my parents' debt, and then make my escape with a healthy bank balance in tow.

Bubbly chatter and giggles come from the female guests. Their eyes, hidden behind oversized shades, obscure what they're whispering about, but going by the oohs and aahs, I imagine it's some juicy topic. At the other end of the pool, the men huddle together, laughing and gesturing like they own the world.

To think I once craved a place in this entitled world of the pampered privileged.

Now, I'm not so sure.

Most of the guests, chewing on carrot and celery sticks and sipping Perrier, are part of Dorian's wellness scene. Some I've met at dinner parties. The wives in airy organic linen shirts and slacks, and their husbands, well, in the same. Gender-neutral wear is how I'd describe it.

It's a rent-a-crowd in a way because my husband doesn't do 'close.' That cockroach party boy Brendan Crib was the only person Dorian seemed close to. But back in New York, my husband drank and partied hard like most Wall Street swinging-dick cowboys. Despite obvious setbacks, given that these men divorce as often as they fiddle with their clients' funds, I preferred that version. At least he was real.

Though my mother's here, holding my hand and supporting me in this performance of a lifetime, my father decided to stay home. Despite my pleading with her not to, she told him all about Xavier. Unlike me, he's not one to pretend, so he chose to stay away.

Of course, the neighbors got an invite. They wouldn't have missed it for the world. Since Dorian and Ana's very public display, we've become figures of interest. I guess one needs the whiff of a scandal to fertilize that unsettling public appetite for good gossip.

I almost asked Jarrad along, but that would have sent the rumor mill into a frenzy. Olivia noticed the little smile I shared with Jarrad during one of her visits, and considering our leaving the bar together that night, I'd say the others know about my growing friendship with the 'hunky' gardener.

That thin skin I arrived with four years ago has thickened over the years, and if they want to think about me and Jarrad that way, they can. I'm not the first unhappily married woman to seek her pleasure elsewhere, even if it was just that one smooch under the moonlight.

I sigh. That warm memory is becoming a little worn out. It needs refreshing.

In need of some respite from all the festivities, I retreat to the nursery upstairs. My mother follows me. She's not exactly enjoying this charade either. But I begged her to come, and Dorian insisted too. While he hates the idea of his mother being in attendance, my socially adept and graceful mom fits the well-adjusted family model he'd like the world to see.

I take a deep breath and massage my face, which is aching from all the fake smiling and feigning how super life is now that this bundle of joy has graced our lives. Though, I must admit, Xavier's growing on me. Like most, I'm a sucker for a cute baby, but I can't imagine growing close. Or I won't allow myself to, given my plans.

Nevertheless, I'm still the mother for now as I watch Xavier in his crib. He's had enough attention for one day. And it's warm out there. Amanda, the nanny we employed for the day, having just fed him, is now on a well-deserved break.

At least Ana's not here. The book club girls would have gone nuts had she been swishing about. And the love in her eyes whenever she's cradling Xavier is heartbreaking and rather revealing. You'd have to be blind not to see it. I also notice the longing in Ana's dark eyes whenever Dorian's close.

I'd swap in a heartbeat.

Wearing a confused smile, my mother stares down at the sleeping baby. This insane arrangement has usurped that happy feeling one would naturally experience around a grandchild.

The nursery also lacks the kind of fairytale embellishments popular in newborns' rooms. If anything, the space is sadly bare. Just a crib, a lamp, and a baby monitor. I haven't had time to go shopping. But then, I'm not into the kind of passion project glowing new mothers normally embrace, like having fairytale characters everywhere or a Disney remake in pink or blue.

"He's a lovely boy. I just hope you know what you're doing, darling. Another woman's child. The maid's baby." She shakes her head. "And why employ her as the nanny?" She wraps Xavier's blanket around him.

I nod wistfully. "I know it sounds crazy. But he's a good baby, don't you think?"

"Of course. But at some point, won't he want to know his real mother?"

"If everything goes to plan, I won't be around for that."

She returns the same apprehensive frown as when I first introduced Ashley while he was going through his morose Radiohead days, getting around in thrift shop clothes and questioning the system.

"What's that plan again?" she asks.

I stare over at the monitor and place my finger over my mouth.

Shit. Were we heard?

My mother's shoulders slump like we've been outed for some crime.

The nanny returns, and we walk out of the room.

"Did they hear?" my mom asks, looking worried.

"It's okay. I'm sure." I'm not. The monitor sounds in the main living areas, our bedroom, and Dorian's office.

She follows me into the bedroom where I change into another blouse. The day's hotter than I expected.

"But what are you going to do? I mean, you are the boy's official mother."

I go into the ensuite and spray on some perfume. "Let's cross that bridge when we get there."

"That doesn't sound like you. You've always been a planner."

I sigh. "I know and look where that got me. I've had to learn to adapt, Mom."

"I get that. We all do to some extent. But this 'let's not think about the future' approach is not a plan."

Don't I know it? I'm in the dark about what my life might look like in a month, let alone one year.

"For now, let's get your bills paid and you back on track, and then I'll think about my own happiness."

She leans in and hugs me. "I hate that you're sacrificing so much for us."

"You would do the same for me. That's what family does. We protect each other. Whatever it takes."

'Whatever it takes,' all right. I never thought that would be my mantra, but it's steadily becoming that.

When we leave the room, we find Dorian's mother lurking about. She gives me a sly smirk. "I just came to see my little grandson."

I can smell liquor on her breath. Yes, she's a heavy drinker and on meds. I brought it up with Dorian the night she arrived.

"How can she drink while on psych meds?" I'd asked.

"She's one of those freaks that can do it."

"You don't look happy about that," I said.

"You think?" He huffed. "You get some healthy housewife who dies after taking one of our supplements, and then there's my mother who can drown in liquor and pop pills like candy and still annoy the crap out of me."

I couldn't find a response given the disturbing subtext to that gripe.

"So the maid's Xavier's real mom?" Dorian's mother slurs.

I'm starting to regret inviting her.

"Just heard you talking. Sorry, didn't mean to eavesdrop." Her raspy liquor-soaked laugh fills the air as I take a step back.

"Xavier's adopted. You know that." I keep my response short and sweet while mulling over how to deal with this unfortunate leak. Won't Dorian be pleased?

I move on with my mother, who's giving me a questioning look. I just roll my eyes subtly as Jenny tags along heading for the nursery.

As she tries to enter, I block her at the door. I can't leave the child alone with my drunken mother-in-law. I'm not that low. Fortunately, the nanny appears just in time, carrying a bottle of milk.

"You should leave him for now," I say calmly. "He's about to be fed."

She pushes past me anyway. "He's my grandson, and I want to be here." Stumbling, she holds onto the wall.

I take her by the arm. "Later."

Staring me down, her steely gaze reminds me of her son's. She might be sloshed, but they share the same stubborn glint in their eyes.

Luckily, she drops the serious act and chuckles. "Sure. I could use another drink."

My mother follows along, looking both perplexed and bewildered.

As we make our way back to the guests, I put on armor thick enough to deal with the next chapter of this shitshow.

THIRTY

Judging by the laughter and animated conversation, the guests are having fun. I'm glad someone is. Even Dorian, chatting with a couple I don't recognize, looks unusually upbeat. He's almost guzzling champagne like he did back in his New York days. He went from overindulgence to moderation the minute we moved here. And while I once marveled at his unfaltering self-control, I've also seen how tightly wound he gets and how the cracks start to show over the smallest things.

People say a lot of folks use liquor to cope. Well, judging by Dorian's sudden personality switch, I can see why. He's even laughing at a joke. He's warmer. Friendlier. Even shooting me the odd smile. I had to look over my shoulder to see if his cheesy grin was directed at someone else.

Olivia finds me in the kitchen, where I'm taking a moment to gather my thoughts after that tense exchange with Dorian's mother. I have a feeling that's not the end of it.

I nod at Olivia and grab a bottle of beer from the fridge, taking a nice long swig as I regard the colorful vegan snacks fighting for space on the marble-topped island. With a plate in hand, I put together a platter for my mom, who's deep in conversation with Shelby Spritz.

I select vegan sushi rolls, avocado chickpea toast, zucchini rolls with cashew cheese, and other bite-sized treats that the guests have been raving about. Even Dorian patted me on the back for finding such a good caterer.

In addition, I baked gluten-free keto cupcakes along with a batch of fluffy carb-rich chocolate versions. Those were the first to go, funnily enough. Still, I was filled with pride as the guests moaned with delight.

I set the tray on the coffee table. "I thought you might like these."

"Oh, how thoughtful," Shelby says. "It's a delicious spread. You'll have to give me the name of the caterer."

Turning to my mother, I say, "Try some; it's delicious."

I read some tension in her smile. She's as concerned about Jenny's outburst as I am.

I head back to the kitchen, where Olivia is sampling a few bites. "Mm... these are great. I can feel cellular renewal with each bite."

I laugh. "You don't like them?"

"No. Really. I do." She licks her fingers, and I pass her a napkin. "You didn't invite Jarrad, I noticed."

"He is the gardener." I shrug. "It wouldn't seem appropriate now, would it?"

"You've still got that maid working here."

What can I say? I know how it looks.

Olivia tilts her head toward Claire and Emily, who are out on the terrace and holding hands. Living up to his 1950s attitude, Dorian didn't hide his revulsion behind their backs after we welcomed the loved-up couple earlier.

"They look happy and comfortable in their relationship." Olivia shakes her head. "Maybe I should hook up with women for a change. Though I'd miss dick."

I chuckle. "There are plenty of ways around that."

"I've got a nice battery-operated boyfriend. At least it can't rip my heart out."

Melodramatic as that comment might be, I fight the urge not to laugh and select a slice of vegan spinach pie instead.

The carb-rich snacks were the first to go. My tipsy, unusually jolly husband couldn't stop eating them. He even polished off a bowl of chips, which had me wondering if I should spike his daily green juice with vodka. I could use a more easygoing vibe around here.

I pass Olivia a slice of spinach and tofu cheese pie.

She takes a bite. "Mm... this isn't bad. What were we saying? Oh, that's right, Emily's a new person. I mean, she's so happy all the time now."

"Happiness hangs around in the most unexpected places." I think of Jarrad, and a flush of warmth wraps around me.

"Then I want to know where mine is hiding." The corners of her mouth turn down.

"Sorry it didn't work with Tommy."

Olivia holds my gaze. "How do you know? Did Jarrad say something?"

"Only what you've told me."

She sighs. "Yeah, well. I guess it was a bit too much introducing the kids."

Natalie arrives and helps herself to a slice of spinach pie. "This is the best food. Ever."

I smile. "Thanks. I'm glad you're enjoying it."

"My aunt's still not out of the hospital, you know."

"Oh, I'm sorry to hear that," I say, almost preferring Olivia's 'woe is me' conversation to one about a family member poisoned by my husband's latest 'cure-all' pills.

Speaking of the devil, Dorian turns up. The kitchen has become the place to be, and going by his sudden frown, he heard Natalie. She sneers at him, and he offers a tight smile in response.

I guess having a thick skin works in these types of situations, and Dorian has had years of training, thinking back to the Brendan Crib days and how he wiggled out of that incriminating situation. The hasty retreat from New York spoke volumes. If I hadn't been so blinded by my own dreams, I might have made a retreat of my own—back to my cozy life in Greenwich, where I would've opened that cupcake café. But hindsight's a bitch, as they say.

Natalie leaves the kitchen to join Sophia and Isabella as Olivia follows her out.

"Why did you invite her?" Dorian asks.

"Natalie's part of my book club. And she's a friend."

"A friend?" He sniggers. "She looks like one of those dumpster people."

"Huh?" I have to stifle a laugh at how absurd that sounds.

"I've seen them, diving into dumpsters, legs in the air scrounging for their next meal."

"Natalie's hardly crawling around for scraps. She's just as wealthy as us. Besides, baggy sweats are all the rage. Billie Eilish set that trend."

"It looks terrible." He drains his glass. Dorian's on his way to being sloshed.

"Her aunt's still in the hospital. She took those supplements. Another victim," I remind him.

"This is coming from someone living with a meth-head."

I can't deny that since Natalie's brother is either a zombie or an excitable clown, depending on what time of day it is. "What's that got to do with it?"

He looks around to see if anyone is within earshot. "Can we not do this right now?"

I leave him just as Shelby Spritz, clutching a glass of colorful juice, joins him.

In search of a heavy dose of positivity and normality, I find Sophia, who's sharing a laugh with her husband. They're the happiest couple there, along with Claire and Emily.

Soon, the conversation descends into doom and gloom again, however. *What is in the water today?*

The subject drifts over to activewear and how poisons are leaching from polyester fabric.

"Oh, stop it. I'm loving my Lululemon leggings to death," Isabella announces, her arm linked with her husband's. "You wouldn't see me dead in organic cotton panties."

"They're very comfortable," I say with a chuckle.

"Sure. For nuns," Isabella scoffs.

Our small talk is suddenly interrupted as someone comes blustering into the living room.

I assume he's connected to Dorian because I don't recognize him.

Only instead of handshakes and friendly greetings, he's yelling abuse and stabbing his finger at Dorian's face.

Then, before I can say anything, it descends into an all-out fight.

It's not even one of those drunken late-night parties notorious for swinging-dick violence. I mean, this is supposed to be a harmless garden party celebrating the joys of parenthood. Isn't it?

The guests have all stopped talking. All eyes are on the scene in the living room, where the newcomer is pushing Dorian's shoulder while yelling expletives.

I think I would have preferred a juggler or sword swallower for some light diversion, but hey, the guests are riveted.

"You're a fucking snake-oil salesman. A fake. My wife's dead because of you and those bullshit pills you're peddling," the man yells.

While Dorian appeals to the muscular server, who doubles as security, I'm kicking myself for not booking a band.

The guests look on in horror as the server removes the disgruntled gatecrasher by the scruff of the neck and drags him off.

The man is thrashing about in the stronger man's arms shouting, "I'll get you, you prick!" before he's pushed out of the front door.

Dorian has gone pale. He rakes his fingers through his hair and heads straight for the bourbon. He pours half a glass and gulps it down in one swallow.

"Turn on some music," he says to the server, who has returned and is rearranging his shirt. "And top up everyone's drinks."

I take a deep breath and look around, spotting Claire and Emily cozied up poolside. I head over to join them.

"Give me some of what you've got," I say.

They both give me mystified looks.

"You look so blissful. I want that." I sigh.

They both reach up to grab my hands. "Things will get better. You just have to leave your douche husband."

"Don't worry, I'm working on it," I mutter.

I guess my happy housewife cover's blown.

I can finally be myself, which is kind of liberating, despite the hell that's about to break loose.

THIRTY-ONE

It's late morning, and I'm fuzzy-headed after yesterday's party. Olivia was the last to leave after I pushed her out the door around two in the morning.

Dorian hasn't been spared either. He arrives from his run looking worse for wear.

"Should you be running? Your eye looks terrible." I go to the fridge and bring out the same bag of peas he applied to his face after the guests left.

Ignoring that comment, he slugs back a large bottle of water, wipes his lips, and, with the bag of peas in hand, plops down in an armchair.

My mother left early. I offered to drive her to the airport, but she insisted on letting me rest and used a cab instead. I think she was eager to get away. Can't say I blame her. The air around here is thick with tension.

Clearly oblivious to any of that, Jenny wanders in looking cheery. "Mornin' all."

The woman's a freak. If I drank as much as she had the night before, I'd need a liver transplant by morning. Must have been all that dancing. After the healthy, well-adjusted guests left, which was five minutes after the angry intruder was thrown out, the party revelers remained. Namely, Olivia, Isabella sans husband, Natalie, Claire, and Emily. They had just one thing in mind, and that was to dance.

I was given the DJ role, and the living room turned into a dance floor. While I was letting my hair down and partaking in shots, Dorian hid upstairs in his study, nursing a black eye.

Jenny shuffles over to a freshly brewed pot of coffee in the kitchen and pours some into a cup along with a shot of whiskey that was left on the bench from the night before.

I peer over at my husband who, despite having his face half-covered, looks horrified. "Isn't it a bit too soon for that?" he asks.

Jenny regards him as though seeing him for the first time. "Wow, he socked you good, didn't he? Fun party." She chuckles.

Though I hate how Dorian has ignored his mother all these years, I'm starting to see why. His mother, who regularly flouts convention—something I once found amusing—strikes me as self-absorbed.

Must run in the family. They also share the same dark, piercing eyes, and high cheekbones. Dorian hated it when I commented on their physical similarities, muttering something to the contrary.

To add to the tension, Ana joins us in the kitchen holding Xavier close to her chest.

Jenny peers over at her with a growing grin, while I feel a stab of sympathy. It's kind of heartbreaking. I know I shouldn't, but I feel for Ana.

I've since learned how she made this huge sacrifice to save her dad, who's being held in Chile by some nasty people.

It seems this whole sacrificing one's happiness for family has become a recurring theme in my life.

Right now, though, Dorian is looking seriously unhappy with his smirking mother, who's acting like she lives here. Something tells me she would move here in a heartbeat.

Not if I can help it. The woman's a drain, not just on our liquor stores but on my energy. Her endless attention-seeking saps me dry.

No, Jenny's not staying. I do wonder what she's cooking up, though, now that she has learned the uncomfortable truth about Xavier's real parents.

"This nanny's prettier than bossy Amanda," Jenny says, turning to Ana, who is preparing Xavier's bottle from milk she had expressed for the weekend.

As Ana moves about holding her son, Jenny adds, "She seems more into little Xavier than you two." She gives Dorian a pointed stare.

Dorian ends a call and then turns to his mother. "Haven't you got a flight to catch?"

Jenny ignores him while topping up her coffee with another shot of whiskey.

"It's at three, I believe," I interject. "I'll drive you."

"Oh?" She frowns. "I thought I might stay a little longer."

"You've stayed long enough," Dorian says, stroking Xavier's little face as he walks off.

Ana gives him a little smile and follows him out.

Jenny watches them leave. "I'd watch those two if I were you. That pretty nanny seems taken with my son. I wouldn't leave them alone." Her sly smile widens. "Oh, that's right, that ship's already sailed." A throaty chuckle follows.

Tension grips my shoulders. "I trust Dorian," I say, almost pushing my chest out. Talk about laying it on thick.

She sniffs. She's not buying it, but I no longer care.

Dorian re-emerges with his checkbook, scribbles a figure, and then hands it over to her. "There. You're leaving today." He turns to me. "I'm having a shower. I need to work from home, so don't disturb me."

He's trying to avoid his office, where I'm told the preying media are swarming around like vultures.

Jenny stares down at the check. I can't tell if she's pleased or unsatisfied. Returning her attention to Dorian, she says, "You've got a few legal suits to deal with, I imagine. That man yesterday came in with guns blazing. And look at that shiner; it's getting darker by the minute."

He turns his back on her, then stomps upstairs. I almost feel bad for him, but then I remember how his face hardly shifted when hearing about that poor woman's death after taking his longevity supplements.

I sense that my husband's heart hides in some dark place. The only time it makes an appearance is for his son. His eyes soften with that unmistakable shine of love, and he becomes unrecognizable.

"Can you run me down to the bank so I can cash this?" Jenny asks, setting her empty cup on the kitchen bench.

I wipe my hands with a paper towel and nod. "We can get some lunch, and then I'll drive you to the airport. How does that sound?"

Her face brightens. "I'll go and get ready. I can see my son's not in the mood for some quality family time."

I bite my lip so as not to laugh.

She points outside to the garden. "You've got a hottie in your garden. A sexy nanny and a sexy gardener. What are you two plotting?"

I turn my attention beyond the pool, where a shirtless Jarrad is digging up a root.

She doesn't miss much. And yes, guilty as charged on the sexy gardener.

"I'll just go and get ready." She staggers off.

I take a deep regulating breath. My chest has been in knots all morning, especially seeing how eagle-eyed Jenny was around Ana and Xavier now that she's stumbled on the whole unpalatable story. Dorian will go nuts knowing that, but I don't care.

I have to toughen up. It's either that or drugs, and I refuse to dull my brain by popping Xanax.

I step outside. The sun is out, and chirping birds make for another perfect day. I wish it were just me and Jarrad alone in the garden right now, without this dysfunctional freak show. Though I wouldn't be pining after the gardener had Dorian loved me. And here I was thinking that with a gentle touch, I could bring out my husband's softer side. I must have missed that seminar on how stubborn people don't change. If anything, they develop deeper roots that even a buff gardener can't dig out.

Oh well, if my husband can cheat, then so can I.

I don't even feel bad thinking that for a change.

I rummage in my emotional toolbox and put on my brightest smile. I wave. "Hey."

Jarrad smiles back and lifts a heavy box away from the path. His tattooed biceps bulge from the weight, and I gulp back a sudden rush of lust.

He rubs his scalp, shaved down to a dark shadow, hinting at the full head of hair. With that perfectly shaped scalp, that buzz cut suits him. "A perfect day for hedging."

I laugh. "It is. You sound like you're looking forward to it."

He shrugs. "I like to work."

"That's admirable." I'm pretty sure I've got stars in my eyes.

If only everyone could be as genuine and easygoing as he is. The world would be a better place without these get-rich-quick scammers my husband likes to rub shoulders with.

Don't get me wrong—I know I wouldn't be living this cozy, privileged existence without him. But that's the irony of chasing happiness because it's the simple things that put a spring in my step. Fancy designer labels and a sparkling House Beautiful home might appeal from the outside, but without the nourishment of warm human connections within, it's just expensive dust.

"I love nature's little surprises. Like that." Jarrad points to a butterfly poised on a red dahlia. "That's a photo right there."

I can't help but agree. Especially if the photo includes him shirtless.

Oh, stop it.

"Can I offer you anything?" I ask.

Now that's a loaded question, going by how a little smile grows slowly on his tanned face. "I'm good."

He looks over my shoulder, and I turn to see Jenny behind the French doors with her suitcase. She's ready to leave. I'm guessing it's because of the extra zeros on that check.

"I better get started," he says, turning away.

I exhale and head back to the promise of an afternoon battling traffic and uncomfortable questions.

THIRTY-TWO

After racing around from one shop to another, Jenny drags me into a dark bar with a bunch of lonely-looking men staring down at their drinks. I wouldn't normally be caught dead there, especially at one in the afternoon.

Jenny's intent on talking endlessly about herself, but at least she hasn't broached the subject of Xavier's adoption. I'm fine with that. She's starved for company, and despite her sharp tongue and unfiltered opinions, I feel sorry for her.

After watching Jenny sink two double whiskies, I finally manage to convince her it's time to leave.

Relieved to finally arrive at the car without visiting yet another shop, I help load her shopping bags into the car, and then we head off to the airport.

Jenny hasn't stopped talking about her time working as a model during the seventies. Over lunch, she showed me phone images of herself as a teenage model. It was like I was looking at a different person. The former svelte beauty is now totally unrecognizable.

Just as we hit the freeway, Jenny brings up her modeling days again.

"I was doing well until..." She stops herself.

"Until?" I ask, sensing something dramatic.

She stares out the window. "There were a ton of snakes in that industry. And we were young. Like really young."

One doesn't need to possess special powers to read between the lines. After all, we are talking about the dark old days when reporting rape was about as uncommon as female politicians.

"When did you start modeling?" I ask.

"Fourteen. While I was shopping one day, this guy approached me. Though my mom told him to get lost, he still handed us a card. I hounded her to see if it was legit, and eventually, she agreed to accompany me to the meeting. When they offered me a hundred bucks for an hour's work, she was pretty accommodating."

"Wait. The men took advantage of you in that way?" I have to ask.

"Yup. I lost my virginity to some forty-year-old jerk. They stuffed us with drugs and alcohol and then took us into rooms, and from there, it was part and parcel of the job."

She just shrugs it off, like we're talking about a backache from heavy lifting at work.

"That sounds terrible," I say, shaking my head in shock.

"We also had a lot of fun, you know. Traveled to Paris and London. I was a popular runway model. That was my thing, prancing about in uncomfortable shoes. I never stumbled once. Not like some of the girls. But they were drugged to the eyeballs." She giggles. All the earlier darkness has now turned sunny.

"And you remained clean?"

"Yeah, well, a bit of sniff for sure. Everyone sniffed. But some of the girls were shooting up."

"And Dorian's dad?" I can't help but ask.

"Oh, that was someone I picked up when I was in my twenties. It was just one night. And then, wham, I got banged up." She laughs again as though reliving the good times.

Weird.

"Your mother, father?"

"My mother tried to get me to abort it. And my dad was dead."

"I'm sorry."

"Don't be. He used to beat my mom."

"Is she still alive?" Dorian's unhealthy upbringing makes me sad and might just explain many things about his rigid attitude toward women and why he chose me and not some sexually experienced woman to be his wife.

"Mom died a few years ago. Dorian didn't even go to her funeral." She shakes her head. "He was horrible to me. Still is." She snorts. "He blamed me for everything that went wrong. And then he left at eighteen. I couldn't find him for two years. I even hired a PI. Dorian had changed his name and was flying high on Wall Street with Brendan Crib, who I hear ended up in jail." She sighs. "I wanted Dorian to finish school. He didn't even go to college, you know."

"People can still thrive without a degree."

"You think he's done good?" She turns to me.

"If doing good is measured by wealth, then yes, he's done well."

"You sound unhappy. Being married to my son can't be easy. He's a cold fish. Even as a boy, he hated being cuddled. He made me promise not to pick him up from school. He was ashamed of me. Still is." Her voice cracks.

We arrive at the airport, and I pull up to the curb and face her. I touch her wrinkled hand. "I'm sorry he's that way toward you."

"It's not your fault." Her face hardens, and I wince from her abrupt mood shift. "That kid is his. You know I know."

The best I can do is a hesitant nod.

"Xavier looks exactly like Dorian. I knew as soon as I saw him."

I open the door. "You're going to miss your flight. I'll help you with your bags."

Despite a queasy feeling, I hurry along, open the trunk, and pass her the suitcase and shopping bags.

"And he's the nanny's kid too," she persists with a deeper twist of the knife. "I saw the look they gave each other this morning."

I lean in to kiss Jenny on the cheek. "Have a safe flight."

She steps away and points. "I'll be in touch. That check won't last a month."

As I stand there watching her walk off, I wonder what she plans to do.

Reading my mind, it might seem, she turns and says, "I've started writing. I've got a few contacts who might like to read about Dorian's perfect life."

And there it is.

I just want to stick my head in a bucket and scream, but instead, I wipe my brow, jump back into the car, and drive off.

It's not my problem.

Or is it?

With that troubling question swishing about like a drunk on a boat hit by a wave, I return home.

Jenny's disturbing story of her life growing up makes me question whether Dorian knows what happened to his mother, or whether I should tell him. Something tells me he'd show nothing but contempt. He'd said on a few occasions how women attract trouble by the way they dress. Of course, I challenged those antiquated views, but my words fell on deaf ears. Once Dorian's mind is made up, he becomes a brick wall.

It really couldn't have been easy growing up with Jenny, but then I also feel for her. It would have been painful having a son who was ashamed of her.

It all makes for sad reading. As will her threats to make public Dorian's fall from grace. Now that's a story that the tabloids would devour: Billionaire supplement guru turned deadly snake oil salesman sires his maid's child.

Whichever way, Dorian needs to set up a monthly stipend for his mother to stop her from talking.

When I step through the door, I notice just how quiet it is.

It's now late afternoon. I pop my bag down on the sofa and head to the kitchen for some coffee.

As I enter the living area, I trip over a broken chair and hold onto the wall to stop myself from stumbling. As I look down at the ground, the floor is stained with blood.

What the...

Everything becomes a blur. My head spins as I follow the bloody stream in slow motion until my attention settles on the grotesque sight on the ground.

My chest turns to ice, as do my legs, which might snap any minute. My mouth drops open, and I scream so loudly that it feels like razor blades cutting into my vocal cords.

Dorian's on the ground, lying in a pool of blood.

I run over to him, kneel, and place my hand under his blood-stained nose. I don't feel any air.

My heart clenches. He's dead.

Or I think he is.

It's after five, and trembling from shock, I pick myself up and race into the front room for my bag. After fumbling for my phone, I dial 911, leaving blood stains all over it.

Taking a deep breath, I give the operator the details.

After she has assured me that help is on the way, I sink into the chair and stare out into space.

Where's Ana?

Just at that point, I hear the baby crying and hurry upstairs.

He's alone in his crib. Nothing looks different. What the hell happened?

THIRTY-THREE

My husband is dead, and instead of crying, I'm a frozen lump. What should I be feeling? Shock, yes. Sadness, not sure. Yes, I know that makes me sound horrible.

It's late afternoon, the day after his murder, and I'm staring out into space.

Jarrad is here. I didn't want Olivia or Emily here, but I couldn't be alone either. I needed someone to hold my hand and not fire off a ton of questions. He's good at reading my mood. Companionable silence is rare in my life. With Dorian, it was always tense silence.

"That disgruntled husband who crashed the party seems like the obvious suspect. He threatened Dorian for all to hear," I say at last.

Xavier cries, and I flinch, having almost forgotten the baby was here.

Jarrad asks, "Shouldn't you go and see him?"

"Amanda, the new nanny, is here."

He nods. "You haven't heard from Ana, I take it?"

I shake my head.

A knock at the door makes me jump.

"I hope that's not Olivia." I wear a guilty smile. "She's dying to know what happened, like everyone, I imagine. I don't want to see anyone."

"Then I should go," he says, rising a little too quickly.

Despite having Amanda there, I needed someone I could trust, so I called Jarrad, and he came immediately.

I touch Jarrad's hand. "No. Stay. Please. I need someone here, and you're the only person I feel comfortable around right now."

He sits again. But I notice he's not himself. Death is an uncomfortable subject, especially when murder is involved.

Amanda shows in a pair of men. No doubt they're here to interrogate me.

I spent the whole night dealing with police while a forensic team swept through the room. They also took my fingerprints and a mouth swab. The floor has only just been cleaned, and the tape removed.

At least the detectives have given me some space to grieve.

The tears I shed had less to do with grief than with the teams of men in space outfits crowding my once-favorite room and the camera-wielding pariahs circling like vultures. The thought of facing a camera and professing undying love for my husband makes me want to crawl under a rock.

What if they dig around and discover that Ana, who's mysteriously vanished, gave birth to Xavier?

That brings up all kinds of scandalous assumptions.

I know how these things are. I've watched my share of CSI. The widow is always the first suspect. Yes, I have an alibi, but they don't know exactly how long he's been dead. Apparently, that's an inexact science, I'm told.

After the pair flash their badges and mumble their names, I direct them to sit at the table where a batch of freshly baked cupcakes is cooling off. I spent half the day baking. Meditation is probably a better way to calm one's mind, but I need to keep myself busy.

"Coffee?" I look over at Amanda, who's not only the nanny but also my new maid—an arrangement she was happy to accept after I doubled her hourly rate.

Jarrad goes to rise when the younger detective, whose name has already escaped me, signals for him to remain. "Who are you?"

Nice. Straight to the point. Not even a smile. Unlike his chubby older partner, who's eyeing the cupcakes.

"Jarrad Hunter. I'm the gardener," he says.

The men exchange a look. Oh God, please don't let them think we're having an affair. It's all too Jackie Collins.

The coffee arrives, and I offer them the banana cupcakes. The older detective, whose shirt is straining at the seams, helps himself, while the younger, leaner cop declines.

For some reason, he reminds me of Dorian. The same serious look in his dark eyes. I sense he's already accusing me, which makes me squirm.

"So take me through the events leading up to finding your husband."

The older cop looks at Jarrad and then his colleague. "We'd prefer to interview Mrs. Gunn in private."

Jarrad rises. He looks eager to get away. "No problem." He gives a curt nod and walks off.

"We'll be in contact, so please remain in the area."

Jarrad looks from the cops to me and nods. "Not planning on going anywhere. Too much work to do."

Jarrad flashes a tight smile and walks off while the younger detective's eyes follow him out with a scrutinizing stare.

"Close, are you?" The younger detective turns to me.

I frown and then smooth it out. Can't have him reading my unease. Eagle-eyed detectives feed off suspects' nervous reactions.

"Sorry, I didn't get your name."

"Chief Investigator Hull."

"Jarrad is a friend as well as an employee."

"Are you friendly with all your employees?" He looks over at Amanda, who's preparing a bottle for Xavier.

"Amanda is new here, as you would know from the statement I made to the officer yesterday. Ana, our nanny, has disappeared."

The older detective, having just polished off two cupcakes, wipes his mouth. "I believe you'd come home after taking your mother-in-law to the airport and found your husband dead. Yes?"

I nod.

"You say that the nanny has run away. What was her relationship with your husband?"

"She was our maid and nanny." Oops, my voice cracked.

"We know differently," Detective Hull declares, looking pleased with himself, like he'd just put in a goal at the buzzer. "We've dug around a little and discovered that your husband purchased the apartment where she's staying. The same apartment we visited earlier. Only she isn't there. The apartment was only recently transferred into her name."

My brows gather. What?

"This is the first I've heard about that." Little beads of sweat slide down my back, and I shift my position.

"Can you tell us a little about the day of the party? Your husband's partner mentioned an angry intruder—the husband of a recently deceased woman—and how he threatened your husband."

"Yes. He'd be the first person you should be talking to. After all, he gave Dorian a black eye. You have a party full of witnesses."

"We'll need the guest list," says the older detective.

"Sure." I take a sip of water. "There's also Ana's ex-boyfriend, who was stalking her. He might have found out about my husband and..."

"Having a relationship with the maid, you mean?" Detective Hull smirks.

I clasp my hands, and he notices, of course.

He adds, "We know about Hector Gonzales. He's gone too."

"That says something, doesn't it?" I ask.

"There are a few suspects with clear motives here, for certain. We've just got to comb through the evidence and leave no stone unturned." Hull stares me in the eye as though to make a point.

I don't like him.

"Resources allowing," says the older cop, revealing an interesting dynamic between a younger eager cop dying to sink his teeth into a case that's got the media in a frenzy and the older, more realistic detective who just wants to focus on the most obvious suspect and close the case.

Both situations don't bode well for me. In the first instance, my life will be ransacked like some burglar pulling drawers apart in search of valuable items. And there's lots to find: bankrupt parents, a prenup offering crumbs, porn on my husband's laptop, and his affair with the maid.

I walk them to the door, and as he's about to step out, Detective Hull turns. "I trust you're not planning a trip."

I shake my head.

"We'll be in touch," says the older detective.

After I close the door, I lean against the wall and take a deep breath.

THIRTY-FOUR

Now that Dorian's body has been released from forensics, I have a funeral to arrange. I flip through laminated pages of themes as though this is some kind of celebration. Dorian left a will expressing his wish to be cremated. He'd rejected the option to donate his organs. How ironic, given his Never Say Die company's mission was all about extending people's lives.

The funeral director's words were, "Think of it as a celebration and not something dark and sad."

Hello, he was murdered.

Dark and sad for those who give a damn. And as the days go on, I'm discovering not so many did.

My husband's friends consisted of business associates who stuck around for what he could do for them. Leeches more than friends.

Then again, Dorian only socialized for business. His buddies were all connected to some kind of profitable enterprise.

The funeral director asked some difficult questions, like what my husband enjoyed.

I couldn't exactly say, "Computer sex with busty brunettes." So I went on to explain how amino acids, diet fads, and the microbiome took up most of Dorian's focus.

He looked a little stumped, as though I'd told him of my husband's predilection for keeping reptiles or something just as weird.

The fact that I made up the answers to the questionnaire highlighted just how little I knew about my husband.

Four years married to a stranger.

Could I have done something more, like shown an interest in Magnolia bark extract or the latest findings on pomegranates?

I pause at the question relating to a eulogy. There are even trending poems. W.H. Auden gets a mention. That's rather highbrow, I think, drifting off in another direction, anywhere but decision-making.

There are trends for everything, so why not funerals?

One can't have a funeral without a eulogy. That's plain enough. But the thought of standing at a podium makes my spine stiffen, recalling my stint at book signings, where I'd have to introduce the author. Even among a room full of motley readers, there mostly for the free snacks, my palms left a damp stain on the hardback I clutched, and my voice quivered.

Yep, I was heading for loser's purgatory back then. A valid justification for becoming a housewife. Look where that's landed me—staring down at a book of morbid themes, playing the part of the grieving widow.

Maybe if it hadn't been such a brutal end, we could smile and listen to some inane pop tune. But this is different.

Hayden Spitz isn't shy when it comes to talking. He's the obvious choice for Dorian's eulogy. The funeral is to take place the day after tomorrow. The sooner, the better. As I dial Hayden's number, I can only hope he'll agree to take the pulpit.

His secretary tells me he is currently unavailable.

"When will he be back?" I ask.

"We're not expecting him back for a while. He's gone away."

I huff with frustration. The douche has run away.

He's probably frightened that some irate family member will come at him with a baseball bat.

I've recently been informed that there was no DNA evidence relating to the disgruntled husband, so he's been struck off the suspect list.

I'm not surprised. Pulling off a murder doesn't always come easy.

After an hour of what appeared to be staged mourning at a venue arranged by the funeral parlor, the guests are now at my home. Some of whom are strangers, but the more, the merrier, I guess. Even if it means nosy journalists masquerading as distant relatives.

The service was a farce. I even hired a director. Actors included.

Dorian's mother looked bewildered. "Who would have thought Dorian knew so many people?"

I had rented a crowd. My neighbors were a bit baffled but just rolled with it. After all, they didn't know my life that well.

The mismatched pair of detectives were in attendance and are now enjoying the free booze and finger food. The media scrum is causing all kinds of chaos for the neighbors, especially during school drop-offs.

As I move around the front room, pausing now and then for that obligatory "I'm sorry for your loss" comment, I see Claire and Emily chatting with Olivia and join them. They all direct their attention to me, wearing the same sympathetic—or pitying—smile they've had planted on their faces all day.

"Thanks for coming," I say as Natalie arrives, dressed in her baggy non-descript clothes that she had previously admitted wearing to avoid male attention.

Will that be me? Or will I swap my upmarket non-descript outfits for something brighter and more fitted?

I think of Jarrad and wonder if I can ask him out for a date, and how soon is too soon?

Like tomorrow?

A frisson of anticipation welcomes me back to the land of the living. Yes, I know it's bad of me to entertain pleasure at such a somber time, but hey, you know the story.

"It was a nice service," says Claire.

She's just saying that because I'm sure she sensed it was make-believe.

I called a bunch of Dorian's friends. The same guys he occasionally invited for card nights, but not one showed his face.

Strange.

What did they have to hide?

The papers hadn't been too kind either. They wrote about my husband's affiliation with Brendan Crib, after which Dorian escaped to LA and set up a wellness company selling supplements promising to extend people's lives, and how people are now suing Never Say Die following a spate of deaths.

I do wonder how that's going to affect me.

I have an appointment with Dorian's attorney in the morning.

"So what now?" asks Olivia. "Will you stay? We'll miss you if you move."

I smile at her feigned look of sadness. "I haven't decided on anything yet."

As though on cue, Xavier cries. I hold up my hand. "Back in a minute."

At least the baby has given me an excuse to escape that perplexing question about my plans going forward.

My heart is tugging me toward Greenwich.

But there is one thing holding me back.

And what am I to do with Xavier now that Ana's mysteriously vanished? Is she still alive?

She was way too devoted to Xavier to leave him.

"Excuse me a minute," I say and head upstairs, welcoming the respite from more questions.

I step into the nursery where Amanda's rocking Xavier.

"He's teething," she says with a smile. "I hope you don't need me downstairs."

I shake my head. "No. I've brought in catering staff to feed the hordes."

She nods. "It sounds like quite a crowd."

Yep. Lots of hungry actors I'll never see again who have signed NDAs. The lawyer I hired to help me navigate this mess arranged it for me. I didn't even know such a thing existed, but he relayed how renting actors was all the rage, especially if the funeral revolved around some loner who'd made a few enemies along the way.

Had my husband made enemies?

Just people like him who were only there for what they could do for each other. I suddenly began to cry. I hated the sad smiles directed at me. Who doesn't hate pity?

I cried through two packets of tissues. Everything hit me all at once. I felt sadness, anger, and regret. What a sham marriage. We were so wrong for each other—both chasing shallow, unrealistic dreams. He wanted some trophy wife who looked good on his arm, from good Anglo-Saxon stock. The thought of this makes me hate him a little more. And me?

Well, we already know the delusions I suffered buying into that whole marriage fantasy. I should have taken a deeper look at myself because I was always going to be that woman who fell for down-to-earth men like Jarrad. Or did I need to meet him first before that self-discovery could be realized?

I return to the party, and Olivia promptly drags me away, saying, "I thought Jarrad might be here."

"He doesn't normally work on Sundays."

Olivia smiles at my curt response. "Oh, don't play coy. You're attracted. Give it a few months, and then it should be okay."

I roll my eyes.

More like days, not months. I need something to dig me out of this endless void. A warm hug will do.

Jarrad is the only male who has hugged me, other than my dad, in a long time. I'm malnourished when it comes to affection, and the thought of a cuddle sends a warm shiver through me.

"So what are you going to do? You'll be a single mother. A widow. Rich, though. That opens up lots of options."

Single mother? Not if I can help it.

I've already decided what to do about Xavier. But I won't be telling Olivia.

Jarrad is my only confidante in this murky affair. My comrade. He's the only one holding me back from leaving.

I can't leave him. Not now.

That kiss glued us together. Or me, at least. Though I can see how he looks at me. I'd have to be brain-dead not to notice the desire in Jarrad's eyes. Or am I wearing rose-colored glasses again?

The line between reality and fantasy can sometimes blur, especially when one is starved for affection.

Sophia joins us. "Are they any closer to finding the murderer?"

Here we go. The question that's been on everyone's lips all day. I just wish everyone would go home so I can drink alone.

"Who do you think did it?" she asks.

"There are a few people with a bone to pick after that supplements scandal."

She nods, looking sympathetic. "I'm glad I didn't take any. Tony put me off them. Wow, liver failure."

"Not everyone experienced that."

According to my lawyer, I'm not responsible. "But what of Dorian's involvement?" I asked him.

He explained that the responsibility lies directly with Hayden Spitz, who oversaw the lab reports, which were scant in detail at best.

I quickly change the subject and ask about Sophia's children instead. That always makes for a happier topic, and right now I welcome anything away from the drama of Dorian's murder.

Two hours later, the last of the guests finally leaves.

I stretch my legs out on the sofa and gaze at the empty wall where I'd always wanted to hang lots of paintings. Dorian's aversion to clutter put a stop to that.

My mother enters the room, joins me on the couch, and takes my hand. "Are you okay, sweetheart?"

I shake my head, and tears erupt again. I didn't even have to dredge up tragic memories of my beloved childhood retriever, Joey, dying, as I'd planned for the service, thinking my eyes would remain dry. It's like once I started crying, I couldn't stop. Four years' worth of tears.

She hugs me. "Don't worry, darling. We're here for you."

"I want to come home, Mom."

"We want you home, darling." She smiles sadly. "What about the baby?"

"If Ana doesn't resurface, I'll arrange an adoption." I pause for a response. "Do you think that's the wrong thing to do?"

She shakes her head. "No, darling. He's a beautiful boy, but I understand."

I study her. "Would you keep him if you were in my position?"

"If I was in a stable relationship with a loving man, I would."

As though on cue, my phone lights up. I see that it's Jarrad, and my chest warms for the first time all day.

THIRTY-FIVE

A WEEK HAS PASSED since the funeral. My mother returned home, and now I'm sitting in a restaurant with Jarrad. Even just hearing him order a steak without questioning everything on the menu brings me joy.

I've never felt so light. Bad of me, I know. Dorian's funeral was only last week, and here I am, smiling like I've just won the lottery.

Jarrad's green shirt complements his soft hazel eyes, which smile back with a reassuring glow. He kept me sane during this whole period. His steady presence flushed me with hope.

We're in East LA, and the media are nowhere to be seen. It's not exactly my choice location, but I love the relaxed atmosphere. Sure, we passed a few alleyway drug deals and streetwalkers doing their thing, but instead of being judgmental, I'm embracing life in all its many shades.

It helps that I'm a multimillionaire, which isn't to say I'm turning my back on those in need. I have plans.

A man with a camera enters, and I flinch.

Jarrad leans in. "He's not here for you."

I'm so relieved when I see the man pick up a menu.

"They probably weren't banking on me heading to East LA. The disguise must have worked." I chuckle.

I'd borrowed Amanda's jacket and have even taken to wearing a baseball cap. If it weren't so depressing having the media stalking me twenty-four-seven, I'd laugh. I was never that interesting.

I'm over LA. But how can I leave Jarrad? What are his plans?

"I didn't realize you live so far from Brentwood," I say, cutting into my sizzling steak.

He swallows his food and then dabs his mouth. "It's all I could afford when I first moved here. I like it, though. The food's not as pricey as in the more affluent suburbs."

I study him for a moment. "Are you needing a raise?"

He shakes his head. "No. But thanks. You're paying me over and above the normal rate, which has helped a lot."

"Are you saving for something special?" I ask.

"No. Just surviving."

"That sounds like you're doing without," I say, knowing full well that any handout from me would be knocked back. Jarrad strikes me as a man who likes to find his own way through life.

"I'm not. I just send money back to New York."

"For your mother, I take it?" I say carefully. We haven't spoken a lot about his life before arriving here.

"Katy, my sister, has just found a new home for Mom, and between us, we're managing. That's why I chose to live in an apartment that could use a renovation." He sniffs. "As long as there's hot water and electricity, I'm good. I don't need to live in a big house to be happy."

"Like mine, you mean?" I tilt my head.

He shrugs. "I'm not judging. And if it weren't for big properties, I'd be out of work." Jarrad touches my hand, and a spark flies up my arm. "I'm glad you accepted my invitation, by the way. I can't imagine what you've been through."

Our eyes lock. I think I read desire in his gaze, but I also see questions and a little bit of something I can't quite put my finger on.

When he called and suggested dinner, I smiled for the first time in days. This was while my mother was in the room. I'm sure she noticed my mood flipping from 'What do I do with my life now?' to something much rosier, like 'Oh what the heck, let's just live each day as it comes.'

In the past, that 'live for the moment' concept would have had me wringing my hands or visiting an advisor on how to make the most of my life. Crazy, I know, when the answer lies in one's heart. It's just a matter of listening and having the courage to trust.

"Do you think us dating..." I pause. *Is that what this is?* "I mean..."

"For me, this is a date." He smiles almost shyly.

His answer gives me a sense of reassurance, like I'm on solid ground.

Maybe I'm allowing attraction to lead the way.

But doesn't love start with attraction?

I notice women checking Jarrad out, like they did that night at the club. The night my life went from beige to technicolor, following a kiss that still makes my knees weak. I think about his soft, warm lips on mine and how they went into ravaging mode within a heartbeat.

As we eat in companionable silence, my appetite's returned, thanks to not having to look over my shoulder.

"I suppose the media are still at your house?"

I nod. "Not sure why. I mean they've already ripped me apart."

"I read the article," he says.

The article exposed it all, including the fact that Ana had given birth to Xavier and that Dorian had purchased her apartment.

"It was humiliating, to say the least. Grubby journalism." I sigh.

Talk about stripping my life naked.

The life I worked so hard to conceal.

I'm sure that article has fed my neighbors' insatiable appetite for gossip. My ears are burning just thinking about it.

"So what now?" Jarrad asks.

"I'll just take every day as it comes, I suppose."

He nods solemnly.

"I have the luxury of not needing to work. So at least I'm not stuck with one of those career curveballs."

"You don't have any career goals, then?" he asks.

I shake my head. "I do like to keep busy, and I love to bake. Who knows, maybe I'll set up a cupcake shop. I know it's not very original, but people will always want coffee and cupcakes."

"Oh yeah," he says. "And yours are spectacular."

I giggle. He makes it sound so sexual.

I'm now a woman of means, and just thinking about it brings a warm, summery breeze my way. Before meeting with Jarrad, I had a meeting with my attorney, who told me that five hundred million dollars would be transferred into my account. On top of that, there's another three hundred million stashed away in an offshore account, and gold bullion worth a hundred million or so in Geneva.

I can't even begin to wrap my mind around it. The sheer scale of that kind of money is beyond anything I could imagine, and I don't even know where to start with it all.

"You're close to a billion," the attorney added. He almost looked apologetic. "There was some reparation, you understand."

"You mean money to the families of the victims?" I was relieved to hear that. All those poor families.

"I'm told that Spitz will be shouldering the lawsuit," the attorney added.

"How much did the partners of the deceased get from Dorian's end?" I asked.

"There were eight in all. Twenty million each."

"Good," I said.

"Then I'll get you to sign these documents for the transfer if all is in order."

I clasped my hands tightly and nodded solemnly, maintaining the whole grieving widow act. I wanted to hug the lawyer, but that would have looked bad, and the last thing I needed was for him to think I orchestrated this.

The best part, however, was handing him a file of my parents' debts, including hospital bills and credit card bills.

"Also set up an account with fifty million dollars in their name," I instructed.

"Of course. I'll get on that right away."

I can finally breathe easy, knowing my parents can now return to living a comfortable, worry-free life, with more than enough money to travel.

If Ana ever surfaces, which I hope she does for Xavier's sake, she'll receive a healthy check. No one will ever know, because that's too weird: a widow giving her dead husband's mistress money? Nah, I'll keep that to myself.

I also instructed the attorney to set up a trust for Xavier. It'll pay for his education, a lifetime of health insurance, and enough to buy his first home. That should see him through.

"You wish to remain anonymous concerning the boy's trust?" the attorney asked, studying me closely. He must have read that shoddy article about Dorian's infidelity.

"Yes," I replied.

I just wanted all this to end, right then and there.

Time heals everything, and though I didn't kill Dorian, maybe my actions played a role. After all, Hector had murderer written all over his angry face that day I saw Ana with him at the supermarket.

The only other thing I had to do was to sign up for the best adoption agency, even though I'd grown a little fond of the boy.

So now here I am, staring into the eyes of the man who can make my dreams come true.

Jarrad insists on paying for dinner, and not wanting to embarrass him, I let him. He's proud, and I respect that.

We stand on the sidewalk, dodging revelers. It's a warm Saturday night, the air calm and soothing, with the full moon quietly shining above.

"Where would you like to go?" he asks, tilting his handsome head.

"It's such a lovely night, why don't we go to the beach?" I suggest. "We can pick up a bottle of champagne."

"What are we celebrating?"

I remove my mask, proverbially speaking. "Freedom."

"Now *that* sounds like a good reason to celebrate." He chuckles, and we head off into the night. Thankfully, there are no pesky media to be found anywhere.

I don't care either way. The dirty laundry has been aired. There's nothing more they can say about me. I hope.

THIRTY-SIX

Ana

The day of Dorian's MURDER

I rock my darling baby in my arms. That party upset me; I'm glad I had the day off. Thinking of Javier being passed around like some cute toy made me cry my eyes out. I couldn't wait to get back to him.

I've never wanted anything more in my life than my son.

What is it with me and abusive men? Dorian's racist views hurt more than Hector's fists.

I see confusion and even disgust in Dorian's eyes, even though he can't take his hands off me. I'm sure if Javi didn't look like him and was darker like my dad's side of the family, we'd be out on the street. Or even worse: me having to bullshit about Javi being Hector's.

I'll never go near that abusive ex again, even if it means living in a shitbox.

At least the apartment belongs to me and my son.

The only positive from this adoption freak show is that Javi will be rich, unless Linley's IVF works.

I can't believe Dorian's staying with her. Something about her making him look good. What crap. You'd have to be blind not to see that they don't like each other.

We still fuck, and yes, I know I'm weak. He even watches me take my birth control to make sure I'm taking it. One baby's enough. For now. Even if I've lost custody of my son.

That's why I accepted the nanny role—if only to be around my boy as much as possible.

Linley goes out a lot, and I'm sure she knows about us still doing it.

How fucking weird is that?

My soul's polluted.

But everything's for Javier.

Now I understand a mother's sacrifice. My mother sacrificed her life by staying with my lazy father. I think back to her slaving away at three jobs. She cleaned people's houses using all kinds of chemicals that I'm sure gave her the cancer that killed her.

When I look back on that dark period, I can't help but ask myself why the hell I made this major sacrifice for my father. Then again, I'm not much better because I'm allowing Dorian to use me.

I'm still attracted to him, which is nuts, I know.

Maybe it's because I'm seriously lonely. Hector isolated me from the outside world. He hated me making friends at work—the same jobs I slaved away at for him.

They say we all make our own choices.

I didn't choose my dad. It all started with him and ends with him. He's responsible for the hell that's been my life from the moment my beautiful mother died, and now I'm losing custody of my son.

Are there any good men in the world?

I have a bad father, a monster for an ex, and now the father of my child, who didn't shed a tear or even look sad when his company's supplements killed those poor people.

I sink into a chair and start bouncing Javi on my leg. He's such a good baby. Hardly ever cries, and his eyes light up whenever he sees me.

After a whole day and night of missing him, I held him so tight I cried as I felt his little heartbeat against my chest.

Linley left as soon as I arrived. Her loudmouth mother-in-law suspects that Javi is Dorian's son. I don't care. I'm not getting involved in that shitshow, not when I've got my own crap to deal with.

They left for the airport, and Dorian locked himself away, dealing with some drama about more people getting sick from those supplements.

I mean, I took some and felt okay. I've stopped, though. So has he; I've noticed.

Funny, it's like I'm acting like his wife. He prefers my meals and always gets me to make his juice, and I'm the one who gets all his supplements together in the morning.

I should hate him, but I want him as much as he desires me. And I know how to please him. But he keeps reminding me that I'll never be the next Mrs. Gunn.

That sucks. But I'm stuck here.

I could run away with Javi, but then the money would stop coming, and I'd be chased by the police since I signed the adoption papers. I also hate the idea of being poor again.

Whoever said money doesn't buy happiness was rich.

I've enrolled in an online stock market course. It's so that I can become rich in my own right and give my boy everything, even if all I'll ever be is his nanny. That thought makes me sick to my stomach. Who knows, maybe Linley will leave soon.

I don't want my boy to ever go through what I went through, and I plan to keep him safe. I won't let him near my dad, who drags those close around him into his shit.

Speaking of the devil, his name comes up on my phone.

I take the call. "What's up?" I ditched the nice daughter act as soon as I lost custody of my son.

"Just ringing my princess to say hello and thank you."

"Yeah, well, it came with a big sacrifice, I hope you realize."

"You haven't had to sell yourself?" he asks. He doesn't even attempt to sound worried.

"One doesn't get that kind of cash without doing something they don't want. And why would you care?"

"Please don't talk like that. I'm still your father."

"What do you need now?" I ask.

"Just wanted to call and say that I'm moving to the States."

"I thought you said Miami was out of bounds," I say, hoping he doesn't want to stay with me. My father's a collector of scumbags.

"I'm heading to California. Your way."

"You can't stay here. I'm making a clean life for myself."

Ha. Who am I kidding?

"I know that. But you managed to get yourself a nice chunk of money. How?" he asks.

There it is. He's after something again, just like I thought. Is there such a thing as a man loving unconditionally?

I'm about to tell him to go fuck himself when I hear yelling in the background.

"I've got to go. And don't ever call me again. You've ruined my fucking life."

Tears burn in my eyes. He's the last person I have who at least speaks nicely to me, even if it's to get something.

Instead of falling into that rabbit hole of self-pity, I run into the living room to see what all the yelling's about.

I stop when I see Hector jabbing his finger into Dorian's face.

"You've been fucking my woman," Hector yells. "You piece of scum."

Clinging onto the wall, trying to make myself invisible, I can feel my heart throbbing in my ears.

If Hector sees me, he'll drag me away.

I'm about to run to get my phone when I hear things crashing.

Why are we the only ones here? Where's Jarrad? He was working in the garden earlier.

I pray he sees and stops the fight.

Sneaking a peek, I watch in horror as Dorian stumbles against a cabinet, sending pictures and vases smashing onto the floor.

He's on the ground, clutching his stomach. His nose is bleeding.

Unable to just stand by and watch him being killed, I yell, "Stop!"

Hector's face goes red. I've seen that same dangerous look in his eyes before he killed someone. That someone had tried to rape me, and Hector became my hero. Only with time, he turned into a monster and is now about to murder again if I don't do something.

It all happens so quickly. A sickening crunch sounds at my feet, and as I look down, blood's pouring from Dorian's skull.

Hector's eyes are wild as he stares down at Dorian. I read fear in his face. Prison is the last thing he wants. He's been locked up before.

Running to Dorian, I bend down. He's out cold.

There's air coming from his nose.

Dorian's still alive.

Scrambling to my feet, I go to run to my phone when Hector grabs me by the waist and drags me off.

Struggling in his arms, I scream, and then Javier starts crying in the background.

My head's spinning. "Please let me call 911. He's still breathing. I can't leave my son. Please let me get him."

Dragging me along, Hector covers my mouth with his hand. "I'm not taking someone else's bastard son. You did this, bitch."

Just my luck, no one's around for a change. Those nosy neighbors are always coming by at the worst times, but not now when I need help.

He throws me into the car and begins to drive off.

I'm crying and yelling for him to stop.

"Shut the fuck up, bitch," he yells.

"Please, I beg you. Let me get my son."

"And what, me bring up that hijo de puta's child? No fucking way. We're getting out. We'll go somewhere they can't find us."

"But my son," I cry.

He turns to me, all crazy-eyed. "How long have you been fucking that rich loser?"

Tears pour down my face. My heart has turned to ice.

At least Dorian is still breathing.

I want him to live so he can protect my boy. Dorian's many things, but I've seen how much he loves his son.

Oh, please God, don't let him die.

"You're nothing but a fucking puta. Look at what you've made me do."

THIRTY-SEVEN

Linley

Two months after the FUNERAL

For once in my adult life, I am breathing in my own skin. It's like the person trapped within has finally stepped out of the shadows and is free to be her best self. It's been a rough ride for sure, but meeting Jarrad was worth it, and he's given me the sweetest time of my life.

The agency found a loving family for Xavier, promising to send an occasional report. After everything that's happened, I need to know the boy's doing well.

Saddened by Ana's disappearance, I can only hope she's still alive.

"But she was cheating with your husband," Jarrad said after I expressed some guilt over the maid.

I nod, the weight of everything sinking in. But in the midst of it all, Jarrad and I are very much in love.

On our first date, we made love. It was like all the pent-up desire burst out of our skin. Under a palm tree, we consummated something so deep and spiritually moving—not to mention, my first-ever orgasm while penetrated. The possibility of being arrested for public indecency never entered my thoughts.

Now I'm packing boxes.

Jarrad holds up some famous basketball player's jersey in a frame. "What about this?"

I point at the toss-out pile. I always hated those ugly frames.

"Are you nuts? A Kobe Bryant jersey? It would be worth thousands." He holds up a container of balls. "And these are from the Red Sox."

I shrug. "Then they're yours. Just put them somewhere I can't see them."

"I'm not into them as a keepsake. I'll sell them. Give the money to my mother's nursing home."

I hold him close and kiss him. "You're a good person."

"I'm doing my best."

"Oh, you're doing well. I'd be happy to write a nice big check."

"She's comfortable. If the home needs anything, I'll see to it."

Jarrad doesn't like gifts, I've discovered.

"I hope I wasn't being too bossy earlier about the frame."

He takes me into his arms. "You can boss me around all you like. I've always had a soft spot for feisty women."

"Then I'd better start harnessing my inner warrior woman. Or read Mary Wollstonecraft again."

"Who's that?" he asks.

"She's one of the first published advocates for women's rights. Her daughter, Mary Shelley, wrote Frankenstein."

He nods slowly. "I've got a lot to learn. And hey, on that note, don't ever change. I like you just as you are."

I toss Dorian's gym gear into the donation pile, smiling like the happiest woman alive, when a knock comes at the door. "I wonder who that is. I hope it's not Detective Hull again. He's such a snoop."

"That's what detectives do," he says.

We've only just discovered that Hector was responsible for Dorian's death. His DNA matched a criminal database in Mexico. They can't find him, however, and have stepped up their search in Mexico.

I told the police all I knew about Hector's relationship with our former maid and how I was concerned for her welfare. They seemed to find that strange, judging by the incredulous expression on the detective's face.

"She was a good person," I'd explained.

"Even though she was messing around with your husband?" Detective Hull asked, tactless as usual.

"It takes two to cheat, and while I was angry about that, I still feel sorry for her. She often came to work with bruises, you know," I told him.

"Why didn't she report him?" he asked.

I shrugged. "The same reason other battered women don't report abusive partners. I take it you've never been around domestic violence in your personal life?"

His swift shift away from that subject left me questioning his attitude about this ugly issue.

Convinced I was responsible for my husband's murder, the detective almost looked disappointed that Hector was now the prime suspect. Hull kept going on and on about my parents' financial predicament and how the prenup wasn't looking favorable, considering four years was up and I was still without a child. He then pointed at the infidelity clause, asking all kinds of tricky questions, like why hadn't I sued my husband once I'd discovered the affair?

I went on to explain how I still loved my husband and wanted to give him a second chance.

Yes, I know that's bullshit, but I wasn't about to tell him how I'd lost my nerve to do just that after Dorian threatened to lawyer up and have the whole cheating thing tossed out as a false allegation and then leave me to pay the legal fees.

The knock sounds urgent as Jarrad follows me down the stairs.

When I open the door, Dorian's mom comes blustering in.

Pecking me on the cheek, she reeks of liquor.

"I wasn't expecting you," I say.

She looks around at the boxes. "No. I can't imagine why." Her mouth twists into a wry smirk.

Like Dorian, Jenny always thinks the worst of people, as if we're all driven by selfish motives and will do whatever it takes to get what we want. That was my late husband's modus operandi. Not mine. That is, until my marriage soured.

Jenny heads straight for the liquor cabinet and fills a crystal glass with bourbon before flopping down on the sofa. "I thought it best to swing by and chat since you're not answering my calls."

"I've been busy."

She signals for me to sit, but I remain standing.

"I like LA, and I want to buy something here. That's why I'm here," she says.

"Hold on a minute," I say. I look around and notice Jarrad is nowhere to be found. Maybe because it's too soon for my former mother-in-law to see a man in my life. That makes sense. "I'll be right back."

I go off to grab a bottle of water and find Jarrad outside. "Why are you hiding?" I ask.

"I'm not in the mood to see your mother-in-law right now."

"How did you know she was Dorian's mom?"

He seems uneasy. Then, before I can figure out what's happening, Jenny comes running out, almost stumbling and pointing her finger at him.

"I know you," she says.

My eyebrows raise. What?

"You came to my apartment years ago."

"I've never seen you in my life," Jarrad says and turns away.

"It's you, all right. You came looking for Dorian. You weren't too happy either."

My jaw drops. Jarrad knew Dorian back then?

They're both from Queens. That's something I recall from our early conversation, and the coincidence did stick in my memory.

But this?

"That wasn't me. You're mistaken." He walks off.

Jenny watches him head back inside. "It's him. He just doesn't want to admit it." She turns to me. "And what's he doing here now? In my son's home, with my son's widow?"

Her mouth turns up at one end as she points in my face. "You both planned it, didn't you?"

I roll my eyes and lead her back inside. That shrill voice of hers travels, and the neighbors have had their fill of drama at my expense.

THIRTY-EIGHT

Jarrad

FIFTEEN YEARS EARLIER

MY DAD walks in, looking exhausted as he lifts his calloused hand to greet me. I hope that won't be me when I hit his age. But if I keep going down this path, that will be me, working my fingers to the bone just to pay rent for some dump.

Our apartment in Queens isn't exactly a dump. My dad's a DIY man, an all-around handyman. He's whipped up some shelves, painted, and wallpapered, so the place feels pretty cozy. My mother contributed too. With her old sewing machine handed down from Grandma, she made the curtains and even matching duvet covers, which are a little too 1980s according to my sister. I can see her point, but it beats living like some of the guys I know. It helps that there's a lot of love here too.

That's something I took for granted until I started knocking around with a bunch of dudes from broken families. I've learned that people are mirrors. They reflect what life looks like when something's missing.

The only thing missing from my life is money and direction.

I'm not so interested in a girlfriend right now. Not like some of my buddies who spend way too much time talking about girls they'd like to... well, you know. I respect women too much to rave about some random girl's body like she's an object. I'd knock someone's teeth out if they talked about Katy, my sister, like that.

I've had my share of women. Not trying to flex or anything, but women seem to want to be around me. The thing is, I've never fallen for any one girl. I'm not in a place to offer much anyhow, so it's just easier this way.

In any case, you can't box me in. I figured that much after one too many drunken fights landed me in prison. Now I'm bouncing at clubs while I save for a horticulture course I have my sights set on.

I'm all about plants. Always have been. I have some growing on the roof, plus a little veggie garden in this wooden box my dad threw together. There's nothing like having my hands in the dirt, watching seeds grow, and besides, the thought of sitting at some desk staring at a screen all day freaks me out.

Dad sets down his work bag and goes to the fridge, grabs a can of beer, and sits down. That's his nightly ritual. Just a nod as a greeting and then he sits quietly at the table. We give him the space he needs to unwind after a long day working as a car detailer—a job he's had since dropping out of school at fifteen.

I don't have much to brag about. I dropped out at sixteen. After that, I messed around with the wrong people, and my life read like that of a loser. Dad didn't sit me down for some big talk. He just looked at me and was like, "Boys will be boys, but don't throw it all away, son." That was it. I didn't need much of a dressing down anyway. That short stint in jail knocked some sense into me. That was never going to be me again.

That's why I'm a disappointment to him; working late-night shifts as a bouncer. He wants more for me. I get that. And I even love him more for caring, but some days I'm not in the mood to talk about my plans.

Standing at the kitchen window, I stare down into the alleyway and its crumbling graffitied walls. Nothing artistic, just tags and angry marks. As a teenager, it was where I had my first kiss. It was where I smoked my first joint and had my first beer. It was also where I learned to fight.

Right now, though, it's just innocent fun. Kids kicking a scuffed ball between puddles and broken bottles. That was me too, once.

What will they become? Will they also be sent to jail at nineteen? It can break you. It didn't break me, though. If anything, prison woke me up with one big slap in the face. However, it helped knowing how to fight. That's one skill I'm grateful for. Learned it the hard way. Got the scars to prove it. But I might not be here telling this story had I not learned how to fight with the big boys.

My mother cleans three days a week, and my sister, Katy, who's four years younger than me, has just started working as a nurse. She's the success story in this family. Not that I'm resentful. She's an inspiration and the reason why I'm working long hours to see myself through this horticultural course, so I can set up a business as a landscaper.

Having that plan has meant the world to me. It kind of freed me up because before that, I tended to run away from the difficult questions. As the prison counselor said, "Often the answer is staring us in the face."

He was right about that. It all comes down to discipline, focus, hard work, and yes, money.

I stare down at my watch; it's my night off, and a few of my buddies want to catch up for a drink. I'm not much in the mood for it, though, but Jack needs me. He's having a hard time at home with his new wife, and he's looking for some of that quality beer counseling: a skill I picked up in prison—listening to a bunch of hard-luck stories. I'm told I'm a good listener.

I go to the fridge, grab a beer, and join my dad at the table.

His eyes go straight down to my bruised knuckles, and a frown appears. He points at my hand. "What happened?"

"Got a bit rough last night at the club." I take a swig of beer.

It's always the same story: a bunch of douchebags in suits out on a big night thinking their gym workouts can see them through a couple of beefy bouncers.

I'm one of those beefy bouncers, and the clowns ended up second-best.

"Do they pay more if you fight?" he asks.

I sniff at that ridiculous idea. "I'm hired as security, Dad. That's what happens. When a bunch of dicks turn up coked out of their heads, thinking they've got the strength of the Rock, and start pushing us around, we do what we must."

"Have you at least put some ice on those knuckles?" he asks, looking worried.

"I'll live. Had worse." I give him a tight smile as I think about the shiners and broken ribs and all the rest of the injuries I've suffered.

One of the pitfalls of growing up in the rough end of Queens.

"At least you've got a night off." He sighs. "Which gives your mother a night off from looking at the clock. Poor woman doesn't sleep well when you're out all night. Wakes me up too."

"Just working, Dad. I'm not drinking like I used to."

"I've got something to tell you," he says, turning his can around in his swollen fingers. He complains of arthritis, and some days he can barely hold a hammer, doing what he loves—making things. It breaks my heart that I can't bring in the kind of cash to support my dad so he can retire.

"I signed up for this today." He lays down a shiny brochure that says, 'Invest in the latest venture development and watch your money grow.'

My mother has just stepped through the door and leans down to kiss my dad and then me.

She's always done that. And while it kind of embarrasses me in front of my pals, I have to admit I like it.

They're still very much in love too, which is nice and rare from what I've seen and heard. Dad's never raised his voice at her once. We wouldn't have allowed it anyway.

"Take a seat for a minute, love," he says.

She smiles at me until her eyes land on my knuckles, and she turns serious. "What happened?"

I lift my palm. "I'm fine. Don't worry. I've got the night off. I'll be good as gold by the morning."

She returns a worried smile.

"So, what does this mean?" I ask, returning to the subject of the brochure.

"Just that I've mortgaged our home and bought into a new development. When it's complete, we'll own a new apartment, and there'll be some left over so that you can do that degree you've been talking about."

My mom, wearing a hopeful smile, doesn't look as concerned as I'm suddenly feeling.

"Have you had this looked over?" I ask.

"Barry and Mike from the garage next door are in. They had a lawyer friend check it out. We all went to the seminar run by this guy." He points to the back of the shiny brochure with some dude named Brendan Crib smiling back with gleaming white teeth.

"So does that mean the bank owns our home?" I ask.

He nods slowly. I can see hope, uncertainty, and possibilities in his faded eyes.

My mom adds, "I'm sure it will be a good thing."

Her eyes are telling me something else, though, as is my heart.

THIRTY-NINE

Jarrad

Present Day

There was no way I could move on in my life while that bastard smirked his way through it. But when I met Linley, I knew I had to change direction. The winds had brought me here, and then a storm hit in the form of desire. Desire like I'd never experienced before.

The first time Linley offered me coffee and cake, I was drawn to her. The soft, warm glow in her green eyes meeting mine so comfortably made it feel as though I'd known her forever.

Like I'd arrived home.

But I had to stay the course. I'd worked too hard to blow my original plan. A plan that, in the end, was simpler to execute than I could have imagined.

When Ana's ex arrived that day, drugged out of his head and hate written all over his sweaty face, I put two and two together. And instead of asking him who he was and why he was jumping over the fence, I turned a blind eye.

Dorian Gunn is dead. And though my original plan was to destroy him before he hurt more people, I never planned to murder him. I didn't have a plan. Well, okay, maybe seduce his wife or something to get back at him.

But then I met Linley, and though seducing her would be more of a pleasure than a chore, I couldn't use her like that.

Dorian Gunn killed my father. Not directly, but through that asshole Crib.

My blood boiled when I saw the article describing Dorian Gunn as one of Queens' rising stars. I nearly threw the magazine against the wall, but I was in a hospital waiting room and had to control myself.

I'd been wanting to leave New York, and now I had a reason.

I never thought I'd fall for his wife.

That wasn't meant to happen.

Then that kiss changed everything.

With that kind heart of hers, Linley's a rare creature in this selfish world. And I could never understand why she was so nice to Ana when it was as plain as day that her ass-wipe husband was screwing her.

And now here I am, facing his mother.

She's not making it up. I visited Dorian's former home. Fists clenched, I was ready to rearrange those chiseled features of his. He wasn't there, she'd slurred. She was as tanked up then as she is now, but somehow she still remembers me.

Linley is back after driving Jenny somewhere. Hopefully to an airport.

"Where did you take her?" I pass her a cup of coffee.

She looks pale, and I'm feeling like a first-rate prick. I've got a lot of explaining to do. That's obvious.

"I booked her into a five-star hotel on Sunset Boulevard and gave her a wad of cash." She falls onto the sofa in the living room and kicks off her shoes. "Just when I was starting to feel good." Linley stares me in the eyes. "You knew Dorian?"

I nod slowly.

"And you were going to tell me when?"

I take a deep breath. "It's a long story. Do you want to hear about it now? You look drained."

"I am drained. But if I want to get a good night's sleep, I've got to know that the man I'm sleeping with is not some conman."

Her sharp response bites. It's the first time I've seen Linley look at me with cold eyes. I'd prefer a slap in the face to losing that warm smile. I can't blame her for being suspicious, though. If the roles were reversed, I'd be demanding answers too.

I join her on the sofa. "As you already know, I grew up in Queens in a small rundown apartment. The same place I was born in. My father came home one day and told us he'd invested our home in some get-rich-quick scheme."

Linley rolls her eyes. "Let me guess, Brendan Crib?"

I run my hands over my prickly scalp and nod. "I asked if I could read the fine print, but he'd already signed our apartment away. A year or so later, he lost everything. I blamed myself in some ways."

"Why?" She opens her hands.

I shrug. "If I'd done better with my life, Dad wouldn't have had to keep working. He'd still be alive." My voice cracks. It's the first time I've ever admitted that.

"But how could you have known about the scheme until he'd already signed up? And what could you have done?"

A knot forms in my stomach. Talking about that troubling experience is bringing it all back—my mother crying, my sister working two jobs to pay off the mortgage, my dad beating himself up, and then us finding him dead in bed after overdosing on sleeping tablets.

My mother was never the same again. That broke my heart, triggering a tsunami of hate for Wall Street cowboys like Dorian Gunn.

"I didn't like myself much. Here I was, a twenty-seven-year-old, just barely scraping by and still living at home."

"Many do it, especially in New York. Rent prices are insane," Linley says, looking more sympathetic, much to my relief.

"School wasn't my thing either," I continue. "Once I'd learned to read and write, I was out of there. Computers and business studies were never my bag. I was more of an outdoors person. I fell in with a bunch of bad dudes, and every night was a party. I couldn't see beyond midnight, let alone my future."

I chug some water. My throat is dry. This is a difficult discussion, bringing up all kinds of demons. I'm drowning in regret. But without all that, I would never have met this red-headed beauty with the kindest and sweetest heart.

"I believe wherever there's love, there's a good home," I say. "And that was true for us. I just should have done better." I exhale. "As you know, my dad took his life, and my mother had a nervous breakdown and never recovered. I had to leave New York, if only for sanity's sake. And to make enough money to see my mother through. I moved close to the beach in a rundown bungalow and worked two jobs: security at a five-star hotel by day and bouncing at a club by night. I managed to get my horticulture degree and set up a gardening business."

I pause for a moment. "My gardening business took off, and then one day, I saw an article about Dorian's wellness business. It brought back the time I confronted Crib on Wall Street when I took him by the scruff of the neck and was about to punch him in the face when Dorian arrived with a pair of burly security guards and had me tossed out on the street like I was trash. I yelled something about my dad's suicide after he lost everything, and Dorian said, 'Shit happens, buddy. Now fuck off.' If there'd been a brick, I would have thrown it through the glass walls."

Linley shakes her head, looking horrified.

"Anyway," I continue, "Crib got what was coming to him and is rotting in jail. I read about his trial and discovered that Gunn got off scot-free. That made my blood boil. There's no doubt he was in on that Ponzi scheme. And that heartless snigger of his has haunted me since." My throat is so dry I guzzle some more water.

"Once I'd gotten my gardening license, I did a letterbox drop advertising my services down your street in the hope of scoring a gig here. It worked. I wasn't sure what I planned to do, but I was going to make sure it involved wiping that smirk off his face."

"He didn't recognize you, though," Linley says.

"No. I kept out of his way on purpose."

"On purpose?" Linley's frown intensifies. "What were you planning?"

I sigh. "Not sure." I sit next to her on the sofa and take her hand. "I met you, and that changed things for me. Out of respect for you, I didn't want to cause a stir. But then, I discovered he was with the maid, and I warned you, but you seemed to be having your own issues."

"So, was your being nice to me part of the plan?"

I shake my head repeatedly. "No way. As soon as we spoke, I just fell in love." My mouth curls up slowly.

"Really?" Her frown melts into the makings of a smile.

I stroke her soft cheek and stare into her pretty eyes, which have softened, much to my relief. "It's the truth, Linley. It was love at first sight."

"Or is that bite?" she asks. "Since you couldn't stop eating my cupcakes."

Welcoming the break, I smile. "The cupcakes were and still are spectacular, but no, I'm a little deeper than that."

She squeezes my hand. "I know you are."

We stare into each other's eyes, and for the first time since discussing my past, the tension starts to ease.

FORTY

Linley

WHILE I'M STILL PROCESSING Jarrad knowing Dorian before and his questionable motivations for working here, I can't help but forgive him. He's always been here for me. Without him, I think I would have lost my mind.

Unless he's one of the world's best actors, I believe that he feels the same about me.

After seeing how Brendan Crib spun his charm and robbed my parents, I can understand Jarrad's need for retribution, even if I'm a little unnerved by it too.

"You should have told me," I say after hearing about his shocking encounter with my late husband.

Dorian had sworn he had nothing to do with Crib's business. I witnessed the shredding machines the day I surprised him at work. Looking stressed, he almost pushed me out of the building. I should have run then and there.

Only I would never have met Jarrad.

Jarrad stares down at his hands. "I should have told you. But I couldn't risk you sending me away. That would have been the sensible response on your part."

My shoulders slump as I exhale deeply. "Maybe. But you've also been my rock this past year."

Life is far from black and white. That much I have learned. Especially when destiny pushes good people to make morally gray choices.

"Did Ana know that you were aware of her involvement with Dorian?"

I shake my head slowly. "All I ever wanted was to start a family and have a nice home. Dorian offered me that. The catch was that it came with a marital agreement that was more like a business contract. And then when my parents lost everything, and with me being unable to conceive, I got a little desperate. An infidelity clause in the prenup offered me half of Dorian's fortune, and not just the two million dollars from not bearing a child."

"Two million dollars is still a fair sum," he says.

"It would have been more than enough for me. But my parents were virtually on the streets, and they had huge medical bills."

He nods reflectively. "That makes sense. Two million doesn't go far when there's illness and a house involved."

"Knowing Dorian and his predilection for girls like Ana, I just had to catch him red-handed, so I employed the prettiest maid."

His brow creases, and my shoulders tense. This confession is making me look bad, I know.

"I told you I saw them getting too close. You could have taken that as proof."

"I didn't expect her to get pregnant and for the adoption to be sprung on me."

"But you could have walked away. Her getting pregnant was proof enough of Dorian's infidelity."

"I know." I stare down at my hands. "I figured if I stayed on for two years and then asked for a divorce, it would have been a clear-cut split, and my parents' bills would have been paid. It seemed like the easiest, least stressful option." I sigh. "Dorian also threatened to bring in a team of lawyers that could circumvent even the toughest of prenups. I just didn't want to risk it. Looking for an easier way, I figured if I stuck out this marriage for two more years, taking care of our new adopted child, I'd have a better shot at a fair settlement." My lips press into a thin line. "Pathetic, maybe. Some would even say it's spineless when it comes to this marriage and how I've handled things."

I tell him about finding Dorian in front of his screen one night on a sex chat site.

Jarrad looks appalled. "That's terrible. Did you talk about it?"

I nod. "He blamed me. He said I was like ice in bed."

He shakes his head slowly. "You're pure fire. Hot."

Standing close to him now, I smile. "You say the sweetest things."

"That's because I'm madly in love with you." He takes me into his arms, holds me tight, and seals that heartfelt admission with a passionate kiss.

I pull away, and as I search for truth, I read something deep and meaningful in his gaze. He's not uttering hollow words to stroke my need for love. If anything, his eyes reflect a silent honesty, touching a part of my soul I'd locked away the day I married Dorian. Jarrad has found the key I'd thought long buried, and slowly the superficial layers I've hidden behind are stripping away, revealing someone I now barely recognize but deeply miss—the free-spirited girl who once ran wild through nature, her heart open to the goodness in all.

"Were you ever in love with Dorian?" he asks.

I take a moment to answer. "At first, I thought I did, but that died quickly the moment I got to know him."

He puffs out his cheek and exhales slowly. "I think we've talked enough for now. I don't know about you, but I'm starving." He cocks his handsome head and smiles sweetly. Suddenly all that matters is just this moment. "How about Mexican?"

A large sunny smile grows on my face. One thing's clear: we're in love, and my heart is full.

I just have to quiet my mind, because I'm not exactly guilt-free.

FORTY-ONE

NATALIE ARRIVES FIRST FOR a change. She's looking sharp and no longer wearing her baggy gear.

"Hey, you," I say. "You're looking different."

She smiles. "These are my work clothes. I've just started working as an assistant to a scriptwriter."

"So no more ghostwriting?" I ask.

"Not if I can help it." She sits in an armchair by the window. "The next thing I write will have my name on it."

"And your brother? How is he?"

She shrugs. "He's better since rehab. He's started an organic community garden and is pretty invested in it. He just has to stay away from a bad bunch of dudes he's known since high school."

The doorbell rings, and I go to answer it.

Olivia is standing there. "I've missed you," she says, hugging me. "So you're moving, Emily tells me," Olivia says, following me into the living room and taking a seat.

"I am." I remove the travel magazines from the sofa and sit down.

"Do you know where you're going?"

"Not sure. Maybe a road trip."

"Oh, that would be amazing," Natalie says.

"What's amazing?" asks Claire as she arrives with Emily close behind. "Sorry, we let ourselves in. You left the door open."

"It's all good." I smile.

As they sit together on the leather sofa, Isabella and Sophia arrive, and with everyone now present, I close the front door.

The women peck each other on the cheeks and are brimming with enthusiasm as always. Though I'm sure I'll miss having such a positive bunch of neighbors, I won't miss the fact that they know all about the sordid details of my previous life.

A move is essential if I'm going to rewrite my life going forward. Nevertheless, I thought it would be nice to get the girls together one more time before we leave in the morning for our road trip. I'm not sure where we'll put down roots. I know where I'd like to go, but for now, I'm happy to live life spontaneously.

Butterflies invade my stomach, and for a change, it's excitement I feel. The unknown promises an adventure and is not something to be feared. Besides, I'd happily live in a hovel if it meant being with Jarrad.

Love is all one needs. The rest is just window dressing.

"I finished the book, by the way," Sophia says, as though it was a major achievement. "I loved it."

"I thought you might." I smile. "I haven't had much time for reading lately, I'm afraid."

Olivia helps herself to some Prosecco. She takes a sip and then, looking pleased, says, "I've got an announcement to make."

Everyone turns at the same time.

"I've met someone." She smiles sweetly, looking the best she's looked in a long time.

After a long pause, Isabella asks, "So are you going to tell us who it is?"

Olivia tells us how they met at a café after he was stood up by a Tinder date.

"He was on Tinder?" Isabella sounds worried, like all of us, going by the wary side-eyes.

"Well, yeah. I mean, don't most people use that?" Olivia looks over at me.

"Hey, if you're happy, that's all that counts." I pour myself a drink.

"So what does he do?" Claire asks.

"He's a lawyer."

"That sounds promising," Claire adds.

"You would say that." Emily giggles at her lawyer girlfriend.

We continue to chat and catch up on the latest gossip. Apparently, there's a new couple who have moved in up the road with people arriving day and night, and we speculate all kinds of scenarios that get darker the more we delve.

While I'm in the kitchen, Isabella comes in looking for some water.

"So, the yoga instructor?" I ask.

She shakes her head and frowns.

"Oh? What happened?"

"My husband found out, and he threatened to leave me, so I've had to put a stop to it. It wasn't easy." She sighs.

"Why don't you just do a trial separation and maybe see how your relationship develops with the instructor?"

"With Max? Mm..." She shakes her head. "He's a gypsy. Max isn't into the whole monogamy thing. No, look, I had my fun. I've got kids and a husband who loves me."

"But are you happy?" I ask.

She shrugs. "Some days I am. I love my family, so what if I'm not turned on by my husband anymore? Isn't it self-indulgent to expect a life of bliss?"

"That's bullshit. I demand it," Olivia says, entering the kitchen.

We laugh. As a hedonist, she would say that.

When it comes to bliss, I'm getting plenty, thanks to Jarrad and his insatiable lovemaking.

Am I headed for a euphoric existence? I didn't expect it before. Even when I married Dorian, bliss was the last thing on my mind.

We return to the living room and spend the next few hours chatting about clothes, marriage, orgasms, and all those special subjects. Not a lot about books, though.

As I stand at the door to say goodbye to everyone, we promise to stay in touch and leave it at that.

A part of me wants to close that chapter on Marigold Boulevard. Once I've read one book, I generally don't go back for a second time.

The house is finally empty. The keys have been handed over to the realtor, who has a few buyers interested, and our bags are loaded in the SUV for our road trip.

I'm not sure where we're heading, but Jarrad, who has been poring over maps for the past week, is set on visiting Mount Rushmore, Yellowstone, and Niagara Falls, along with other famous natural wonders. I'm just happy to be along for the ride. I feel like clicking my heels in the air, only I'd probably hurt myself doing it.

Just as we're about to drive off, the police arrive and pull up in the driveway. My heart sinks. What now?

Detective Hull steps out with two uniformed officers and, true to form, skips any greeting and just points at the car. "Going somewhere together, I see?" He directs his attention to Jarrad. "Step out of the car."

Heavy with uncertainty, I stay rooted in place as Jarrad touches my hand and whispers, "Don't say anything."

Before I can speak, he climbs out of the car.

I'm not just going to sit there and let them take him away.

The detective seems to have his attention solely on Jarrad, and my heart is squeezing into a knot.

I get out and lean against the car, and of course, Olivia is just returning from school drop-off. Looking stunned, she opens up her hands.

Hull gestures to Jarrad. "You need to come with us for questioning."

"He wasn't even there," I say.

Hull turns to stare me down like he's finally noticed me. "And you would know how?"

"I reported it, if you remember," I say, trying hard not to shrill. "I was told our former maid's boyfriend is responsible. That his DNA was found on the scene and that his car was caught on CCTV entering our street that same day."

"Hector Gonzales is a person of interest. We have yet to find him, however."

My heart pounds so hard it might break a rib, while Jarrad stays expressionless. I turn to him, struggling to think straight.

"But you closed the case," I appeal.

"We've since found some DNA evidence that was overlooked at the time. Staff cuts, you know how it is. But I've been working on this case in my own time." He gives me a smug grin.

I can't believe this is happening. "What kind of DNA evidence?"

Hull doesn't need to tell me; I know that much, but I sense he's enjoying my suffering.

"Hair was found on the victim's shirt that belonged to someone else. We ran it through our criminal data system, and it matched Jarrad Hunter's DNA." He turns to face Jarrad, who is being flanked by a pair of officers. "It seems you have a criminal background. Pulling punches being your specialty."

Really? I look at Jarrad. He didn't tell me about that. What am I to make of this? Have I fallen for a criminal?

Not Jarrad. Not that soft, beautiful man who would drop everything to help children and the elderly. Not that I'd ever seen him do that, but you get a sense about people. Rose-colored glasses again?

"You need to come with us for questioning," Hull says again, nodding at the officers as they take Jarrad away.

My legs are trembling. What now?

As they start to pull out of the driveway, Jarrad looks out the window at me and shakes his head.

Is that him saying he's innocent?

FORTY-TWO

Ana

I HAVE TO PLAY nice because of Javier. Hector is threatening to have my son killed. I tried running away in New Mexico at a gas station, but he came after me, and I was so weak that I almost collapsed.

The people there just ignored us as he dragged me back to the car. Unbelievable. Hector's a little scary. I get that. But still, what's wrong with people? Can't they help a woman in obvious danger?

We finally arrived at Hector's auntie's place in Mexico. She knows my dad. We're kind of family, and she was always nice. She made me feel comfortable and at home and cooked enchiladas like my mother used to make, but I was still miserable.

She listened to my sob stories and said, "Hija mía, you have to follow his orders. You know this family. The men have always ruled."

Yep. Men ruled until they needed something. My dad called again, and this time Hector took the call and told him to fuck off.

I'm not talking to my father anymore, so I couldn't care less.

I have no family. Only my son. My heart is heavy. But one day soon, I will find a way to escape and get my boy back.

I even tried jumping out of the window, but his auntie's dogs barked and alerted Hector.

They have the windows barred too. It's crazy. But there's a long history of violence surrounding Hector's family. A cousin was murdered only a month ago, Hector's auntie told me while crying her eyes out. Related to the drug business, of course.

Those horrible drugs. I hate what they've done to my family, to my life. I always refused to take them, even weed.

I pray my son never goes near them.

It's now early morning, and Hector walks into the room and pulls off the bedcovers.

"Come on. We're going," he says.

I cross my arms and shiver. "Can I at least have a shower?"

"No time. You sleep too much. Lazy bitch."

I groan inside. Here we go again. I'm lazy? I'm the one who had to work while he all but became part of the couch, smoking crack and playing on his Xbox.

"Where are we going this time?" I say, pulling on my pants.

"Where you can't escape."

I toss the few clothes that Hector allowed me to buy along the way into a bag.

His auntie is waiting at the door and hugs Hector and then me. She whispers to me, "Stay strong."

I nod. "I will. Thanks."

At least the women in this family have some heart.

Suffering will do that to people. Sadly, you have to experience pain before you can fully understand people's sad stories.

Dorian once said that when something bad happens, the person involved is the one to blame. That they somehow caused it, as if they brought it on themselves.

I disagree. I wasn't responsible for my father looking for an easy way out in life by joining the Gonzales family's drug business. He couldn't do it properly and ended up pissing people off and putting us all in danger. I was his bargaining chip. They only kept him alive because Hector fell in love with me.

Huh. Strange way to show love by bashing me around.

I would never have fallen for Dorian had Hector treated me nicely.

My heart hurts. Now Dorian's dead. I know he wasn't a good man, and I was bad too. We were both cheaters.

And now I've lost my son. I can hardly breathe from the ache in my heart. I miss him so much. And my breasts are heavy. Lactating. Staining my tank top, which I have to hide. Any mention of my son and Hector growls like a monster.

We've been driving for a few hours, and I get the feeling we're going to his family's hacienda in the middle of Sierra Madre.

I'm truly fucked. No one will ever find us. It would be easier to escape jail in the States than that place they call a compound, which is more of a fortress than an estate.

As we're driving, Hector says, "They arrested the gardener, you know."

"Oh?"

"He's a person of interest in the murder of Dorian Gunn." He smiles, looking happy about that. "That means I'm fucking innocent. Great, huh?"

I shrug. "You knocked him out."

"That cheating asshole's dead. That's all that matters."

My eyes drown in tears again, overflowing with grief like the milk in my breasts with no mouth to feed. My poor darling son, being deprived of his mother's milk.

"You'll never escape now. You'll be mine forever," he says.

He's already raped me twice since dragging me away from a life that looked like Disneyland compared to the hell I'm now living in.

After stopping for tacos and a soda, we drive in silence. The day is warm and sunny.

As we descend into a valley, the spiked mountains swallow us up. We're hidden from the world. Not even the police can find this place.

There are secret roads to the hacienda that only those close to the family know about. The only time they leave is in a coffin, should they piss the cartel off. Cocaine makes people violent and do crazy shit, like murder, rape, and playing with their guns like they're toys.

We drive down a bumpy road as bushes scrape against the car. It's the same track I used to ride my bike on when I was young.

"This is where we first fucked. Nice memories, eh?" He smiles.

I hate him so much that I can't even bring myself to crack a fake smile. I know that will land me a slap.

"What's the matter? Is it because I'm not some hotshot gringo?"

I roll my eyes, and a sudden slap stings my already bruised cheeks.

"You're my bitch. You get that? You're mine." His black eyes are wild. He's been using the stuff his cousin gave him last night.

I know I'm being punished by God for cheating.

We finally get there. The high walls have barbed wire on top, and through an iron gate, the large white mansion with a red roof comes into view. My prison.

Dogs growl and bark. They're not the cute kind. Señora Gonzales has a few of those inside, but these beasts will tear you to bits.

Glad to at least be able to stretch my legs, I take a deep breath of the mountain air, which smells of pine, as Hector hits the buzzer.

Set up by his grandfather, the compound has belonged to this family since the fifties. The Gonzales family has a long line of drug dealers and murderers. It was my father who introduced me to this world. I'm sure it's what killed my mother. Toxic people shorten your life.

The gates open, and a security guard leads the dogs away.

The place looks like a luxury resort straight out of a magazine. The paved courtyard is surrounded by pots of flowers and plants, and around the side is a large patio with a swimming pool.

Here, cocaine money buys everything but freedom.

Guards holding weapons stand at the entrance, and instead of giving in to fear, I focus on a rocky stream running by the house that I would paddle on as a girl.

All kinds of memories come flooding back. Some good. Some bad. Like seeing those guns pointed at my dad's head, and my mother on her knees pleading for mercy. Not to mention Hector leading me by the hand and ripping my virginity from me when I was just fifteen.

I liked him despite the painful sex, which I confused with passion.

A cool wind blows through my hair, and I cross my arms as Hector pushes me along. "Come on."

We enter the house, which looks more like a palace.

Vibrant, oversized artwork covers the walls between television screens showing CCTV images of the property.

There are leather couches, marble floors, and sparkling chandeliers. Along the wooden staircase sit life-size framed photos of the Gonzales family. Their scary eyes say, 'Don't mess with me, I'm rich and powerful.'

I walk up the stairs to greet Hector's mom, Gloria, the woman who can turn you into ice with just one glance.

Hector's very close to his mother, and I sense he's told her about my little adventure.

Whatever. From this point on, I am not going to let anything get in my way. Not until I find my son. That is all that matters. If it means I have to sleaze onto one of the security guards or whoever to help me escape, then I will. Or murder Hector by feeding him poisonous mushrooms.

I will do anything to get to my son.
Anything.
Nothing's off the table.
If I thought I was bad before, then I'm even badder now.

FORTY-THREE

Linley

PRESENT DAY

IT'S BEEN THE longest forty-eight hours of my life. I haven't slept a wink.

After I booked a room in a hotel, I headed straight to the county jail, where Jarrad spent two nights locked up. Hull refused to answer any of my questions.

It breaks my heart to think of Jarrad locked up like that. I know he can look after himself. He's not exactly the type of person who would get picked on. But the thought of him holed up in such a place haunts me.

But did he kill Dorian?

I recall Hull's comments about Jarrad being arrested for fighting. My mind is swirling with questions, flying around like seagulls at a picnic.

There were no marks on Dorian's neck. That much I do remember.

I've since discovered, after speaking to my lawyer, that hair on a victim's garment is hardly enough evidence to convict someone.

I breathed a little easier after that.

I explained to the lawyer how I'd hugged Jarrad the same day I had contact with Dorian. Hair could have quite easily been transferred from me.

We didn't hug, but I had to say something to fight for Jarrad.

The attorney explained how it would be very surprising if the DA called the case in for a trial. They normally need skin cells from under the nails or more substantial DNA to be convinced of someone's involvement in a crime.

Now I'm tapping my foot, impatient, as I wait at this correctional facility in the poorest part of town.

After over an hour's wait, I see Jarrad and sigh with relief.

He's even looking rested. More so than me.

I go over and hug him. "Are you okay?"

"I'm fine." He unravels from my arms. "Let's get out of here."

We step out onto the street, and I'm so lost in the moment I'm nearly mown down by a scooter as Jarrad gently moves me away.

A call comes through, and expecting word from my attorney, I answer my cell.

It's Hull, however, and in his typical curt manner, he says, "Don't go too far. This isn't over yet. I'm not convinced."

"Talk to my lawyer." I end the call abruptly. Then, signaling Jarrad to wait, I say, "I want to call the lawyer. The car's just over there." I press on the key fob.

Leaning against the car, I tap on my phone.

"Rossiter," the lawyer answers.

"I just took a call from Hull. He's demanding we don't go far."

"Ignore him. He's got his head on the chopping block. I know how the LAPD works. They need someone to take the rap, and it's a headline case."

"Then they have to work harder to find Ana's ex."

"Hector Gonzales is in Mexico, and it will be nearly impossible to find him. I'd say Hull is looking for anyone at this stage to get his chief off his back."

"We're good, then? I mean, can I leave this with you? I imagine Hull is going to keep at us."

"Yup. Send him my way. The DA has tossed it out. Insufficient evidence. So unless they find something significant, they have nothing on Jarrad Hunter."

I wipe my brow and sigh with relief.

I couldn't have handled the love of my life locked up for a crime he didn't commit.

Or did he?

FORTY-FOUR

Jarrad

Everyone's entitled to a dark secret. And I have one I plan to keep. Yes, it's true love with Linley, and secrets contaminate relationships, but I'm not about to jeopardize what we have.

I'm hooked on her loving smiles and can't stand the idea of Linley looking at me like I'm some kind of killer.

Her beautiful, warm green eyes make me feel at peace with the world. She makes me want to be a better man.

I promised myself back in New York that I'd never go to prison again, and after two days locked up in that shithole, a lot went through my mind.

I can't tell her what I did.

She's holding onto something too.

That's okay. As I said, everyone's entitled to a dark secret. Not everything has to come out in the open.

In my case, Pandora's box will remain locked. I've seen what truth can sometimes do to people. It's like tossing an ember onto a gas leak.

As I sat in the cell that smelled like a toilet, I relived the events of that day.

I was there, all right. Saw it all. Enabled it, one might say.

Some drugged-out guy jumped the fence with murder in his eyes. I was ready to take him down. He didn't scare me. There were a ton like him in prison—full of piss and vinegar that one punch could fix.

"What the fuck do you want?" I asked, blocking him.

"I've come for Ana. She's my girl, and that rich asshole has been taking advantage of her."

His face was greasy, and he stunk of bad choices.

I let him go inside and then hid behind a bush and watched the show unfold.

Dorian didn't know what had hit him as the intruder charged at him like a bull. It didn't take much to knock the prick down, and then Ana came running in.

The way she cried over Dorian made me see how much she loved him.

Then it all happened quickly, and her ex whisked her away. I should have jumped in at that point to save her, but I didn't.

I don't like cheaters. Don't give a crap if they're men or women. They're all bad in my eyes. Weak.

Sure, I kissed Linley that night, and it took the strength of the Rock to not make love to her. But we both knew it was wrong. That's the difference. And while Linley might have hired Ana in the hope of her maid luring her husband, I still believe Ana was just as guilty as Dorian.

I've worked at plenty of wealthy homes and have seen how stuck-up they can be. How they look down their noses at the staff who are often working for peanuts.

That was never Linley. She treated Ana well. Too well.

Ana took advantage of Linley's kindness by plotting to steal her husband. At least, that's how it looked to me.

Linley's bad luck was marrying one of Satan's sons. And there's only one way to deal with the devil—match him at his evil game.

After Hector dragged Ana away, I saw Dorian shift on the ground.

I was hoping the hit had done the job, but it hadn't.

His "life sucks, get over it" comment in response to my father's suicide flashed before me in neon lights.

And a force pushed me inside. Maybe it was my dad's spirit. Who knows? But this evil son of a bitch wasn't going to be around to hurt any more people. I did it not just to free Linley but to avenge my father. After all, that's why I went there looking for a job in the first place. That was always the plan.

"Help," he cried, struggling to lift himself off the bloody floor.

"Remember me?" I asked, standing over him.

I could see he was in agony.

"Let me remind you." I picked him up by the scruff of the neck, and he cried out in pain.

"You laughed in my face when I told you how my dad took his life after your scumbag buddy, Crib, robbed him blind. You then had me tossed out on the street like I was nothing but a piece of dirt."

His eyes went wide with fear, and he started to beg. "Call 911. Please. I'll give you whatever you want."

"Oh, I already have what I want. Your beautiful wife. The woman who you've treated like scum from day one."

"You can have her. You can have anything." His eyes were cold, despite his desperation to live.

A lot of things flashed through my mind. Those few seconds felt longer as I reminded myself how guys like Dorian Gunn have lawyers who can pull off magic tricks, and by that, I don't mean rabbits out of hats. But more like locking me up in the slammer and greasing a few palms to dodge paying Linley.

Nah, the prick had to go. No good would come from him sticking around.

It was time to put him out of his misery.

I grabbed a cushion while holding him down and smothered him.

Would I do it again?

You bet.

I'd kill to protect those I love.

Anger that had been seething through me since that day on Wall Street left me on his final breath. It was like I'd exorcised some demon possessing my soul.

My father had been avenged. My mother would never know, but I sensed she would've patted me on the shoulder and given me a nod of approval.

If anyone comes near those I love, I do what has to be done.

The law doesn't understand the pain and suffering these Wall Street pricks inflict. They're vampires feasting on the blood of hard-working Americans. The law's always on their side.

Sure, Crib's rotting away in some hellhole, but Gunn was just as fucking guilty.

I washed my hands, walked away, and looked forward to giving my heart and soul to Linley.

That's all that matters now.

FORTY-FIVE

Linley

After leaving the correctional facility, we ate burgers. I wanted a real meal, but the only thing around was a burger barn. My appetite had returned too, and my stomach groaned with delight at such a simple but delicious feast. The simple pleasures of guilt-free eating. It's not nice to talk of the dead, I know, but Dorian would have spent the next hour lecturing me on how cows are fed hormones and all kinds of appetite-killing tidbits.

I could finally put my feet up and enjoy life. Though there were still questions, those could wait. All that mattered was Jarrad being with me.

We step onto the marble floor of the opulent hotel when Jarrad says, "This is next level."

"We can afford it." I link my arm with his.

A subtle smile is his response, and yes, he's too proud to allow me to support him financially. But hearing the 'we' exit my lips still feels amazing.

We enter the elevator, and then he takes me into his arms. "I'm sorry, I might not smell so good."

His lips touch mine, and like every time we kiss, I'm transported to some sunny island. By the time the elevator opens, I'm breathless, my fingers clutching his shirt, and the air between us is electric.

Jarrad waltzes me to the bed, our arms entwined. "I might need a shower first."

I push him onto the bed. "And spoil the moment?"

Yes, we've become insatiable.

He makes love to me like it's our first time again. As tears burn into my eyes, he makes me see stars.

We're now free to love each other without boundaries.

Jarrad walks out of the bathroom with a towel around his waist, rubbing his head with another towel. "I hope you don't mind, but I need to crash."

I smile. "You do that. We've got the rest of our lives." I study him for a response because that's virtually me proposing. "Am I being presumptive by saying that?"

He shakes his head slowly. "I would only add that we have the rest of eternity. That's if there's an afterlife." Jarrad strokes my cheek affectionately. "You're my soulmate, Linley."

He smiles tightly, and before I can say anything, he adds, "Oh, and about my prior convictions..." He rubs his neck.

I can see it's not an easy subject and jump in. "Hey, not now. Let's do this later."

"It's not a long story. Just that back then, in my early twenties, I drank too much. Someone said something about my sister, and I knocked him out."

"I would have done the same." I take his hand and kiss it. "To me, you're a good man."

After leaving Jarrad to rest, I decide to do some shopping.

Two hours later, I'm sitting in a café with a latte and a slice of Black Forest cake. I do my best thinking when sinking my teeth into something sweet and delicious.

As wonderful as things feel, there is still that big question spoiling my party: Did Jarrad kill Dorian?

I'm not guilt-free myself, and it's a secret I plan to keep tightly locked away.

You see, the first time I saw Ana wasn't at my home but at a supermarket. Along with others, I watched in horror as her boyfriend, drugged to the eyeballs, pushed her around.

He yelled, "You're a whore. I saw how you looked at him." And then he dragged her away. No one stepped in. He had knife-wielding psycho written all over him.

When she arrived for the interview, I instantly recognized her and employed her on the spot. It wasn't out of pity either, but something more calculated. She was Dorian's type, and that infidelity clause had turned me into a schemer.

When Hector arrived one day, shortly after we'd adopted Xavier, he demanded to see his son. Instead of threatening to call the cops, I told him Xavier was Dorian's son and not his.

Two days later, he came back, and as they say, the rest is history.

Can I live with myself and this secret?

Time will only tell.

I know Jarrad is holding something back too.

But we love each other. That's all that matters.

It's been two days, and after a bit of shopping and packing, we've decided it's time to go. We're going to drive off somewhere and carve our future in stone.

The car is packed, and we're about to drive off when Jarrad asks, "So what now?"

"We get to finally live our 'happily ever after.'" I smile. Little does he know, a big surprise came earlier that day.

He returns the smile. "I meant where to?"

"I'm thinking Greenwich. A large colonial with a big garden," I say. I'd already seen the house online. "A very big garden that will require lots of upkeep."

"Lead the way." He strokes my cheek with so much affection in his eyes that I can see he's loving that idea.

The dazzling lights of LA are just not our thing. I'm a Connecticut girl through and through, and Jarrad, I know for certain, will be in his element there.

I take a deep breath. "Oh, and by the way, I'm pregnant."

He stops driving, pulls up at the curb, and turns sharply to look at me. "How long? Is it from IVF?"

I shake my head. His surprise matches mine after I read the results on the stick. I did three tests to make sure. "I never went ahead with IVF. I'd say I'm about two months. That was roughly the last time I had my period."

His face lights up. "Our first time? Under the full moon."

He's such a romantic. I love how he always stares up at the sky and points out planets.

"Yep. The heavens decided it was our time. Magic."

He nods with a big smile that just keeps growing. "It sure is."

We hold each other, and after kissing me all over, he says in a deep heartfelt drawl, "I love you."

"I love you, too," I say as tears of joy slide down my cheeks. He starts up the engine, and off we go, driving into the sunset.

THE END

jjsorel.com/amora-sway-thrillers/

Printed in Dunstable, United Kingdom